It is time. The debt is due.

'Not yet. Please. I need some more time. Just a little more time.'

You wouldn't attempt to cheat me, would you?

'No, absolutely not. I just need a little more time.'

How much time?

'Six months.'

Six months. Six full cycles of the moon. It will cost, of course.

'Of course.'

I will grant you the time, then: six full cycles of the moon. But you know the rules. The final payment will fall due, then, and I will collect.

'I know that.'

Six months, then. Interest is payable at the full of the moon. And you will make your payments in the traditional manner. I will have my pound of flesh.

IMP

Michael Scott

WARNER BOOKS

A *Warner* Book

First published in Great Britain
by Warner Books in 1993

Copyright © Michael Scott 1993

A CIP catalogue record for this book
is available from the British Library.

ISBN 0 7515 0156 5

Photoset in North Wales by
Derek Doyle & Associates, Mold, Clwyd
Printed in Great Britain by
Clays Ltd, St. Ives plc

Warner Books
A Division of
Little, Brown and Company (UK) Limited
165 Great Dover Street
London SE1 4YA

Chapter One

MADDY stepped naked from the bathroom, pausing to hang over the banisters to listen to the muted sounds of the television percolating up from below. She heard the snap and fizz as a beer can was opened, and smiled with grim satisfaction: she'd deliberately chosen this night, knowing that the semi-final would keep Christy busy for a couple of hours.

Stepping over the squeaky floorboard on the landing, she slipped into the bedroom, then gently turned the key in the door so she wouldn't be interrupted. Checking that the curtains were closed – she'd caught that old bastard across the road peeking again – she switched on the bedroom light, even though it wasn't eight yet, and the August sunshine still burned warm and orange against the curtains.

Now, what was she going to wear?

Maddy Riggs opened the wardrobe and looked at the full-length mirror on the back of the door. Putting her hands on her hips, she regarded her body critically. She was only twenty-five, but two years of marriage had added weight to her hips and across her stomach, and in a couple of years she would be fat. Her breasts were still good, though, still firm, the nipples large and dark against her pale skin, and her legs were good, with smoothly rounded knees and neat ankles.

She ran her hands across her large breasts, feeling the nipples harden beneath her fingers. The simple touch set her heart pounding, and muscles fluttered deep in the pit of her stomach into her thighs.

Jesus, she was excited! She'd been like this all day, in a state of almost constant arousal. She hadn't been able to settle, to concentrate on anything.

Maddy tried to calm herself. This had to be one of the longest days of her life, but there was just another hour left. Just another hour. What was she going to wear? What would please Richard?

No bra. She knew he liked her breasts. Maybe it had been their swell and movement beneath her blouse that had first attracted his attention. He'd been looking at her breasts when she'd spotted him two weeks ago in the bookshop.

My God, was it only two weeks ago? She felt as if she'd known him all her life.

Maddy pulled open a drawer and looked at her underwear. What would he like? Sexy or simple?

Both, she decided. Richard Jager was unlike any of the other men she'd known. He was a lot older, for a start, sophisticated and cultured. Not particularly handsome, but distinguished and with the self-assurance that comes with both wealth and age. He always dressed well, and his manners were impeccable.

She chose a pair of white, silk panties and stepped into them, relishing the sensuous feel of the material against her thighs, feeling it cupping her groin like a hand.

Richard would prefer stockings to tights; tights were a great passion killer, but she'd already decided that she wasn't going to wear stockings, not tonight anyway. She'd had her legs waxed the previous day –

Christy would kill her if he knew how much it had cost – and she wanted nothing between Richard's hands and her flesh.

She'd already picked out the dress, a simple, black, off-the-shoulder copy of a designer label that came to mid-thigh. She'd bought it six months previously for her sister's wedding, but Christy hadn't allowed her to wear it when he'd seen how much cleavage and thigh it revealed.

Well, she was wearing it tonight.

Sitting at the dressing table, she turned on the bedside lamp, tilting the shade to spill light onto the mirror. She stared at herself in the glass, before she nodded fiercely. She was pretty. Two years of marriage hadn't taken that away from her. Yet. Christy obviously didn't think so; he spent more time looking at the box than he did at her, and he usually needed a couple of pints inside him before he bothered groping her in the dark. Christ, what had happened to the days before they were married when he couldn't keep his hands off her, when they'd make love in the morning before they both went to work, and then again in the evening, when they'd come home? Where had those days gone? Now, if they made love, it was once a fortnight, and then not always successfully.

Was that why she'd fallen so easily for Richard Jager? Maybe she'd just been waiting for someone like him to come along. Someone who'd show her a little interest, someone who'd look on her as a woman, rather than just another object, another part of the house, a cooking or cleaning machine.

Leaning into the mirror, she started to work on her enormous brown eyes.

His eyes were a pale, almost colourless grey, that tended to pick up the colours from the surroundings.

She'd met him two weeks ago, in the bookshop. She'd been bent over, sorting a pile of pamphlets on the long table at the back. Intuition had warned her that someone was looking at her, and she'd looked up suddenly. He was standing right at the other end of the shop, but she could tell that he was staring straight down the front of her blouse at the tops of her breasts.

But he hadn't turned away – maybe that's what had interested her in the first place – he hadn't suddenly dropped his eyes and pretended to be busy looking at something else. He hadn't even flushed in embarrassment. He had continued to look at her for a few moments before walking down the shop towards her. She had straightened, automatically pulling her blouse taut, until she realised that that accentuated her prominent nipples.

He's going to ask me a dumb-ass question, she thought.

Instead, he'd said, 'I generally don't make a habit of staring at women ... except when they are very beautiful.'

And while she'd gaped in astonishment, he'd nodded curtly. 'It's very difficult to pay a woman a compliment today without it being misconstrued, but I hope you'll take it as such.'

And then he'd turned and walked out of the shop.

That might have been that: except she saw him later in the pub where she usually got a beer and a sandwich. He was sitting in the corner, busily scribbling notes in a jotter. She could have walked away, but she didn't. There was an empty bottle of Coke on the table in front of him. Buying a Coke for herself, she carried her tray over and slid it onto the small round table.

'Do you mind . . .?'

He'd barely bothered to glance up . . . until he'd realised who was sitting opposite him, and she felt a curious glow when she saw the genuine look of delight in his watery eyes.

And that's how it started. He'd introduced himself as Richard Jager, and she'd reached across the table and shook his hand, impulsively giving him her maiden name, Madelaine Horner, suddenly glad she wasn't wearing her wedding ring.

With her face now made up, Maddy sat back, turning her head from side to side, pleased with what she saw. She rarely got the chance to make herself up properly.

This was their first real date. Oh, they'd met every day for the past two weeks in the pub and the shop. He'd taken to coming in late, just before five-thirty. Mr Soper left around four, and on weekdays the shop was usually empty when he arrived. She'd kissed him for the first time three days ago, catching him unawares, wrapping her arms around his head, drawing him close, pressing her breasts against his chest, forcing her tongue between his teeth. Her sudden passion had seemed to surprise him – just as it had surprised herself. But his response, his lips and tongue hard against hers, his hands against her breasts, had taken her breath away, leaving her shaken and trembling.

Sitting in front of the dressing table, she pressed her hands against her breasts, imagining the touch of his fingers against her skin. As she stepped into the skimpy dress, she wondered where he would take her. A surprise, he said.

Getting out of the house had been surprisingly easy.

Christy was still sitting in front of the TV, now on his third can as she came down the stairs, moving silently on bare feet. She'd thrown a light raincoat over the dress and had opened the front door when she called, 'I'm just popping down to see one of the girls. I won't be long.'

She heard a grunt that might have been a goodbye, but she wasn't sure. She knew that getting back in might be a problem, but she'd cross that bridge when she came to it. She'd thrown a change of clothes in the washing machine. If she got in late, she'd simply change, throw her dress into the machine, and then remain up for the rest of the night. Since he'd lost his job, Christy didn't get up until around noon anyway; he'd probably never even know she hadn't come home.

At the bottom of the road, Maddy hailed a passing taxi. Sliding back onto the seat, she slipped out of her flat shoes and into the black high-heels.

'Where to, love?'

'Victoria and Albert, please. Exhibition Road entrance.'

It was just like him to meet her at the V&A. She wondered if the gallery was open tonight – and then had a moment of panic when she suddenly wondered if he'd been going to take her to a special opening. Was she dressed appropriately? Overdressed? Underdressed? A smile curled her full lips. Too late now.

Although she was nearly thirty minutes early, he was already waiting on the low steps of the V&A, casual in a cream-coloured linen suit, arms folded across his chest. He was moving even before the taxi pulled in to the side of the road, pulling open the door, helping her out – his eyes lingering appreciatively on the length of bare leg – and before she could get to her purse, he'd paid the driver with what she suspected was a tenner, even though the trip hadn't come to half that. And as the driver was counting out change, Richard shook his head, and muttered 'Keep it.'

'What would you like to do tonight?' he asked, catching her elbow and manoeuvring her back down towards Kensington Road.

'Whatever you like,' she said, feeling a wave of giggling giddiness wash over her. She had actually done it! She slipped her arm through his, pulling him close, allowing his forearm to brush against the side of her breasts. Her nipples hardened immediately.

Jager smiled, showing small, slightly uneven teeth. 'Thank you for coming,' he murmured.

'Why, did you think I wouldn't?'

'Something could have come up,' he shrugged. 'I'm glad it didn't.' He glanced at a flat, gold wristwatch. 'I was thinking that we might go to the theatre and then have dinner, what do you think?'

'Sounds marvellous.'

'But first an aperitif. I live quite close. Would you care to come up to my apartment for a drink?'

'Yes, I'd like that.' She was sure he could feel her heart thundering against his arm.

Jager turned left, down Imperial College Road, onto Queen's Gate, crossed the road, then turned into a small mews.

Maddy was intrigued to discover that Richard lived in one of these. She hadn't really known what to expect, but she'd been expecting somewhere grander, not one of these boxy, post-war, rather plain-looking buildings. However, this was an SW7 address; she hated to think what it cost.

While Jager fished in his pocket for a key, Maddy looked at the illuminated bells. Only four of the eight slots were filled: Jager was on the ground floor; the other three were doctors.

Richard caught her looking at the plates. 'They're all physicians,' he said lowering his voice to a whisper.

Maddy nodded, and then remembered she didn't know what Richard did. As if reading her mind, he turned and said, 'I suppose I should put "doctor" on my nameplate too.' He tilted his head towards the corner. 'I lecture at the Royal College of Music, just down the road.'

Maddy smiled as she followed him into the dry, slightly musty-smelling hallway. She should have guessed he was an academic; he had that air about him.

Jager's apartment was at the bottom of the short corridor. 'This is the best flat in the building,' he confided, 'no stairs.' He threw open the door and allowed her to precede him into the room.

Maddy stopped. The room was bare, plastic sheeting covering the floor, even pinned to the walls.

'Decorators,' Richard said with a tired sigh, 'I don't think they're ever going to go.'

She heard the door close with a solid click, then Richard was standing behind her, easing her coat off. She remained still, allowing him to see the full effect. Then he stepped close – she could smell his musky aftershave – and his arms slid around her waist, resting on the flat of her stomach, his mouth at her neck.

'Thank you for coming,' he said again.

Maddy pressed herself back against him, feeling his erection through the thin material of his suit and her dress. She rested her hands over his, then dragged them upwards to cup her breasts. His thumbs pressed against her nipples, sending a shudder through her that set the muscles in her thighs quivering. She threw her head back and Richard bent his neck, tongue flicking at the column of her throat. His hands moved up her body, across her shoulders, down her back, catching the narrow black zip, easing it downwards, then pushing the dress off her breasts, and it hissed onto the floor.

He cupped her breasts, squeezing gently, short fingers probing the flesh, tracing designs and patterns over the skin, returning to stroke and caress her nipples until they were stiff and aching.

His left hand moved away and she could hear it busy with his belt.

She ran her hands across her stomach, hooking thumbs into her panties, pushing them down, wanting him to see her naked, to touch her.

He brought his mouth back to her throat, licking at the faintly perfumed flesh, moving upwards, his breath warm on her ears. 'You're perfect,' he breathed . . .

. . . And cut her throat right to left with a razor-sharp, ten-inch, double-edged blade.

'Absolutely perfect . . .'

There was no pain, only surprise, and she realised then why the room was covered in plastic.

With infinite precision, he pressed the blade of the razor into the woman's breasts. The skin parted silently, the wound opening up like a flower blossoming. She had been dead for three days now, so there was no blood, only a pale, viscous fluid.

With quick, deft strokes, he began to carve the signs of the zodiac into the blue-white skin. When he was finished, he pressed his lips to the wounds, breathing into them, bringing the magical zodiacal signs to life.

When he could feel the corpse trembling with magical life, he bit off the nipples, and added them to the others . . .

9

Chapter Two

'I think it disgusting, revolting, perverted and obscene.'

Katherine Norton pushed the thick bundle of manuscript across the cluttered desk. 'If you hadn't insisted I read it, I would have given up on it a long time ago. I felt physically sick reading parts of it. I mean, where he bites off the dead woman's nipples . . .' She shuddered.

Tony Matthews sat back in his creaking leather chair, laced his fingers together and wrapped his small hands around the back of his completely bald head. 'I know.'

Katherine Norton tapped the manuscript with a blunt finger. 'I know it's a mistake to equate the writer with the writing, but this guy is sick!'

Tony Matthews sat forward. He rested his hands on top of the pile of paper and turned the bundle around so that it was facing him, fingers automatically squaring up the paper. Without looking up he said, 'We haven't really been fair with you, Katherine.' He too tapped the manuscript. 'This book has been published.'

Katherine frowned and shook her head slightly, brushing strands of her chestnut hair off her high forehead. 'I don't see . . .' she began, but Matthews raised a hand and stopped her.

'You've been with the Image Press for how long now . . . three years, four?'

She nodded. 'Something like that.' A panicked fluttering began in the pit of her stomach. Had this horrible book been some kind of test? And had she failed? She couldn't afford to be out of a job. With the cutbacks in the publishing trade, finding another post as an editor would be next to impossible.

'You're the best editor we have,' Matthews continued.

Katherine blinked in surprise. Coming from Tony Matthews, this was high praise. Matthews was one of the most respected publishers in the business. He had been editorial director of the Image Press for the past ten years, had survived four owners and two heart attacks, and had managed to keep the publishing house afloat while bigger and better funded companies had gone under. He put his success down to a talent for knowing exactly what the market wanted – and then supplying it.

Matthews tapped the manuscript again. 'I asked you to read this because I wanted your objective reaction.'

'You've got it.'

'No, you've given me an emotional response. Now, give me an editorial decision. Is this a good book?'

Katherine glanced down at the sheaf of typewritten notes she had prepared. 'It is well-written, has a cohesive storyline, strongly developed three-dimensional characters, good pace and tension is held throughout. The climax is superb.' She paused and looked up, her deep brown eyes flashing good-humouredly. 'Having said all that, I should add that I found the characters amoral, the plot highly implausible, the sex and violence incredibly graphic – so much so that I actually began to wonder if the writer had actually done some of the things described in the book. It certainly feels as if he's writing out of personal experience.' She sat back into the chair and shrugged. 'Perhaps I'm just old-fashioned, but it worries me to think that the youth of today are actually reading this rubbish.' She sighed. 'My God, I sound like my mother. I must be getting old.'

Matthews pushed back his chair and stood up. 'We're all getting old.' Crossing to the window he pushed it open a fraction, allowing the hot, metal-tasting London air to waft into the small, cramped office. 'If it's any consolation, my considered opinion is that this is a piece of shit – well-written shit, mind you, but shit. And if you think this is bad – wait until you read the next one. Christ!' He shook his head. 'Parts of it are *disgusting*.' He nodded at the manuscript on the table. 'You've just read *Zodiac* by Robert Hunter . . .'

Katherine nodded. 'The Master of Terror.' She shrugged. 'I know the name of course, but I don't read horror.'

Matthews reached over to the bookshelf beside the window and pulled off a thick hardback, which he dropped on top of the manuscript. The cover showed a zodiacal wheel dripping blood. 'We published this in the middle of last year. To date it has sold just under eighty thousand copies – in hardback! It comes out in paperback next month. The initial print-run is two hundred and fifty thousand copies. Our reps have pre-sold two hundred thousand copies in the bookshops.'

Matthews slumped back into his chair and stared at Katherine as if expecting a response.

'It will make you – and him – a lot of money,' she said eventually.

'That's an understatement.' Matthews fished a huge, florid handkerchief out of his pocket and patted his face. 'We've published all eleven of Hunter's books. We were his first publishers, and although other publishing houses have attempted to lure him away with bigger contracts, he's stayed with us for some reason. His twelfth title, *Tarot*, will be published in hardback when *Zodiac* is released.'

Katherine reached for the coffee cup on the editor's desk, grimaced when she realised that it was cold. 'Tony, can I ask you why you're telling me this? I mean, I know Hunter's name. I know he's one of the Image Press's most important authors.'

Matthews leaned across the desk, his pale blue eyes blinking rapidly. 'He's more than that. He is probably our single most important author at the moment. Warner Brothers have bought the rights to *Zodiac*, and they're talking about De Niro playing the role of the killer.'

'He'd be right for the part.'

'Perfect,' Matthews agreed. 'And you know what a movie like that would do for the sales of the book.'

Katherine nodded. The hype for a major motion picture would give the book a second lease of life, guaranteeing enormous sales not only of this title, but also for the backlist, the author's previous works.

'About a year ago, we signed a contract with Hunter for another book, his thirteenth. It was provisionally entitled *The Earl of Hell*.' Matthews took a deep breath and added grimly, 'It was due for delivery last month.'

Pieces of the jigsaw began falling into place. Katherine sat up straight. Matthews continued. 'For the first time in his life, Hunter didn't deliver. He's having problems with the book. He's got a plot, sub-plots, characters – everything – but he just needs someone to hold his hand, point him in the right direction . . .'

He stopped. Katherine was shaking her head. 'Not me. I didn't like this example of his work, and I certainly don't want to spend a couple of weeks or longer working with the guy who'd written it.'

'I've met Hunter. He's rather charming. Married with two lovely daughters. Around about the same age as your own,' he added.

'I don't care, Tony. I hated *Zodiac*. It gave me nightmares. It's still giving me nightmares.'

'It's supposed to do that. It's a horror novel.'

'I won't do it,' she said finally.

Matthews's expression hardened. 'We need to have this book delivered. Hunter signed for an astronomical amount of money, most of which has already been paid over. Hardback and paperback deals have been put in place across the world . . . all subject to a completed manuscript, of course. The movie people are sitting there with mouths open, tongues hanging out, waiting for a copy. And they're beginning to get a bit edgy. If Hunter fails to deliver, it could hurt Image badly. Very badly.'

'Tony, I don't want to do it.'

'You went freelance because you wanted more time to rear your three children,' Matthews said quickly.

Katherine nodded, surprised. She swallowed hard, realising that the threat was coming up.

'If you were to refuse this commission, I'd have to find someone else. You're my best editor . . . but I'm not sure if there would be any more work for you with Image Press.'

'Oh Tony, don't do this. Don't pull this shit, please. We've worked together for a long time. You know I need this job, you know Peter has been out of work for six months.' She was surprised – and annoyed – at the note of pleading in her voice.

Matthews wouldn't meet her eyes. 'Will you do this job? It's three weeks' work; a month at the outside. I'm not asking you to like the book, I'm not even asking you to like the man. I'm simply asking you to get the book out of him. I'll pay a bonus,' he added. He looked up quickly, a smile curling his lips. 'And a holiday. How about a holiday for you and Peter and the kids? Get the book finished in four weeks' time, and I'll send you all away somewhere warm and hot, where the only horrors will be the mosquitoes.'

Katherine sighed. 'Do I have a choice, Tony?' she asked tightly.

'You have a choice,' he said slowly.

'Exactly,' Katherine replied. 'I've no choice at all!'

Chapter Three

ROBERT Hunter sat back in the high-backed, leather armchair and listened to Tony Matthews's voice on the answering machine. *'Bob . . . Bob. I know you're there. Godamnit. Answer the phone. This is important.'* The slender, grey-haired man hesitated a moment before snatching the phone off the cradle. The answering machine whistled with feedback before he managed to switch it off.

'You know I never answer the phone in the morning, Tony,' Hunter said pleasantly. He leaned forward and tapped his computer keyboard, saving the few paragraphs he'd managed to write in the past two hours.

'I know that, Bob, but you know I only phone you when it's important. Anyway, it's ten minutes past noon; technically, it's not morning any more. How are you?' he continued.

'I'm fine, Tony,' Robert Hunter said patiently. He knew Tony Matthews had called to see if he was any closer to completing *The Earl of Hell*. While he waited for the publisher to continue, he ran the counter over his morning's work: 625 words. When on form, he usually managed at least two thousand before lunch.

'How is the book coming along?' Tony asked after an embarrassingly long silence.

'Slowly. Look, Tony, why don't you save us both a bit of time and tell me the real reason for your call?'

'You always did believe in getting straight to the point.'

'I was a teacher for far too long. You quickly learn to cut through the bullshit. So tell me . . .'

'All right, Bob. Cards on the table. *The Earl of Hell* is late, very late and getting later, and every time I ask you about it, all you say is, "soon". Well, soon isn't good enough any more. We've got a lot riding on this book, Bob, so I'm assigning one of our best freelance editors to work with you. And when I mean "work" with you, Bob, I mean she'll be calling at your house every morning, working right alongside you, editing, correcting, making suggestions as you go along. You should fly through the remainder of the book.'

Hunter sat back and allowed himself to consider the possibilities. Finally, he nodded; this could be good.

Matthews misinterpreted the silence as disapproval and hurried on. 'We've used this technique with some of our other authors when they've hit a bad patch. It works wonders,' he finished lamely.

'Who are you sending?' Hunter asked.

'I've assigned Katherine Norton to work with you on this. She works on all the big-name authors . . .'

'Why have I never worked with her before?' Hunter said immediately.

'Well, that's because your books have never needed that much editorial assistance.'

'Until now,' Hunter added.

'This is a different case. You've never been late with a book before.'

'That's true. But then, I've never written a book like this one before.'

'So you keep saying, but I wish you'd let me read

17

what you've done so far . . .'

'No. That's not how I work,' Hunter said quickly. 'Does this lady know my work?' he continued.

'She's just finished reading *Zodiac*. I have her report on my desk now.'

'Did she like it?' Hunter asked.

'She was very impressed,' Matthews replied. 'She described the ending as superb.'

'I look forward to meeting her,' the writer said. 'When will she arrive?'

'Well, I wanted to get things clear with you first. So, if it's all right with you, I'll have her report for duty tomorrow. Now, if you've any problem with her – a personality clash, something like that – let me know immediately, and I'll find someone to replace her.'

'I'm sure she'll be fine. Goodbye, Tony,' Hunter said, and put down the phone.

He tried to work out the implications of this woman's arrival. He wasn't sure . . . but he thought it might be very good news indeed.

Chapter Four

'THE bastard!' Peter Norton snapped. He rolled over in the bed to look at his wife.

'Ssh, you'll wake the children,' Katherine chided him gently. She pushed her glasses up onto her head and dropped the manuscript she had been correcting onto the floor. Pinching the bridge of her nose between thumb and forefinger, she sighed. 'Yes, that's what he said. Either I do this job or I don't work with Image again.'

'But you hated that shit you read. You told me so yourself. Christ, how many times did I have to wake you from nightmares?'

'I know, I know, Peter,' Katherine said tiredly. 'So what was I going to do – tell him to take his job and shove it up his ass?'

'There are other editorial jobs,' he said quickly.

But Katherine shook her head. 'Not really. They're thin enough on the ground, and they're not easy to get. I've got a good deal with Image. I've worked hard to get where I am. I don't want to risk blowing it just now.' She reached over and switched off the light. 'Even if I walked away from them and did manage to get a job with another company, I'd be starting from the bottom again.'

'Did you tell Matthews that reading that shit made

you feel physically sick? Christ, I read some of it myself, and I was revolted.'

'I told him,' she said staring up into the darkness. The outline of the window slowly appeared out of the gloom as her eyes adjusted to the dark. 'And he agreed with me. But he said that if I can bring the book in within the next month, he will pay for all of us – you, me and the kids – to go on a long holiday.'

Peter rolled over onto his back. He locked his hands behind his head and stared at the ceiling. Passing car lights brightened the curtains.

Katherine felt her husband's tension and rolled over to lay her head on his chest. His heart was pounding so hard she could feel his skin trembling with each beat. 'What's wrong?' she whispered.

'I hate to see you doing this.'

'It's what I do. It's my job,' she said simply. In the darkness she squeezed her eyes shut, instantly knowing she'd said the wrong thing.

'And if I had a job you wouldn't have to do this,' Peter said, not quite making the statement an accusation.

'I worked when you had a job,' she reminded him.

'But you didn't *have* to work then. You do now.'

'I don't have to work,' she said quickly. 'We still have your redundancy money, which we haven't touched. But that's our emergency fund. We don't want to start dipping into that yet.' Katherine moved upwards along her husband's body and kissed the base of his neck. 'You'll get a job soon. With your qualifications someone is bound to snap you up.'

'I've been unemployed for six months,' Peter said quietly. 'I've called in every favour I thought I had, contacted all my old friends and, even with my qualifications, I can't get a job. The longer it goes on, the harder it's going to get.'

'Something will come up,' Katherine said.

Peter Norton had been a junior partner in an established firm of accountants. Eight months previously, the firm had been absorbed into a national accountancy firm, with branches all over Britain. He was 'surplus to requirements' and received two months' notice almost immediately. With the redundancy and bonus payments, he had walked away with close to twelve thousand pounds.

Peter had talked about setting himself up as an accountant in private practice, but London had more than its fair share of professional and private accountancy firms, and looking at the situation logically, he realised it would be throwing his money away. Even if the business was a success, it would mean pumping all the redundancy money into it, and then waiting at least three years before it showed a return.

After a lot of discussion, they had both decided that he would take six months – although they were both certain that it wouldn't take six months – to look for another job. In the meantime, Katherine would take on a little more work as a freelance editor to bring in some cash.

Peter shifted in the bed, his right arm moving down to stroke his wife's back. 'What are we going to do if I don't get a job?' he asked.

'I can go back to work full time,' she said simply. It was the answer she had been giving him since he had begun to lose confidence. 'We'll role-reverse. You can be a house-husband. Wear a pinny, do the dusting and the ironing. I've always wanted a maid,' she added, sliding her hand up along his bare ribs to tickle him under the arm. He squirmed, caught her hand in his, pulling it away from his body. 'You should be enjoying your time off,' she continued. 'We've been married ten years, and all you've ever had is two-week summer holidays. Now you've got this great opportunity to enjoy the glorious weather.' Peter nodded, and she felt the tension seep out of his shoulders. She rolled over, hitching her nightdress up so that she could straddle him. Dipping her head, she allowed strands of her chestnut hair to trail across his face. 'And look on the bright side: at least it's giving you more time with the children. You were always saying that you didn't get to spend enough time with them.'

Peter slid his hands up along the nightdress's silky material, moving across her flat stomach, over her breasts, touching frills, then the warmth of her flesh.

'We haven't had this much time together since we were in college,' she said, leaning down to kiss the tip of his nose.

'Long ago and far away,' he breathed, tilting his head back so that her lips trailed across his. 'I do love you.'

'I know.' Straightening, she pulled her nightdress over her head and dropped it onto the floor. She could feel him harden beneath her, could feel her own body beginning to respond.

Peter kissed her, tongue touching the surface of her lips, her mouth opening to receive him. Pressing herself against him, her breasts flattening against his chest, she raised her head as his tongue traced a moist line down her throat . . .

teeth ripping into flesh, tearing into the jugular vein

. . . and across her chest, flicking at her hardening nipples, then encircling them, taking them into his mouth . . .

teeth closing on the hard points of flesh, biting through

22

them, shaking his head to tear the buds from the breasts.

Katherine jerked back with a whimper of horror.

'Oh Jesus, love, I'm sorry. Did I hurt you?' Peter rubbed her breasts gently within the palm of his hand.

'It's all right. It's . . .' She stopped. The images were from Hunter's book, *Zodiac*. But she wasn't going to tell Peter that. 'My breasts are a little tender.' She attempted a smile, but realising that he wouldn't see it in the darkness, lifted her breast and, leaning forward, rubbed the nipple across his lips. 'Gently, gently,' she whispered.

They made love slowly and tenderly for the next hour, ten years of marriage having taught them almost all there was to know about each others' bodies. But the grotesque and sickening images from Hunter's book had completely destroyed Katherine's mood. She faked orgasm moments after Peter had spasmed into her, then lay with him until he slipped into a contented doze.

When she was sure he was asleep, she slid out of the bed, and stepped into the en suite bathroom. Blinking in the harsh light, she squinted into the mirror . . .

the glass exploding, shards gouging flesh, ripping into the lining of her stomach, lacerating the soft flesh of her breasts

. . . and barely made it to the toilet before she threw up. As she squatted on the floor before the toilet bowl, she swore she would phone Tony Matthews tomorrow morning and cancel.

Chapter Five

THERE was no bell and the door knocker was shaped in a snarling demon's head. Katherine Norton stared at it for a moment, before snatching it and hammering twice on the solid door. When she let go of the knocker, she unthinkingly wiped her hand on her skirt. She thought the demon was in appalling bad taste – but hardly surprising for the man who had written something like *Zodiac* – and oddly down-market. However, the address was anything but. Pushing her sunglasses up onto her hair, she turned and looked around the small private square. Eaton Square was off to her left, Sloane Square to her right. The white stone house was three storeys over a base-ment, and she suddenly wondered if Hunter was only renting a flat in the building. With the way property prices had been shooting up in London over the past few years, she wouldn't have been able to guess at a price, though she knew of two-room flats in the area selling for one hundred and fifty thousand plus.

'You must be Katherine Norton.'

Katherine spun around. The door had opened silently, and she found herself facing a young, blonde-haired woman, dressed in a fluorescent pink leotard that showed off her golden, tanned and healthy-looking body. There was a thick, fluffy towel

around her neck, which she used to pat her face. Maid
. . . nanny . . . daughter? Daughter, probably.

The young woman held out her hand. 'I'm Emma
Hunter, Bob's wife.'

Katherine put down her briefcase and shook her
hand. 'I'm delighted to meet you.'

'Come in, come in, please.' Emma Hunter stood
aside to allow Katherine into the long, bright hallway.
'Did you find us all right?'

'I did, thank you. I took the Tube to Sloane Square,
then got a cab, because I wasn't sure of the address. It
took the cabby about three minutes to drive up from
the station. It was only when he left me outside that he
told me it was a thirty-second walk straight down the
road. As I was paying him, he asked me if I was
coming to see the writer. When I told him I was, he
said to be sure to tell him that *Zodiac* was the best yet.'

Emma smiled. 'Most of the cabbies know Bob. We
don't have a car, you see. So we either go by Tube or
cab.' She pointed to a door to the right of the stairs.
'Why don't you come and get a cup of coffee before
going up to see Bob?' She glanced up at the hideously
ornate Swiss clock on the wall. 'It's just gone nine.
He's probably still answering his mail. He likes to get
that out of the way before he starts writing.'

Katherine followed the young woman down the
hall, watching – with a certain amount of envy – the
pattern of her muscles, clearly outlined beneath the
thin fabric of the leotard. Emma, like the exclusive
address, was quite a surprise. The girl was in her early
to mid-twenties and although she was pretty, she
wasn't beautiful: her bright blue eyes were too close
together, her mouth too small, lending her face a
slightly pinched expression. Her blonde hair was
scraped back off her face and tied into a thick ponytail

25

that reached almost to the base of her spine; and her tan was so perfect, it could only come from a sunbed. Her tiny feet were bare, Katherine saw.

'Tea or coffee?' Emma asked as they entered the kitchen.

'Tea, please.'

The young woman moved silently to the other side of the kitchen, her feet leaving tiny misted impressions on the highly polished wooden floor.

'I wish I had a room like this at home,' Katherine said, looking around.

The kitchen was bright with early-morning sunlight, which reflected off the golden pine cabinets, the matching table and chairs, burnishing the rows of copper pots standing on the old-fashioned dresser. Bunches of dried herbs hung from the exposed rafters. Through two enormous windows, Katherine could see out into a beautifully kept garden, still blazing with summer colour, despite the hosepipe ban.

'Milk, sugar?'

'Milk, please. Don't tempt me with sugar. I'm trying to give it up.'

'Why don't we have this in the garden?' Emma suggested, loading a small teapot with matching cup and milk jug onto a circular wicker tray. She added a tall glass of orange juice.

'That's a lovely idea.' Katherine dropped her briefcase and handbag onto the floor. 'Can I help you with anything?'

'No thanks. I have everything.'

Katherine followed Emma out into the garden. She breathed in the scents of herbs and the perfume of the dozens of varieties of flowers. She wasn't a gardener – she loathed gardening – but she recognised the amount of work that had gone into creating this garden. She admired the way a combination of trees, bushes and decorative latticework combined to create an area of sheltered privacy around a sunken patio area. Water trickled nearby.

'You have a lovely home, and a beautiful garden,' Katherine said admiringly. 'Did you do all this yourself?'

'A lot of it was here when we bought this place four years ago,' Emma said, sinking gracefully into a wooden patio chair. She poured tea into the single cup as Katherine sat down facing her. 'It was a bit formal and severe then, and I've really concentrated on breaking up the rigid lines, making it softer, more comfortable.' She looked around the garden. 'I've done a lot of planting, trying to keep some colour in it all year around. The hard part is the weeding.'

'You must be a keen gardener,' Katherine smiled.

'I wasn't – until we got this place, that is.' Emma lifted her orange juice and sipped it slowly. 'But Bob has no interest in gardening, and if I hadn't gone out and done it, it would have meant bringing in a gardener, and neither of us wanted that. We're very private people,' she added, glancing at the editor.

'I really am sorry for intruding,' Katherine said.

Emma shook her head quickly. 'No, no, I didn't mean that; I wasn't talking about you. You're not intruding – far from it. I think it will be good for Bob to have someone to help him get over the hump of this book. What I meant was that Bob is very self-contained; he has his writing, he doesn't need anyone or anything else. I don't have many friends – not around here, anyway.' She lowered her voice. 'They're all a bit snooty; I think they look down on Bob because he writes *horror*.' She made a face as she said the word. 'And maybe they're a bit jealous because while they're renting a couple of rooms, we own the whole house.'

'Have you any children?' Katherine asked, drinking her tea, recognising the distinctive taste of Earl Grey.

'Two girls,' Emma said, her face lighting up. 'Violet, she's six, and Rose, who'll be four soon.'

'The little flowers,' Katherine said, suddenly remembering the dedication in *Zodiac*. '*To the little flowers . . .*'

Emma smiled delightedly. 'We had actually given them their names long before we realised they were flower names. If we have another girl, we'll call her Jasmine,' she said decisively. 'Have you any children of your own?'

'Two girls and a boy,' Katherine said. 'Elizabeth is ten, Mark has just turned eight and Jody, the youngest, is five. Sometimes it frightens me when I realise how quickly time has slipped away. It only seems like yesterday when Lizzie was born.'

Emma nodded. The two women sat in silence. It was so peaceful in the garden that the droning of insects and the chirrupping of birds sounded almost unnaturally loud. Katherine found it difficult to believe that she was sitting in the back garden of a house in the centre of London.

'Will you be able to help Bob?' Emma asked suddenly.

'I'm sure I will,' Katherine said. 'I'm really here to facilitate things and hurry the book along. I'll be working on the manuscript as he completes it, help him get through the rough patches.'

'You've done this sort of thing before?'

'Often,' Katherine smiled.

'How long will it take?'

Katherine shrugged. 'I don't know. It depends on how much Robert has written and how much work there is to do on that, and then we need to see how much remains to do. However, I have a deadline in four weeks' time.'

The young woman nodded. She ran her index finger around the rim of the tall glass, now streaked with orange peel. 'I'll be pleased when this book is finished,' she admitted. 'This one has caused him a lot of problems.'

'Writing doesn't get any easier, no matter how many books you write,' Katherine said.

'Bob is always distracted when he's working on a book. Sometimes he becomes so wrapped up in the writing that he loses contact with the world around him. He won't speak, won't leave the house, works all through the night, falls into bed as I'm getting up, barely eats. And then, when the book is finally complete, he'll fall into a deep depression until he starts working on something else.'

'Many writers are like that,' Katherine murmured.

'I haven't read any of this new book,' the younger woman continued, 'I don't even know what it's about. He tells me it's the best yet.' She looked at Katherine, bright blue eyes searching her face carefully. 'What I'm trying to say, I suppose, is that you'll find him difficult. Probably rude, uncommunicative and moody, maybe even aggressive. He told me you were coming, and seemed almost pleased about it, but he can be very difficult to read sometimes. He may resent your presence.'

'Don't worry, Mrs Hunter . . .'

'Emma, please call me Emma.'

'Emma. Don't worry, Emma. What you've told me is nothing new. Robert is a professional writer, doing a job. I'm sure he'll simply look upon me in the same way.'

Emma nodded. 'I hope he will.' She stood up. 'If you've finished your tea, I'll take you up to him. Tell me,' she asked, 'do you like Bob's work?'

Katherine considered for a moment before answering. 'He's a very powerful writer,' she said eventually, 'but horror is not a genre I'd read for pleasure. What do you think of the books?' she asked in return.

'I think they're disgusting,' Emma said with a quick shake of her head, and then smiled. 'Sometimes it worries me to think that I'm living with a man who has an imagination like that.' She attempted a laugh, but it rang falsely in the early-morning silence. 'It makes me realise that I don't know him at all.'

Chapter Six

'SO you're the woman who's going to save my life? Well, you're younger, and certainly prettier than I'd been expecting.' Robert Hunter smiled, taking the sting from the words as he extended a surprisingly small-fingered hand.

'It's a great pleasure to meet you, Mr Hunter,' Katherine said, slightly breathless after the long climb up to the top of the house.

'Call me Bob. Only my solicitor and bank manager call me Mr Hunter. Here, sit down, get your breath back. Those stairs can be a killer.'

Katherine sank into a hanging wicker chair and attempted to regain her composure. This was obviously a morning for surprises. Having read Hunter's book and from her conversation with Matthews, she'd formed the impression that the writer was a big, robust, vulgar man. Instead, she found herself looking at a rather slender man in his mid-forties. A long, narrow, thin-featured face was topped by iron-grey hair, cropped close to his skull, and an equally sparse beard. His eyes were pale grey, almost colourless, slightly magnified behind circular glasses. He was casually dressed in battered jeans, a stained teeshirt advertising a two-year-old rock concert, and tartan carpet slippers that had seen a lot of wear. Katherine looked around the room, envious of the amount of space.

Robert Hunter's study took up the entire top floor of the house. Two large bedrooms had been knocked together to make one enormous room. Windows at both ends and a large square skylight gave it a bright, airy feel, and the room had been decorated to emphasise the wooden floorboards and original stonework. There were books everywhere. Floor-to-ceiling bookshelves ran the length of the room; broken-spined paperbacks mingled with antique leather-bound volumes, magazines stuck in alongside rows of hardbacks.

There were three long desks in the room. One held Hunter's large computer, printer, phone and fax, while the other two were scattered with open books and magazines.

'You probably think it's a mess,' Hunter said, sitting down in a battered leather armchair opposite Katherine. He stretched out his legs, crossing them at the ankle and folded his hands into his lap.

'On the contrary,' she smiled, 'I imagine you're able to put your hand on any single book or article at a moment's notice.'

Hunter grinned, showing small, slightly uneven teeth. 'That's what I keep saying. But it's only true some of the time.' He shrugged. 'The truth is I hate throwing anything out. You never know when it's going to be useful, so I tend to squirrel things away. I'll have a clear-out soon. Maybe when this book is finished.'

Katherine grasped the opening. 'Well, I'm here to help you do just that. And I'll be out of your way as quickly as possible.'

'Good. I'd appreciate that, Miss Norton.'

'Please call me Katherine. And it's Mrs,' she added. Hunter bowed. 'I know this must be a terrible intrusion, Mr Hunter – Bob,' she corrected herself. 'But I didn't really have much say in the matter. My brief is to render you every assistance to complete the manuscript of *The Earl of Hell* as quickly as possible.'

'I understand that, Katherine. It's just that I'm not used to working with anyone else in the same room as me. It's been too many years since I had a real job.'

'I don't think I'll actually be here as you write,' she smiled. 'I won't be snatching every page as it rolls off your printer. And you won't see a lot of me for the next few days, anyway. First, I'll need to read what you've written so far – and I'll do that at home.'

Hunter nodded. 'Don't get me wrong, Katherine. I don't resent your being here. Far from it. Perhaps you'll help me finish this book, free me of this particular *demon*, if you'll pardon the expression. I think what I resent is being forced to realise that I actually need help. That hurts.'

'You shouldn't look on it that way. I'll simply be doing here and now what would normally take place after delivery of the manuscript to the offices. I'm just shortcutting that process.'

Hunter stood up and strode down the room, his ridiculous carpet slippers flapping slightly on the wooden floor. Katherine hesitated a moment, before easing herself out of the hanging chair and following him.

'I presume you've read my books, Katherine?' he asked without looking around.

'I've just finished *Zodiac*,' she said carefully. 'I haven't read *Tarot* yet.'

Hunter sank into his chair before his large-screen computer. He pulled the keyboard onto his lap, and swivelled around to look at the woman, while his fingers moved swiftly across the keys.

'When Matthews told me he was sending an editor, I thought it would be Chris Kamen. How is Chris?' he asked.

'Chris is fine,' Katherine said cautiously. 'I don't know why you didn't get Chris. Possibly he was busy with another project.'

Hunter's fingers stopped moving on the keys. 'Katherine, I don't need to tell you how many copies of my books have been sold. I have made the Image Press a great deal of money. I don't think – in fact, I *know* – that Image has not got a better-selling nor more important writer on their lists. I expected to find myself working with someone I knew' – he paused and added coldly – 'and someone who knew my work.'

Katherine nodded, lowering her head so he would not see the smile that curled her lips. This was what she had been expecting: an author's ego. While seeming to welcome her, and despite his words to the contrary, Hunter secretly resented her presence.

'I am the best editor Image has,' Katherine said. 'I specialise in top-selling books. In the past two years, I have worked on two bestselling royal biographies, a very controversial Bush biography and a Vatican exposé the Church hierarchy tried to ban. The last fiction writer I edited spent forty-eight weeks on the *New York Times* bestseller list, went on to be published in sixteen languages and motion picture rights were sold for an undisclosed sum, in excess of five million dollars.' Katherine smiled thinly. 'You haven't worked with me before, Mr Hunter, simply because you weren't big enough. You are now.'

Hunter stared at her for a moment, then his fingers

began tapping the keys again, his shoulders shaking, his head nodding. It took her a few moments before she realised that he was laughing softly. When he looked up, his eyes were damp with unshed tears. 'I think we're going to get along fine, you and I.'

'I'm sure we will.'

Katherine Norton spent the next hour transferring copies of Hunter's work onto the small Compaq laptop computer she had brought with her. There was a slight hitch when they discovered that they used two different word-processing programs; Hunter used Wordperfect, while Katherine preferred Wordstar. However, Hunter converted the files to plain ASCII format, which Katherine's program recognised.

Sitting back in a chair with the A4-sized computer on her lap, Katherine created a directory entitled HUNT and dumped all Hunter's files into it. When she ran a word-count, she discovered that he had written just under seventy thousand words; the contract called for one hundred and fifty thousand.

'Less than half-way there,' she said quietly.

Hunter looked up from his own machine. He was busy copying his lists of characters, a timeframe and other relevant notes which he thought might be of some use to the editor. 'I felt sure there would be more. I've put a lot of work into this book,' he said, tapping the keyboard. 'But it didn't come easily. The basic idea of the book is a simple one: raise the devil, bargain with him, then cheat him. Unfortunately, it just wouldn't come straight.'

'Do you have a synopsis?' Katherine asked.

He passed across a single sheet of paper. 'The whole book synopsised into four paragraphs.' He then passed across three A4 pages held together by a paperclip. 'Here's a slightly more complete synopsis. You'll see how I intended to develop the story.'

'Do you have a hard copy of what you've written so far?'

The writer leaned across his desk and lifted a thick bundle of manuscript. 'I can give you this: it's a first draft. It's a bit rough in places, but it'll give you some idea where I'm going with the story.'

'Have you a second or third draft done yet? I don't want to edit stuff you've already corrected.'

'There's a more recent draft still in the machine.'

Katherine nodded. 'I presume that's what you've given me. Would it take long to print up a hard copy?'

Hunter nodded. 'A while.' He did a quick calculation. 'About an hour or so.'

'Leave it then. I can print it up at home. I'll come back to you when I've read what you've written. In the meantime, I would prefer it if you didn't actually do any work on the book.' Hunter looked at her in surprise. 'That doesn't mean I want you to stop writing. I'm sure there must be bits in your book that are generally unrelated to the rest of the story. I noticed in *Zodiac*, for example, that you had little chapters that told mini-stories – which usually ended in someone being killed,' Katherine added with a wry smile.

'I know what you're talking about,' Hunter nodded. 'Body chapters.'

'Perhaps over the next day or two, then, you could write a chapter like that. Give yourself a break from the storyline. Have a bit of fun with a body chapter.'

Hunter nodded again. 'I could do that. In fact I think I'd enjoy doing that.'

'Good.' Katherine copied the new material from the computer's hard disk onto a floppy disk and ejected it from the machine. She held the disk between thumb and forefinger. 'I'll be doing my corrections on floppy. So, instead of my writing to you with suggestions for rewrites, then your doing the new work and sending it back to me, we'll be doing it here. When we're finished, I'll send the disk directly to production, who will format it, print up bromides and send them on to the printers. The printers will have page proofs two days later. You and I will both read through them, make whatever corrections are necessary, and I will personally deliver the corrected proofs to the printers. The finished book will be available two weeks after that.'

'Remarkable,' Hunter shook his head. 'I'm used to seeing my books appear six or nine months after I've delivered to your people.'

Katherine turned off her computer and closed down the screen. 'This is a special book. We're pulling all the stops out for it.' She stood up and slipped the laptop into her briefcase. 'I'll go home, and do some reading. I'll probably phone you tomorrow, and may see you on Thursday.'

Hunter accompanied her to the door, and smiled. 'Enjoy your reading.'

Chapter Seven

THE unmarked car nosed its way through the crowd that had gathered outside the abandoned quayside buildings, drawn by the police, ambulance and fire tenders, red, blue and yellow lights strobing off the walls and the sweating, wide-eyed faces.

The inspector leaned forward, eyes scanning the crowd, looking for familiar faces. It was not unknown for the guilty to return to the scene of the crime to mingle with the crowds, listening to the hushed conversations, taking part in the speculation, enjoying the secret knowledge which he or she alone possessed.

The young driver sounded the horn, attempting to clear a path through the crowd. The onlookers parted slowly, reluctant to give up their hard-won places against the tall mesh fence that surrounded the dilapidated building. In the inspector's experience, the size of a crowd was in direct relation to the horror of the crime . . . and if the size of this crowd was anything to go by, then the initial reports, which had said that this was the worst yet, were probably correct.

In nearly twenty-six years as a police officer, Inspector Margaret Haaren had learned that no matter how graphically incidences of violation and death were described, the descriptions were no match for the awful reality. You learned to deal with it, though; you had to if you wanted to survive in the force. Some officers bottled up their feelings only to explode in sudden senseless rage. Others found solace in alcohol. Some cultivated a cynical detachment bordering on callousness. Exposure to brutality and violent death blunted the sensibilities, but you never got over the initial horror – that sense of shocked outrage. You learned to deal with your feelings, compartmentalise them . . . and then go for lunch.

Somehow she didn't think she'd be eating lunch today.

Sergeant Stuart Miller pulled open the door even before the car had come to a stop. The big West Indian's face was grim, lips drawn into a thin line, and as the inspector climbed out of the car, she caught the sour smell of vomit from the younger man.

'Bad, Stuart?' she murmured.

'They don't get much worse,' the sergeant replied.

The officers and technicians standing outside the building fell silent as Inspector Margaret Haaren approached. Highly respected – though not always well-liked – the inspector enjoyed a formidable reputation in the force. A tall, stocky woman in her early forties, her otherwise plain, almost masculine face was relieved by a pair of startling green eyes. Her short brown hair was cut in a vaguely mannish style. A third-generation police officer, she had never married, and had worked her way up through the force the hard way.

She had come to public notice three years previously when she had shot the mass-murderer Jonathan Frazer. Her reputation had been further enhanced when she had suffered severe injuries while rescuing thirteen newborn babies who had been snatched for an occult ritual. The policewoman had enjoyed a celebrity status in the months that followed, and had appeared in a series of highly successful recruitment campaigns for the Metropolitan Police. She was widely tipped to be the next Chief Inspector.

'What is this place?' she asked, stepping through a rotting, graffiti-scrawled door into a darkened hallway that stank of urine.

'A warehouse, once upon a time,' Stuart Miller said. 'This is the office entrance. The other side opens directly onto the river.'

A suite of small offices was situated off the hall. They had all been vandalised, and the wall of one was streaked with smoke.

'Squatters moved in for a while,' Miller continued. 'Then junkies used it as a shooting gallery. Some of the local working girls used to bring their clients around if they only wanted a quickie.' He opened a door that led out into the warehouse. 'However, about six months ago, the site was bought for redevelopment, and the new owners erected barbed-wire fencing around it. It's been fairly secure since then.'

The two police officers walked across an enormous empty space, reminiscent of an aircraft hanger, footsteps echoing flatly. Broken-paned windows shed a dirty light over the filthy floor, shimmering off oil-scummed puddles. The air was heavy with the stench of the Thames, now overlaid with a sweeter, cloying odour: a mixture of putrefaction, faeces, and urine.

A group of plainclothes officers stood at one end of the wide room, grey wisps of cigarette smoke coiling straight into the air above their heads. An ambulance crew waited patiently behind them, a black body bag opened on the stretcher. The only sound in the unnatural silence was the whirr of the police photographer's flashgun.

Margaret Haaren dug into her pocket and pulled out a small tester bottle of cologne. She smeared some on the ball of her thumb and then rubbed it onto her upper lip, just beneath her nose. Her eyes watered with the sharp, bitter odour, but she knew it was infinitely preferable to what was awaiting her.

She passed the small plastic container to Stuart, who glanced at the label before he too rubbed some in. 'Four-seven-eleven . . . a classic cologne.'

'Healthier than cigarettes,' she remarked. Even non-smoking officers lit up in the presence of an old corpse, to disguise the stink of decay.

The officers turned as the inspector approached, and silently moved aside. The photographer spotted the movement out of the corner of his eye and glanced over his shoulder. Seeing the inspector, he stepped away from the back wall; for the first time Haaren caught sight of the body.

The reports had been wrong. They said it was bad, but it was worse . . . much worse.

The inspector dug her hands into her pockets so that the other officers wouldn't see her fingers curling into tight fists. Her square face remained impassive; only her eyes betrayed her revulsion.

She took care to breathe through her nose, the sharp Four-seven-eleven not quite disguising the bitter-sweet stench. Haaren crouched down before a crucified corpse.

It was impossible to guess the woman's age: she could have been anything from twenty to thirty. Most of the flesh on her face was gone, carefully lifted away to reveal the muscle and sinews beneath. Her eyes were missing and, in the black hole of her mouth, the inspector could see the bloodied stump of the tongue. Her throat had been torn open in three savage gashes –

41

the killer was left-handed, the inspector realised – but the woman had been long dead before she had been crucified upside down with long masonry nails driven into the wrists and crossed-over ankles. Her body was unmarked, except for the occult symbols carved into the flesh of her breasts . . . and the gaping holes where the nipples had been bitten off.

Haaren lifted a series of polaroids out of her pocket. They showed five female breasts, all of them carved with the curling, twisting and circular symbols, and in each case the nipples were missing. The symbols were identical.

Straightening, the inspector deliberately turned her back on the corpse, forcing the officers to look at her. 'What do we have, gentlemen?' she asked, her voice rock steady.

'She wasn't killed here,' Miller replied.

Haaren nodded. There was no blood beneath the corpse.

'Any local people reported missing?' the inspector asked.

'We're looking into that now, ma'am,' one of the older men said.

'Who reported the incident?'

'A security guard,' Miller said. 'He calls on this place once a week. When he saw the body he put a call in to his office, and they called the police, fire and ambulance.'

'I was wondering where they'd all come from,' Haaren muttered.

'He's down at the station now. I thought you'd like to speak to him yourself.'

Haaren looked over the assembled officers, and nodded at the two ambulancemen to include them in her statement. 'I don't think I need remind you that there is a press blackout on this case. If I discover any leaks, I will personally bring disciplinary charges against the officer concerned. Someone tell our two friends from the ambulance service that this case is covered by the Official Secrets Act.'

She turned around to look at the corpse again, fixing it in her memory, absorbing the surroundings. In the weeks and months to come, she would close her eyes and visualise this stinking warehouse with its desecrated human body; she would still be able to recall her anger. When every other aspect of the case had faded, the anger would remain. She would use that anger – that energy – to drive her on to solve this case, and bring the murderer to justice.

'How many is this, Stuart?' she asked, as they moved away from the body.

'Six,' the sergeant said, although he was aware that the inspector knew the answer.

'One a month for the last six months, all women, all with the flesh gone from their faces, and those symbols cut into their breasts.'

'The full moon was six nights ago,' the sergeant reminded her. Forensics had placed the five previous murders on the nights of the full moon.

'Nothing further on the occult symbols?' she asked.

'Mostly signs of the zodiac; you'll find them in every newspaper and women's magazine,' he shrugged. 'We haven't been able to identify the others.' He allowed the inspector to precede him up the metal stairs. 'I think you should know that the lads at the station have a name for this case . . .' he began.

'I'm not sure I even want to know . . .' The inspector sighed. It was difficult enough keeping the lid on this case; the press knew something was up and were sniffing around. The last thing she wanted was the killer seeing some fancy name splashed across the tabloids. She pulled open the door that led into the offices. 'What is it?' she asked, when the sergeant said nothing.

'The Horror-Scope Killings.'

Chapter Eight

'AND how was the beast of Eaton Square?' Tony Matthews sounded jovial, but Katherine detected an underlying tension in his voice.

'Very charming, actually.' Tucking the portable phone in beneath her ear, she carried the kettle over to the sink. She looked at the breakfast dishes still piled in the sink, and felt the first flickerings of anger. 'Very professional.'

'So you got on well with him?'

'Fine. Hang on a sec'.' She waited while the kettle filled, then plugged it in before returning to the call. She knew she'd get a call from the publisher some time during the day; she just wasn't expecting him to ring the moment she stepped in through the front door.

She went on. 'There was a slight moment of unpleasantness when he asked why Chris Kamen wasn't doing the editing.'

'And what did you tell him?' Matthews asked.

Katherine shrugged out of her linen jacket. 'I told him I was a better editor than Chris.'

Matthews laughed wheezily. 'Good answer.'

'Now tell me why Chris *isn't* editing,' she said.

'Well, you *are* the best . . .' Matthews began.

'The truth, Tony,' Katherine snapped. 'Come on, you owe me that. Chris is a damn good editor, he's used to Hunter's work and he's read a damn sight more horror than I have. He's far more qualified for the job than I am.'

Matthews sighed down the phone. 'I'll admit it, he was my first choice – but only because he knew Hunter's work,' he added.

'So why didn't he do it?' she persisted. She tossed her coat over the back of a chair and stepped out of her low heels, pressing her hot feet onto the cool lino. Catching her shoes in her hooked fingers, she made her way upstairs. She knew the portable phone would buzz and fade on the stairs and infuriate Matthews. 'I can't hear you,' she said when Tony started speaking.

'I was saying that Chris told me he wanted a break from Hunter's books. I did the best I could to persuade him, but he was adamant he wasn't working on the new book. I'm only speculating now, but I think he might have had an argument with the writer.'

'Hunter didn't seem to think so,' Katherine said slowly. She opened the bedroom door, and was vaguely disappointed – though not entirely surprised – to find Peter still in bed. Lately he'd taken to returning to bed when the children had gone to school. He rolled over and opened his eyes, blinking short-sightedly at her.

'How much work has Hunter done on the book?' Matthews asked quickly, in a transparent attempt to change the subject.

'Just under seventy thousand is almost ready to go,' she said, making a mental note to drop into the office soon and speak to Chris Kamen personally.

'Jesus, that's not even half-way!'

Katherine unzipped her skirt and allowed it to puddle around her feet. Stepping out of it, she began unbuttoning her blouse, juggling the phone from ear to ear. 'Apparently, he's got a lot of the work done. I'd imagine it's simply a matter of organising it and then putting the words down on paper. I'll have a better idea what to do with it when I've managed to read what he's done so far.'

'You'll keep in touch?' Matthews said, almost anxiously.

'Every day, Tony. Goodbye.' She turned the phone off before Matthews could say anything else and tossed it on the bed.

Peter sat up, running his fingers through his thinning grey hair, pulling it back off his face. He groped on the bedside locker and found his glasses. 'How did it go?' he asked.

'Fine,' Katherine said shortly, unable to disguise the annoyance in her voice. 'I thought you'd at least have had the breakfast dishes done.' She pulled off her blouse and dropped it on the end of the bed. Unselfconsciously, she unclipped her bra, pulled down her panties and walked naked from the bedroom.

Peter followed her. She could see his distorted reflection through the frosted glass of the shower stall and knew that any moment he was going to slide open the door and step in with her.

Turning on the water, she mixed it down to tepid and turned it up full, allowing the stinging jets to wash away the city grime. The Tube always made her feel dirty. She pulled her short hair back, and tilted her face to the water, closing her eyes, feeling it pound off her eyelids and run in rivulets down her cheeks.

The shower door clicked open. Cool, smooth-skinned hands slid around her body to cup her breasts, thumbs pressing against her nipples.

Long, filthy nails pinching the hard points, digging deeply, tearing them from her body . . .

Katherine jerked suddenly, slapping her husband's hands away, her heart racing. 'Not now, Peter. I haven't got the time,' she said. Then, deliberately, she added, 'I've got work to do.'

Peter backed out of the shower. She saw the hurt in his eyes, the wounded look on his face, and felt her own anger swell. She reached out – saw him begin to smile – and pulled the door closed. He stood in the bathroom for a few seconds, then turned away.

Katherine squeezed liquid shower gel onto her hands and began scrubbing furiously at her shoulders and across her chest. Christ, he needed a good kick in the arse. OK, he had lost his job. So had countless thousand others. And at least they were better off than a lot of other families in the same boat. And she had a job. So, while their standard of living had fallen, at least the change in circumstances wasn't as dramatic as it could have been; they weren't going to lose the house or anything like that. But there was no way she was going to be able to hold down a job and do the housework at the same time. She had supported Peter – now he needed to support her. If she was going to bring this book in under the deadline, she'd need time to herself, to devote to the manuscript. She knew he'd probably sulk about it, but once Hunter's book was finished and they went on that holiday, he'd thank her for it. Katherine nodded fiercely; that's what they needed now: a holiday.

Peter Norton pressed his fingers to the kettle. The hot metal stung his flesh. 'Fuck!' Katherine had obviously filled it before coming upstairs. He held his fingers under the cold tap and stared out into the garden, blinking in the brilliant noonday sun.

Katherine's words had hurt. Maybe she hadn't

meant to sound quite so harsh, but she had still hurt. It wasn't his fault he was unemployed. He had worked all his life, going out to work when he was sixteen when his father had died, supporting his mother, brothers and sisters, continuing his studies at night. His whole life had been regulated by his work, clocking in, clocking out, one hour for lunch, fifteen minutes' break in the morning, fifteen in the afternoon, the seven-fifty train in the morning, or the eight-ten if he missed that, then the five-thirty train, or the six-ten in the evening. All his friends were associated with his work, friends he played squash with, swapped books and CDs with, gossiped with, went out once a week with to a club in Soho.

And when he lost his job, all of that stopped. He hadn't just lost a job, he had lost a way of life.

The whole rhythm of his life changed dramatically. He no longer had a reason to get up in the morning, to wash and shave, bolt down a minimal breakfast and race for the Tube. He missed wandering around the city at lunchtime, keeping up to date on the magazines, books and CDs. He missed his friends. Friends – shit, none of them had even bothered phoning since he left the job.

He felt tired a lot of the time, bone-weary with a heavy sleepiness behind his eyes. He knew it was a lack of exercise. Unconsciously, he patted his stomach; he was putting on weight, too.

'We have decided that cutbacks are necessary . . .'

Nice, safe phrases, the little bald bastard not looking at him as he'd passed across the single sheet of typed paper. 'Cutbacks are necessary . . .'

They weren't letting him go because of cutbacks. The new owners were disposing of him because he knew too much about the old business, because they feared his knowledge about the deals, the backhanders.

'Cutbacks . . .'

They weren't cutting back, they were cutting him out. Now he was dependent on his wife to go out and earn a living. Little by little his manhood, his pride, was being stripped away from him. And that look in her eye when he'd reached for her in the shower, that look of loathing . . .

Peter poured hot water into a fat-bellied teapot, swilled it around and emptied it into the sink. He added two spoonfuls of Earl Grey, then poured water in on top of it. He disliked the slightly scented tea, but it was Katherine's favourite and he was making it for her sake. He suddenly wondered if there were many things she did for him which she disliked.

He reached for the mugs hanging on their hooks over the sink when he caught sight of Robert Hunter's *Zodiac*. It had been stuck in on top of the cookbooks on the top shelf. He pulled it out and looked at the cover. An embossed silver Zodiacal wheel dripped blood onto a background of stars and astrological symbols. Hunter's name and title, the Master of Terror, had been picked out in silver lettering. There were quotes on the back from Stephen King, Clive Barker, Dean R. Koontz and James Herbert. The names meant nothing to Peter, except Stephen King's, but he guessed that the others were also horror writers. Peter didn't read horror . . . nor did Katherine; with so much good literature around, why waste time with this shit?

He stood on the pedal bin, popping open the top, holding the book over the milky remains of soggy cornflakes and crusts of burnt toast. This piece of sickening rubbish had actually given Katherine nightmares . . . and yet now here she was actually editing this writer's new book.

She hadn't wanted to. But she'd been forced to. Because he had no job.

Peter Norton pushed the thought away and looked at the cover again. He hadn't read a book in a long time.

Chapter Nine

WITH infinite precision, he pressed the blade of the razor into the woman's breasts. The skin parted silently, the wound opening up like a flower blossoming. She had been dead for three days now, so there was no blood, only a pale, viscous fluid.

With quick, deft strokes, he began to carve the signs of the zodiac into the blue-white skin. When he was finished, he pressed his lips to the wounds, breathing into them, whispering the myriad names of God into the cuts, bringing the magical zodiacal signs to life.

When he could feel the corpse trembling with magical life, he completed the ritual and bit off the nipples, then added them to the others piled onto the flat metal plate.

The scales were ancient, the brass thickly coated with verdigris which almost concealed the ornate scrollwork on the metal. He had bought them in an antique shop on a day-trip to Brittany, paying a wizened crone way over the odds for them. He had always promised to come back and pay her . . . in full.

But the scales were necessary.

Libra, the Scales.

Like a miser counting out coins, he carefully lifted the plate of severed nipples and slid them onto the scales. The older pieces of flesh had shrivelled and dried to twisted, dark nuts, and were practically weightless. But the weight was important. He was bitterly disappointed when he added the one-pound weight to the opposite scale and looked at the imbalance. He was going to need much more flesh to balance the scales.

The devil wanted his pound of flesh . . . and only the tastiest morsels were acceptable.

Chapter Ten

MARGARET Haaren moved around the small, cramped office she had been given for the duration of the investigation, opening the windows, allowing sluggish air into the hot, dusty atmosphere.

Why did every police station smell of coffee and sweat?

She took off her jacket and tossed it over the back of the chair, then grimaced at the damp patches beneath the arms of her blouse. With a sigh, she pulled the jacket back on. So much for the deodorant that works as hard as you do. Then again, looking at a week-old corpse probably wasn't one of the many things its designers had counted on.

A WPC tapped on the open door and looked in. 'Records sent these up, ma'am.'

'Thank you . . .' The inspector didn't remember the constable's name. 'Thank you. Any chance of a cup of tea?' she asked quickly as the WPC placed a thick file of brown folders on the corner of the desk.

'Yes, ma'am, of course,' the WPC said.

Margaret Haaren saw the brief flicker of resentment in the young woman's eyes as she turned away. 'I would have made the same request if it had been a male constable,' she said.

Colour touched the WPC's cheeks. The inspector

had read her mind: she resented being asked to make a cup of tea. She hadn't joined the police force to be a skivvy, but seemed to spend a lot of the day making tea and coffee for fellow officers or distraught women, with damn-all real police work in there.

'Something to get the taste of a week-old corpse out of my mouth,' the inspector added, in the same quiet voice, sinking into the creaking swivel chair.

'Yes, ma'am. Sorry,' the WPC said.

The inspector waited until the young woman had left the room before turning to the files. She had ordered a search on all possible combinations of sex/occult/ritual killings in the past three years, which contained at least two of the things unique to the case: the fact that the corpses were kept for a period of three to six days before being mutilated, the type of mutilations, the lunar cycle, the use of a knife, and the curious anomaly that, despite the sexual nature of the crime and mutilations, none of the women had actually been sexually assaulted.

The inspector ran her index finger down the files, quickly counting them: twenty-two. Dearest Jesus, twenty-two files, twenty-two killers, and each had killed at least once. How many ruined lives did this pile of folders represent? When a killer took a life, they took more than the life of the victim: the lives of family and friends were irrevocably altered, sometimes destroyed.

The WPC returned and set a steaming mug of tea down in front of the files. The inspector smiled her thanks.

Margaret Haaren had been five years in the force before she had seen her first dead body, and even then it was a case of natural causes, an old woman who had died peacefully in her bed. But the times had changed, the crimes had changed; in the last few years, she had been viewing bodies with monotonous regularity.

Sipping the tea, scalding her tongue on the thick liquid, she lifted the first folder off the pile.

Two hours later, she had managed to whittle the pile down to eleven. Of the twenty-two convicted murderers, twenty were male, the remaining two were women, both convicted of sacrificing their own children in satanic rites. Both were in their teens.

Some had been easy enough to dismiss. Six of the males were black or Asian. Studies had shown that serial killers tended to hunt within their own ethnic group, and so far all the victims had been white. Of the remaining group of fourteen, three were under five-foot seven, and the autopsy reports had concluded that, judging from the angle of the knife thrust into the throat – the fatal blow – the killer was at least six feet tall.

That left eleven. Realistically, she knew that the chances of any of these eleven being guilty were very slim, but at the moment, they had nothing else to go on. Of the five identified victims, there were two students, a waitress, a supermarket check-out girl and a clerical assistant in an insurance office. And now one more. Haaren wondered who this poor woman had been. In her cabinet, she had files on the five dead women, and in the last six months she had come to know them intimately. She didn't relish adding another file to the bundle.

A dark-skinned shape loomed up outside the frosted glass door.

'Come in, Stuart,' she called before he had time to knock.

The West Indian smiled broadly as he stepped into the office. 'That's a great trick.'

'Only works with people of colour,' she smiled. She pushed the eleven folders across the desk in front of her sergeant. 'Bring this lot in for questioning. They've all been involved in similar crimes at one time or another. They've all served time, but what terrifies me,' she added, 'is that they were allowed out again.'

'I'll get on it right away.'

'Have we discovered anything about the victim yet?'

'Nothing.' Miller glanced at his watch. 'Autopsy's in about an hour. Do you want to be there?'

'No, I don't. But I don't think I've any choice,' she sighed.

'We're still holding the security guard who discovered the body,' Miller continued. 'You said you wanted to speak to him . . .'

'I suppose I should do it now. How's he holding up?'

'He's ex-Army. Did two tours in Northern Ireland, seen a couple of dead bodies over there, so on the whole, I'd say he's in pretty good shape.' Haaren got up, and moved towards the door. The sergeant held it open, allowing her to precede him out into the controlled chaos of the outer office. They threaded their way through the maze of desks and filing cabinets into a long, brightly lit corridor.

'We're going to get a lot of heat from this one,' Haaren said. 'Six bodies and we're no closer to solving the crime than we were six months ago.'

Miller nodded. 'And the chances of keeping details from the press become slimmer with every crime. They'll have a field day when the news breaks. The fact that you're heading up the investigation will spark all sorts of speculation.'

'I know. I didn't want to take this case for that very reason, but the chief insisted.'

'Maybe we'll get a break with this body.'
'God knows, we deserve one.'

Three of the four interview rooms were busy, sobbing, shouts and laughter dimly audible as they walked past. The inspector had long ago realised that it was possible to experience or witness the full range of human emotions in any one day in a busy city-centre police station. She presumed that was true if the station was in London, New York or Hong Kong.

Sergeant Miller pushed open the door of the last interview room and followed the inspector into the room. Two men, both in blue uniforms, came to their feet. The inspector smiled; the security guard's uniform was almost identical to the constable's.

'This is Jeff Nichols, who discovered the body in the warehouse. Mr Nichols, this is Inspector Margaret Haaren.'

The inspector saw the guard's eyes widen as he recognised the name. His handshake was firm and confident.

'It's a great pleasure to meet you, inspector. I've read about you, of course. I wrote you a card when you rescued those babies, bravest thing I ever heard.'

'Thank you very much, Mr Nichols . . .' There had been hundreds of cards.

'Jeff, call me Jeff.'

'Jeff.' He was older than she expected, late forties, or early fifties, and even if she hadn't known he was a soldier she could have guessed his military background. His iron-grey hair was very short and he sat ramrod straight in the uncomfortable plastic chair. 'Before we begin, I want to thank you, Mr Nichols – Jeff – for agreeing to help us.'

Nichols nodded curtly. His eyes were the same

colour as his hair, she noted.

'Would you like some tea . . . coffee?'

'Nothing, ma'am.' His hands, big and square, were clasped on the table in front of him.

'Would you have any objections if we taped this interview?'

'None at all. I take it,' he smiled, 'that this is not the first of these bodies to have turned up?'

'What makes you say that, Mr Nichols?' the inspector asked, not looking at him, pretending to fiddle with the controls on the double-cassette recorder.

'You're very organised,' he shrugged. 'I was an Army man for thirty years. I know enough about organisations to know when they're caught on the hop . . . and also when they're simply waiting for something to happen. It was like that in Northern Ireland,' he added. 'You knew that sooner or later there was going to be a bomb; so everything was in place waiting for that bomb to explode. I saw the way the police moved into the warehouse; everything was in place.'

Haaren smiled. 'You're very perceptive. And, off the record, you're right. This is not the first body. Young women murdered and mutilated in the way you saw today. However, this case is covered by the Official Secrets Act. As a soldier, you will be aware of the need for secrecy to avoid panic and also to prevent operational details from becoming public.'

Nichols nodded curtly. 'I understand.'

'I would like you to tell us in your own words exactly what you saw today. Please include anything which you feel might be useful, no matter how incidental.'

'Yes, ma'am. My name is Jeffrey Nichols, and I'm a security guard in Four Square Security. I've worked with them since I left the Army three years ago. Four Square have a policy of employing ex-Army men,' he added. 'We're trained, disciplined, and used to taking orders.' The inspector nodded, encouraging him to go on. 'I have a mobile patrol which covers sixty properties across London. These properties are reasonably low priority, empty office blocks, tenement housing, warehouses, derelict factories. Most of these properties will eventually be pulled down and the sites built upon. I visit the warehouse at least once a week. It's really just a matter of ensuring that there are no vandals or junkies hanging around and with a big warehouse, like the one in question, there's always a possibility that it could be used for one of these house parties or raves.

'When I visited the warehouse a week ago – that would be Monday, the first of the month – I noticed that the wire mesh over the door had been cut. I made a thorough search of the building, but it was empty and there were no signs that the building had been entered. I wrote up the incident, reported it in, repaired the mesh, and resolved to pay more attention to the place, but a bunch of students moved into one of my other properties in Hackney, and it took me a couple of days to eject them.

'When I got to the warehouse at about nine this morning, I noticed that the mesh had been cut again. I dismissed it as nothing more than kids, messing. I was making my inspection, checking through the building, when I spotted the *thing* on the warehouse floor. I think it was the smell which alerted me even before I got close: if you've breathed it in once, it's a smell that never leaves you. I radioed in on my walkie-talkie, told them I'd discovered a dead body – but I didn't give any details,' he added quickly. 'I asked them to phone the police.' Nichols shrugged. 'That's it. Sorry I can't be more helpful.'

'On the contrary, Mr Nichols – Jeff – you've been most helpful.' Haaren came to her feet, reached across and shook the older man's hand.

'How?' he asked blankly.

'We may speak to you again,' she said, ignoring the question, and stepped outside the door. Miller followed her. 'What did I miss?' he asked her.

'The warehouse was interfered with a week ago – before the body was deposited there. That was obviously our murderer checking the place out. All the victims have been discovered in derelict buildings. We assumed the buildings were chosen at random ... obviously, they weren't. Let's start looking at the buildings, eh, see if we can establish some sort of pattern. Let's assume our friend won't want to carry a body too far from the killing ground.'

Miller shrugged. 'It's a long shot.'

'We haven't got any other.'

Chapter Eleven

THE intercom on the wall buzzed. 'It's nearly seven, Bob.'

Robert Hunter looked at the square plastic box. 'Seven?' he repeated. His thoughts were muddled, bloody images from the chapter he'd just written still confusing him.

'It's Tuesday night,' Emma reminded him. 'Didn't your magic-machine warn you?'

Leaning across the table, he thumbed the call button. 'I'm shutting down the machine now, love. And no, my magic-machine didn't warn me. Katherine Norton was transferring files off this machine at around the time the alarm should have gone off. We've got plenty of time. Anyway,' he added, 'Carlo'll keep our table.' He released the call button and Emma's voice crackled back.

'I want to hear the machine go off now.'

'Listen carefully.' Hunter parked the hard disk, then turned off the screen and processor. It powered down with a long descending whine. 'Satisfied?'

'Satisfied.'

Hunter sat for a few moments staring at the blank screen. He could still see the words glowing, fading slowly, some words lingering . . .

Blood . . .

Knife . . .
Sacrifice . . .

Hunter squeezed his eyes shut and looked away. He knew it was nothing more than overtired eyes. Propping his elbows up on the chair, he rested his chin on interlaced hands. The room seemed unnaturally silent after the constant humming of the machine. Faintly, very faintly, he could hear children's high-pitched giggles.

The writer shuddered suddenly. The sound reminded him of . . . something else. Shaking his head, still hearing the echoes of the laughter, he stood and pressed his hands into the small of his back, rotating his head and shoulders, easing stiffened muscles. Usually, he tried to avoid sitting at the machine for too long, but he had taken Katherine's advice and written a self-contained chapter that had no reference to the characters and situations in the rest of the book: chapters where someone was violently and graphically killed – body chapters.

Hunter's books always had a high body count. This afternoon, in two thousand five hundred words, he had brutally and descriptively butchered an innocent young woman. He had actually written the scene where the murderer bit off her nipples when he realised that he'd used that trick in *Zodiac*. He grinned, smiling humourlessly: he had reached the stage where he was now plagiarising himself. Anyway, how many new ways were there to kill a human being?

Leaning over his machine, he turned the key on the processor, locking the computer. Although the machine was password protected, he didn't like to take any chances: this machine contained his entire life. He popped the key into the empty eye-socket of a shrunken head pinned to the side of a bookshelf. It was probably the last place anyone would look – and certainly the last place they'd stick their finger. Pausing to take a look round the room before he left, he checked that the fax and answering machine were on before pulling the door shut behind him and locking it. He knew DeeDee, their babysitter, occasionally brought a boyfriend along with her; he didn't want anyone wandering around his room.

Emma was in the bedroom when he got there, standing in white cotton bra and panties while she fiddled with her hair. Robert came up behind her, running his small hands across her flat stomach, moving up to cup her breasts.

'DeeDee's here,' Emma said, ignoring him.

Robert bent his head to nuzzle at her neck, tasting the soft, scented flesh. Emma twitched and wriggled away, strands of hair coiling down around her shoulders.

'Now look what you've made me do!' She pushed him away playfully. 'Come on, it's nearly twenty-past.'

Undressing quickly, Hunter stepped into the en suite shower and turned it on full, lifting his face to the water, then turning around, allowing the lukewarm needle spray to massage his neck and shoulders. Images from his day's writing flickered at the edges of his consciousness. He allowed them to come, knowing that if he attempted to shut them out, they would bother him for the rest of the evening.

The scene where the young woman stood at the top of the stairs, knowing that someone was in the room downstairs needed to be worked upon. It was too short. He needed to concentrate on her fear . . .

The killer's perception needed to be heightened; he needed to be able to smell her . . .

The mutilation of the body needed a new twist,

something unusual, something unnatural . . .

'You're daydreaming!'

The images fled, faces of killer and victim blending together, dissolving into a bizarre, eyeless mask. He turned off the shower, then stood for a moment while water coiled from his body and dripped onto the tiles. He smiled suddenly: he hadn't written a shower scene for a long time. Maybe one of the victims turning on the shower and blood, thick and viscous, pouring down . . . He nodded; he liked that.

'Robert!'

'I'm coming.'

Stepping out of the shower, Hunter plucked a towel off the rail and rubbed vigorously at his thin body. His wet feet left perfect footprints on the white bedroom carpet. 'I'm paid to daydream,' he said. 'This house was bought and paid for with a daydream.'

'A nightmare, more like,' Emma said. She was sitting in front of her dressing table, applying dark eyeliner. 'Don't you ever have nightmares, Bob?'

He crouched down and rested his chin on her shoulder, staring at her in the mirror. 'Never,' he said simply, 'I sleep the sleep of the innocent, completely at peace with the world. I just give other people nightmares.' He kissed her shoulder.

Hunter dressed quickly in a casual, open-necked shirt, slacks and a light cotton jacket. Emma was more formally dressed in a light, two-piece emerald-green cotton suit. As they left the bedroom, Hunter locked the door behind him. Emma saw him slipping the key into his pocket.

'You're paranoid,' she whispered.

'Not paranoid, just practical.' He had no illusions about the babysitter; DeeDee came highly recommended, with good references from the neighbours who used her . . . but she was only sixteen, with all the idle curiosity of a sixteen year old. He knew she wandered around the house when they were out because Violet, his elder daughter, had told them so. He'd no doubts that she'd tried to get into his room.

Hunter waited by the open hall door while Emma looked into the kitchen where DeeDee and the girls were watching TV. 'Bed by eight at the latest,' she said. 'We'll be back around ten, DeeDee.'

'All set?' Hunter asked.

Emma tucked a purse beneath her arm. 'I'm ready.'

The square was quiet, with little traffic and few passers-by. The Hunters made a handsome couple as they strolled arm in arm across Eaton Square, making for Elizabeth Street. A maroon taxi slowed as it drove past, pulling away when Hunter waved it on.

'Did you get much work done today?'

'Some. A chapter, in fact.'

'That's good,' Emma said. Lately Robert had only been managing a couple of hundred words.

'It was an idea that editor gave me,' Hunter continued. 'She suggested I stay away from the main story and write a self-contained chapter – almost like a short story. So I did.'

'When did she say she'd be back?' Emma asked.

'A couple of days. She wanted time to read what I've written so far. Then she'll come back with some suggestions about how I should continue.'

'She seemed like a nice lady. Will you be able to work with her?' Emma was unable to keep the tone of concern out of her voice.

Hunter squeezed her hand. 'I will. And, according to her, it'll be all over in a month.'

'And this is the last book, Robert?' Emma asked anxiously.

'I swear it,' he said solemnly. He was about to say more when Emma suddenly pointed to the red-white-and-green striped Italian flag draped across the windows of Little Italy.

'There must be something special on tonight.'

Carlo Cipriano hurried forward to greet them both, his hands extended. Although he had come to England at the age of four, he still spoke English with a strong Italian accent. Robert was quite sure it was put on, and almost expected him to slip into a Cockney twang at a moment's notice.

'My friends. It's good to see you both.'

'You don't have to sound so surprised, Carlo,' Robert said with a grin, 'we've come here practically every Tuesday night for the past four years.'

'My most loyal customers, my best friends.' The tall, elegant Italian swept up Emma's hand, pressing the back of her fingers to his lips.

'We actually thought you were closed when we saw the sign up on the door,' Emma said.

'We are. Tonight is for family . . . and a few close friends. Tonight is a special night,' he continued, dark eyes sparkling. 'Tonight, my mother has come from Roma to see how her son is doing in this country. You must meet her.' He led them through the untidy jumble of small circular tables towards the window where a large square table had been set up. All the tables were piled high with food and bottles, and the room was filled to capacity with voluble Italians. Some looked curiously at the newcomers.

'Silence, my friends, silence, please.' The hubbub gradually diminished, though from the kitchen Gino the chef continued to sing at the top of his voice, unaware that the noise outside wasn't drowning him out. 'I would like to introduce some special friends.'

The crowd before the large table slowly parted to reveal a small, white-haired woman in a plain grey dress. Her skin was deeply tanned and so wrinkled that it was almost impossible to guess her original appearance. Her snow-white hair was pulled back severely off her head, emphasising her dancing eyes. Her pupils were tiny, polished black marbles surrounded by yellow-tinged whites. They drifted over the newcomers . . . and fixed on Robert Hunter's face.

Carlo turned to Hunter and Emma. 'You will excuse me if I speak Italian. Mamma doesn't speak any English.'

'Of course,' Hunter murmured. He was watching the expression on the old woman's face, something about her fixed expression disturbing him, reminding him of something he'd encountered only once before.

'Mamma, I would like you to meet two of my closest friends. Every week, every Tuesday night, for the past four years, they have come to my little restaurant . . .'

The Hunters were almost up to the table now, with fixed, slightly embarrassed smiles on both their faces.

'They come to my home for Christmas, they invite me to their home for Christmas . . .'

With a sudden jerky movement, the old woman came to her feet. A glass of red wine toppled over, staining the linen table-cloth a deep bruise-coloured purple.

'Mamma . . .?' Carlo began.

But the old woman ignored him. Leaning across the table, she spat in Robert Hunter's face.

Chapter Twelve

'BOB . . . Bob . . . What happened?' Emma hurried to catch up with her husband, high heels skidding on the pavement.

'Nothing happened,' Hunter snapped, 'the old woman had too much to drink, or she's senile.' He scrubbed at the thread of sticky saliva on his cheek with a paper tissue, then tossed it into a litter bin.

'But the look on her face. Did you see it? She was . . . I don't know. She looked terrified,' Emma whispered, remembering what she'd seen on the old woman's face: terror. And there was something else . . .

'A senile old woman, nothing more!' Hunter said icily.

'It was almost as if she recognised you.'

'She thought she recognised me. She mistook me for someone else. Obviously someone she doesn't much care for,' he added wryly. He was breathing deeply, great gulps of the warm London air, attempting to calm his flapping heart and still the cold, bubbling rage that had exploded inside him.

'And what did she do with her hands?' Emma persisted. 'When she shook her fist at you?'

Hunter stopped and caught his wife's arm, turning her to face him. 'I didn't see that. What did she do? Show me!'

Emma shrugged. 'She made some sort of fist with two fingers pointing out at you. Like this.' Closing her left hand into a tight fist, she extended the index and last fingers straight out, pointing them at Hunter. He flinched, as if she'd struck him, caught her hand and gently folded away her pointing fingers.

'What does it mean?' she asked.

'I don't know,' he lied, 'I've never seen anything like it before in my life.'

DeeDee was standing at the door when they turned into the small square. A long-haired youth was standing on the doorstep, both hands dug deeply into the pockets of baggy jeans.

The babysitter stiffened when she spotted the Hunters and muttered something to the youth that made him turn.

Both Hunter and Emma saw the look of disappointment that flowed across his face when he spotted them.

'Is everything all right, Mrs Hunter?' DeeDee asked quickly.

'The restaurant was closed. A family celebration,' Emma said. 'Carlo wanted us to stay, but under the circumstances . . .'

The young woman nodded. Her eyes flickered nervously from her boyfriend to the writer. She was still very much in awe of Robert Hunter, with his cold, watery eyes and chilly smile. And he didn't look at her the way a normal man would. There had been days when she'd come to the house wearing tops and cut-off jeans that showed a lot of flesh – and while a normal man wouldn't have been able to take his eyes off her, Hunter's eyes had slid over her as if she hadn't been there. He was married, so she didn't think he was gay – though you could never tell nowadays – but it had only begun to make sense when her boyfriend had persuaded her to read some of Hunter's books. In the two books she'd read, the women were all treated the same way: used, abused, then mutilated and killed.

As they came up the steps, the long-haired youth stuck out a hand. 'Mr Hunter . . .' He pulled a slightly dog-eared paperback from his back pocket. 'I'm Matthew Elliot; I'm a great fan of yours. I've read everything from *The Possessed* right up to *Zodiac*.'

Emma smiled at them as she went into the house, then shot a warning glance at Hunter. She knew he was often incredibly rude to his fans, but she didn't want him upsetting the babysitter. Reliable babysitters were hard to find.

Hunter looked at the young man, saying nothing. Elliot was sixteen or seventeen, his educated accent belying his scruffy jeans and sneakers and the wrinkled Greenpeace teeshirt.

The young man glanced sidelong at DeeDee. 'I mean, I think you're the best,' he tried again. 'Better than King, better than Barker . . .'

Hunter silently took the book out of the young man's hand, turning it over to look at the cover: the American edition of *October Moon* – his fifth, sixth book? – a snarling beast-man's face glowering from a full moon.

'That's my favourite. Maybe because it's the first I read.'

Hunter nodded, trying desperately hard to remember the plot. Something about a werewolf . . . 'I remember it well,' he said, looking into the boy's dark eyes. 'It's one of my personal favourites.'

'I don't know how many times I've read it. Four, five, more probably. I've been giving your books to

DeeDee. I mean, when you're working for a celebrity, you should know what he writes, that's what I say.' Hunter could almost see the boy swelling with pride; what a story he was going to have for his friends tomorrow.

'And what does DeeDee say?' Hunter asked, turning to look at the babysitter. 'What do you think of my books?'

The young woman couldn't disguise the quick flicker of disgust – of fear – that darted into her eyes. 'I've only read two, Mr Hunter,' she said. From behind her Emma's voice echoed slightly as she chased the two girls into bed.

'Which two?' He was watching her now, his pale eyes locked onto her face, reading her every expression, perversely enjoying her embarrassment.

'*Zodiac* and *Blood Passion*,' she said quietly.

'The serial killer and the lesbian vampires,' Hunter murmured, smiling at Elliot to include him in the private joke. 'Nice, light, bedtime reading. And what did you think of them? You can be honest with me. Writers have very thick skins,' he added.

'They were very ... powerful,' the girl said eventually.

'I think I'll take that as a compliment.' He was about to hand the book back to Elliot when the youth asked, 'Would you sign it for me, please? I'd be very honoured.' He pulled a pen from his pocket.

Robert folded open the cover and scribbled, '*To Matthew, a lifelong fan. Till death us do part.*' I'll leave you two to your chat. We won't be needing you tonight, DeeDee,' he said, pulling out a five-pound note and a pound coin. 'However, it's not your fault, so here's your pay.' He nodded at Elliot, who was still reading the dedication, a wide grin on his narrow face, before stepping into the hall and closing the door behind him. Emma was standing on the stairs.

'Where's DeeDee?'

'I've paid her,' he said shortly.

'Where are you going?'

Hunter looked surprised. 'Work, of course.' He walked away before he could see the hurt look in Emma's eyes.

The long study was hot and still, dust motes circling in the slanting sunlight coming in through the window at the front of the house. For an instant he got the impression that the room had just been vacated; he thought he smelled the faintest hint of . . . perfume . . . flowers. He shook his head quickly, convincing himself that it was the perfume of night-scented flowers from the garden below. He fished the computer key out of the shrunken head, stuck the key in the machine and turned it. Then he hit the switches on the processor and screen, pulling off his jacket and draping it over the back of the chair while the machine powered up.

PASSWORD REQUIRED

Hunter tapped in 'GRIMOIRE'. The word was more usually used to describe a collection of magical spells, a book of magic. When he'd first got a computer, Emma had called it his magic-machine; when he finally decided to create a password, it seemed the obvious one to use.

Calling up the processor, he logged onto the working directory and opened up a new chapter. He'd already completed a body chapter, but the evening's events – the old woman's expression, the babysitter's grimace of disgust – had given him an idea. He hadn't killed an old woman in one of his books for a long time, not since *October Moon* in fact.

His fingers moved slowly over the keys. In his novels, a young woman's death was always associated with sex, but how should he handle the death of an older woman...? He smiled quickly, his fingers beginning to dance across the clicking keys. The older woman's death should be associated with dreams of remembered sex, of loss, of age...

Sofie Cipriano lay in the centre of Carlo's enormous bed, her tiny hands folded over the top sheet, her rosary, polished smooth by over sixty years of prayers, moving slowly through her arthritic fingers.

Carlo, standing at the foot of the bed, was distraught. 'How could you, Mamma?' he demanded. 'How could you?'

Sofie Cipriano ignored him, her lips moving in the familiar litany of prayer, taking comfort from the words. She hadn't wanted to come to London; it was a godless place, she had read that, a place of sin and debauchery...

'Mamma!'

... but Carlo had insisted, and then he had sent the ticket and money for new clothes. And she was old now, she knew that, and it might be her last chance to see him...

'Mamma!'

The old woman's gaze shifted off the ceiling, falling to look at her son. Poor Carlo, the youngest, always the fool. He thought he had done well for himself here in this city which once ruled the world. He had money, a nice house, a big car, but nothing else, no values, no honour: he was empty inside. It would have been better if he had remained at home in Roma. He might never have amounted to much, but it would have been more than he was now.

'Who was that man?' she asked very softly.

Carlo wrung his hands. 'Mamma, he is a very respected writer, very rich. He has been very good to me. A friend.'

Sofie moved her head slightly. 'He is not your friend,' she said simply.

'Mamma, how can you say that? He comes to my restaurant every week; he brings many important people here. I have been a guest in his home; he has been a guest in mine. We have exchanged gifts at Christmas.'

'He is not your friend. He is a friend to no man . . . except perhaps himself.'

Sofie had seen men like him before. Cold, empty men, soldiers in the Cosa Nostra. He reminded her of Mario. The beads stopped in her hands. Mario. My God, how long had it been since she had thought of Mario? Ten years, twenty, more, surely more? Mario, dead and rotten in his grave. He had been buried in a closed coffin because the shot-gun that had killed him had taken away much of his face. Her head moved slightly. Mario: that's who the writer had reminded her of.

And yet this writer had looked nothing like Mario. Tall, blond Mario from the cold north of Italy, perhaps some German or Swiss blood in him. Her first lover. So gentle, so strong. His hands, always moving, touching, caressing. His lips, always moist, sliding across her body, kissing her where no man had ever kissed, ever touched her before.

It had taken her a while before she discovered what Mario was: a Mafia soldier. She later learned that he liked to work with a knife, that those hands which had held and caressed and stroked her flesh had also sliced throats, cut out tongues, castrated men, mutilated women.

He was like that writer. Cold. Still. Empty inside.

And when that writer had walked up to her, with his hand outstretched, and turned his dead eyes on her . . . it had been like turning the clock back fifty years and more, feeling once again the cold touch of evil that emanated off the man. Which man? Mario, or the writer? Both.

'He is different. He looks at people with dead eyes,' she said softly, her voice surprisingly firm, although she could feel the erratic flickering of her heart.

'He is a writer, Mamma. Maybe he is a little different, a little strange. He creates worlds and people. He lives inside his imagination.'

'His imagination must be a dark place,' Sofie Cipriano whispered.

Carlo stopped. He frowned; he didn't think he had told his mother that Hunter wrote horror. She wouldn't have understood.

The old woman caught the momentary hesitation. 'Are his books dark?' she asked shrewdly.

Carlo had only read one of Hunter's books, although the author had given him signed copies of all the first editions. He vaguely remembered the story had been about vampires, but the violent and erotic imagery had disturbed him. For weeks after reading it – and he hadn't actually finished it, he remembered – whenever Denise, his beautiful English wife had touched him, he had imagined the vampires' long talons sinking into his flesh. He'd wondered how such a nice man as Robert had thought up such vile scenes.

'His books are dark,' Sofie said, interpreting her son's prolonged silence. 'They give you a glimpse of the true man. Avoid this writer. He is as dark as his writing.'

'Mamma . . .' Carlo began, attempting to laugh.

'He reminds me of Mario,' she continued quietly.

Carlo shook his head, but suddenly realised that his mother wasn't talking to him any more.

'He would write to me. Letters from all over the country, wherever his business took him. I didn't realise it then, but his business always ended in pain and death. He would send me these letters, lovely letters, long letters, with little pictures, scribbles, doodles in the margins. When I looked at those doodles, I should have realised I was looking at the true soul of the man. They were evil, foul, obscene. Just like the man. Mario.' She closed her eyes.

Headless bodies, skulls, swelling breasts with daggers through them. She remembered the tiny drawings, she'd often wondered about them. Had Mario even been conscious that he'd been drawing them, or were they simply unconscious outpourings as he composed the letters?

Mario.

When she opened her eyes again, he was standing at the end of the bed. Tall, blond and cold-eyed, just the way she remembered him, in a linen suit that cost more than she earned in a year. And he was smiling, showing his perfect, even teeth.

The black-bladed knife in his hand was very long.

'You should have been mine, Sofie.'

'No, Mario. I would never have been yours.'

Distantly, very distantly, a voice said, 'Mamma?'

'But you went and married that baker. A baker!' Mario spat bloody phlegm onto the coverlet. *'He couldn't give you a tenth of what I'd have been able to give you.'*

'He loved me, Mario. Without question.' Digging her

heels into the mattress, she pushed herself up in the bed.

'*I loved you too. I had a great future in the organisation . . . only someone betrayed me. Maybe you know who that was, eh, Sofie?*'

'I don't know what you're talking about.'

'Mamma? Mamma? Please . . . Mamma?'

The flesh was peeling away from Mario's face, falling onto the bed in stringy gobbets. The raw muscle beneath was torn, speckled with black pellets, one eyeball gone, exploded into liquid, the blond hair – so fine, so soft – scorched and burnt, the skull beneath an ugly wound.

Mario leaned forward across the end of the bed, and Sofie attempted to push herself further away.

'Mamma!'

Mario began to crawl up the bed, the flesh on his face sloughing away, revealing the grinning skull beneath. '*I took your virginity, do you remember that, in the attic of that house on the Via Napoli? I was your first lover. The things I taught you; the things we did . . .*' It was hard to make out what Mario was saying now, because the torn mouth and throat couldn't form the words. '*And how did you pay me? You betrayed me. And a white-handed baker shoved a shot-gun in my face.*'

Sofie shook her head. She hadn't known that. Perhaps in the secret places of her heart she had suspected . . .

The knife flickered out, inches from her eyeball.

Sofie Cipriano screamed and lashed out.

Carlo Cipriano watched in revulsion as his mother writhed and spasmed on the bed, arms flailing, eyes wide, staring and terrified. He was afraid to touch her as she thrashed about, entangling herself in the covers. Then, suddenly, she stiffened and lay still, and he breathed a sigh of relief. The fit had passed. He would have Denise call a doctor; obviously the strain of the trip and the excitement . . .

He was tucking the blanket in around his mother when he noticed the trickle of blood that curled from her ears . . . that gathered and dribbled from her nose . . . that squeezed from between her tightly closed lips.

Robert Hunter sat back in the chair, pleased with what he'd written. He especially liked the bit where the dead lover climbed up onto the bed.

Chapter Thirteen

PETER Norton slid a cup of coffee across the desk in front of Katherine. 'How's it going?' he asked gently, perching on the edge of the desk, tilting his head to read the computer screen.

Katherine sat back into the creaking typist's chair and pushed her glasses up onto her forehead. She pinched the bridge of her nose between thumb and forefinger. 'Slowly,' she said. She hit the sequence of keys that saved the text glowing white on blue on the computer screen. Stretching, she could feel her neck and shoulder muscles creak. 'What time is it?'

'Close to midnight. I was just about to go to bed,' Peter said softly. 'Are you coming?'

'I think I'd better finish this chapter first.' She shook her head. 'Jesus, it's grim.'

'Which – the writing or the content?'

'The content, the subject. The writing's fine. It's nothing special, it'll win no literary awards. It's very direct – but that's why it works; it's so powerful.'

'I know,' Peter said. 'I've read a couple of chapters of *Zodiac*.'

Katherine looked up in surprise. 'You don't read horror.'

'Neither do you,' he reminded her. 'But if you can do it, I don't see why I shouldn't do it with you. Share the burden.' He leaned forward and kissed her gently on the forehead. 'Don't be too long,' he said.

Katherine waited until he had left the room, pulling the door firmly shut behind him so that the clicking keyboard wouldn't disturb the children, before she lifted the coffee and sipped, grimacing at the bitter taste. Peter always made it just that bit too strong. She also knew if she drank it, she would remain awake for the rest of the night, and be fit for nothing in the morning, but right now she needed the caffeine just to keep her going into the small hours.

Cradling the cup in both hands, she stood up, easing muscles stiffened by sitting too long in the uncomfortable chair, and paced across the room. Like Hunter's study, hers was lined with books, but whereas the author's were scattered and piled indiscriminately, Katherine's books, magazines and journals were carefully categorised. Sitting in his study today, she'd dearly wanted to get up and start tidying his shelves . . . she smiled suddenly, that was precisely what she was doing to his text: tidying it up.

Pushing open a window, she leaned out, breathing in the cool night air, the odour of coffee suddenly sharper, cleaner. The night was quiet, the distant motorway an orange glow on the horizon, the sounds of the cars a low, but not unpleasant drone. The fresh air helped clear her head. Another hour; she'd give it another hour, then go to bed. Finishing the coffee, Katherine returned to her desk and picked up the bundle of manuscript.

Before she'd started working on Hunter's text earlier that day, she'd copied the files from her laptop computer onto the larger desk machine. Although the colour screen was easier to read than the liquid crystal display on the laptop, Katherine still preferred to work from a hard copy. Formating the text into a readable typeface, she'd printed it up on the laser printer. In double-spacing, it came to just over 260 A4 pages.

She'd skimmed through the pages as they cycled through the printer, but had discovered no obvious or glaring errors. She'd read both of Hunter's synopses, so she knew the main thread of the story: a young woman desperate for success sells her soul to a demon. When her time is up, she bargains another year out of the demon, but only on condition that she sacrifices a soul to it every week. In the end, she fails to sacrifice the last victim and the heroine – or central character, since she most definitely wasn't a heroine – is torn apart by the demon.

Katherine had immediately identified a couple of faults in the book. The opening was very strong. Hunter had dwelt in almost morbid detail on the discovery of a flayed and eviscerated human body in a shallow grave in the New Forest. When Katherine had reached the part where a putrefied arm had come apart from the corpse, spilling white maggots onto the ground, she had almost thrown up.

However, the next couple of chapters were a little weak, and the development of the main female character was poor. The woman wasn't properly described, remaining almost a cipher, and although she was now four chapters into the book, Katherine still hadn't a clear idea just what she looked like. She realised this might be a deliberate ploy by Hunter: allowing the reader to associate any face, any woman, with the main character.

She'd carefully worked her way through the early chapters, familiarising herself with Hunter's style, his phrasing, his sentence construction, until she felt she could begin to write in his simplistic, though straightforward style. Whatever corrections she made now would have to be invisible to the reader. She was tempted to tone down the nauseating detail, but decided that wasn't part of her job. And besides, this was what Hunter's readers wanted.

Chapter Five was turning out to be a nightmare; there was so much she wanted to change, but daren't. Here, in flashback, the heroine recalled how she raised a demon from a medieval manuscript she had discovered amongst her father's books. After several pages of almost tedious description about the preparation of the pentagram and what Katherine concluded was a fairly complete invocation – that would have to go – the demon appeared. The description of the demon was almost matter-of-fact: a straightforward traditional demon with horns, cloven hooves and a tail. And naturally, because this was a Robert Hunter book, the demon sealed his pact not in blood, but in sex. In an episode that took up six manuscript pages, Hunter described in vivid detail the couple – woman and beast – having intercourse.

Katherine slumped in the chair and looked at the bundle of manuscript, then consulted her page of notes. How was she going to handle this? How much could she change; what should she leave in? Maybe she could edit out the preparations for the calling, and then the invocation itself – did that have to be so detailed? And the sex. She knew there was graphic sex in Hunter's books, but where was the line between erotica and pornography?

She made a few tentative changes on the printed pages, then called up the chapter on the screen and began moving text around . . . only to replace it.

She'd been staring at the screen for close to thirty minutes when she realised that she hadn't got a clue what she was going to do with the chapter. She didn't know enough about Hunter's previous books. How graphic *was* the sex; how detailed were the occult bits? She was going to need a lot more information before she could proceed. With a sigh, she saved the work onto a floppy disk, parked the hard disk, and turned off the screen and processor. The machine died with a low, subsiding whisper. Lifting her watch off the table, she looked at the time. One-thirty.

Flicking off the lights, Katherine pulled open the curtains so that the room would be bright with morning sunshine when she came into it in the morning. Pulling the door of her study closed behind her, she moved quietly down the corridor, pausing to peer in at the girls. Lizzie and Jody shared the larger bedroom at the back of the house. As usual Lizzie was curled up in a neat, tight ball, while Jody lay sprawled across the bed, with the covers on the floor. She tucked them in, then kissed them on the forehead. Mark slept in the box room. Looking in she could make out his shape on the bed, his arm stretched straight out – just like his father. He was snoring softly.

There was a light on in her own bedroom and, for a moment, Katherine thought that Peter was still awake. but when she stepped into the room, she discovered that the radio was hissing soft static, and that Peter had fallen asleep sitting up, *Zodiac* still open in his hands. Using a tissue to mark his place, she gently eased the book from his hands and turned it around to look at the page. She was surprised to find that he'd read nearly a third of the book.

Katherine sat down on the side of the bed, feeling a wave of exhaustion. Her eyes were gritty, and there was a dull throbbing in the front of her skull, the result of two many hours' concentrating on the screen. She looked at the book in her hands . . . then turned it over when she realised that the bedside light, catching the lurid cover, brought the blood-soaked zodiacal wheel to trembling life.

Switching off the light, Katherine stood up, pulled open the curtains, and looked down onto the quiet, suburban street. There were lights on in only two of the houses; in one she could see the flicker of a television screen through the parted curtains, and she knew there was a new baby in the house across the road.

She undressed slowly, her eyes on the street below, breathing in the cool air through the open window. She needed a shower, but she was too weary even to think about it. Pulling on a long, candy-striped teeshirt, she checked to ensure the radio-alarm was set before she slipped into bed.

The troubled images from Hunter's book, the awkward words and phrases from Chapter Five, swarmed and buzzed at the edges of her consciousness. She allowed them to come, knowing that by the morning she would have a solution to be her problem. Once she'd got over that hump, she'd fly through the rest of the book, and then it was simply a matter of encouraging Hunter to get his act together and complete the manuscript. She had a vivid image of him working now – she knew he often worked on into the night – sitting in a darkened room, with the glow from the computer screen white and ghastly against his face, tongue moist against his lips, fingers dancing across the keys as he created another scene of mayhem. Was it possible to write that sort of shit and *not* be affected by it . . .? Was it possible to read it . . .?

Peter shifted in the bed beside her, rolling over on his side, his arm flinging out, coming to rest on her stomach. He was breathing fast, his spread fingers twitching, and she wondered what he was dreaming about. Since he'd lost his job he'd had a lot of nightmares, usually simple anxiety dreams, dreams of falling, of drowning, of being trapped in a locked room, of walking naked down the high street. They'd laughed about them over breakfast, but some of them had brought him awake bathed in icy perspiration, and once or twice she'd been forced to shake him awake because he'd been crying in his sleep.

Peter's outstretched hand began trembling, as if he was clutching at something. Katherine shifted in the bed, tilting her head to listen to him, but there were no cries, no whimpers. The movement brought his hand lower onto the pit of her stomach, directly above her groin. His twitching fingers tickled and she carefully lifted his hand and moved it away. Peter sighed and seemed to relax. Leaning forward, she kissed him gently, tenderly. He wasn't the man she'd married ten years ago, but then again, she didn't think she was still the same woman. If she was asked if she loved him, her answer would have been an emphatic yes, but there were times, like now, in the dead of night, when she realised that the answer was purely automatic. It wasn't as if she didn't love him – it was simply that they had become used to one another. Much of the magic had gone. Turning her back on her husband, Katherine Norton rolled over, her eyes fixed on the gently shifting curtain.

She was dreaming, and she knew it. The dream was confused. Pleasure and pain. Flickering impression of faces . . . figures. Some she recognised: family, friends, Peter. But there were strangers also, half-glimpsed faces, characters, caricatures, figures from novels . . .

Katherine swam up from the depths of unconsciousness, dimly aware of the heat of another body lying close to her, then abruptly – terrifyingly – aware of the moistness between her legs, the taut pressure of her nipples. Peter was lying wrapped into her body, one of his hands draped around her waist, resting on her belly, another hand between her neck and the pillow clutching at her breast. Her teeshirt was bundled up around her neck.

And he had penetrated her.

Her immediate reaction was to push him away, to slap his hands off her for violating her . . . but the waves of pleasure were shivering through her thighs, flooding her lower body with warmth, sending electric tingles through her arms, right down into her fingertips. She reached down, not to push him away, but rather to pull him in closer, to press herself down onto him, grinding her buttocks into his lap. He was moving gently now, his whole body shifting, drawing her into a gentle, effortless rhythm.

His head was on her left shoulder, his breath warm and moist against her ear. He was breathing quickly, great heaving gasps that filled his chest, pushing it against her back, the coarse hair brushing her skin.

Her first orgasm took her quickly, shuddering through her, forcing her down onto Peter, driving him deeper into her body as she clutched at his thigh, her nails sinking into the flesh, her right hand splayed across her stomach.

Peter was close to orgasm now. His breath was harsh in her ear, cool and faintly foul. His movements had become ragged, rougher, now pounding into her with short sharp strokes, his right hand clutching at her breasts, pinching the tender flesh.

They came together in a quick convulsion. The

instant of pleasure turned to pain as Peter's nails scored her breasts and across her stomach, his left hand catching the soft flesh around her hip and squeezing, his teeth closing onto the flesh of her shoulder, nipping her painfully. She attempted to push him off, but he was shuddering inside her now, the long muscles of his thighs spasming.

Ice blossomed in the pit of her stomach.

The cold was so intense it burned, sending long daggers of pain across her stomach and into her chest. She jerked away from Peter, feeling the ice-cold liquid flow down her inner thighs.

She was flailing for the bedside light when she fell out of bed.

The fall awoke her.

Katherine sat on the floor listening as her heart began to slow and she realised she'd been having a nightmare. The details were still appallingly clear. Pieces swam up from her unconscious and slotted together. Hunter's book. The nightmare had been inspired by Hunter's book, where the demon sealed its pact with the heroine by penetrating her. The devil's seed was always described as ice cold.

Coming slowly to her feet, surprised by the trembling in her legs, the tenderness in her breasts and the pressure in the pit of her stomach, she wondered briefly if she'd actually had an orgasm in her sleep.

Moving around the bed in the dark, she made her way into the bathroom, hitting the switch with the palm of her hand, blinking as the sudden light hurt her eyes. When she sat on the toilet, she discovered livid scrape marks across her thighs and stomach, and bruising around her nipples.

Chapter Fourteen

'WHAT time is it?'

Without looking at the clock, Robert Hunter said, 'Just after three. I'm sorry I woke you.'

'You didn't wake me.' Emma Hunter rolled over in the bed to watch her husband, silhouetted against the window. 'Rose was awake earlier. A bad dream.'

In the darkness, Hunter grimaced.

'Is she OK now?'

'She's fine. She dreamt that an invisible monster was chasing her. Probably something she saw on television; a cartoon maybe.'

Hunter slid naked into bed beside his wife, feeling her flesh, warm and soft, brush against his. She kissed him lightly on the lips before turning her back on him. He settled into her, wrapping one arm around her waist, sliding the other around her neck to cup her breast. Her buttocks settled onto his lap and he hardened immediately.

'I've been waiting for you,' Emma whispered, lifting her leg, pressing herself onto him, grinding her buttocks into his lap as she pulled him in closer.

Hunter began moving gently, his whole body shifting, drawing her into a gentle, effortless rhythm, that built to a convulsive orgasm.

. . . and the demon settled into the woman, wrapping one

arm around her waist, sliding the other around her neck to
cup her breast . . .

They usually made love in this position now; effortlessly, gently. He had written the scene into one of his books – *Zodiac*, he thought – where the heroine mates with the demon in this position. He'd started making love to Emma in the same way shortly afterwards . . . or had it been before?

Which had come first: the imagining or the experience? Had he used his imagination, and then made it a reality, or had he drawn the image from some previous experience and woven it into his book? He shook his head; he had learned that the line between fantasy and reality was gossamer thin. Too often, fantasy could become reality.

Chapter Fifteen

'HELLO, Chris. This is Katherine Norton. How are you?'

There were a few moments' hesitation on the other end of the line, and Katherine guessed that Chris Kamen was mentally asking, 'Who the fuck is Katherine Norton?' The editor was never at his best first thing in the morning.

'Chris, wake up! It's Katherine Norton. I work with you, remember? I'm one of the freelancers,' she continued, glancing sidelong at the clock on her desk. Three minutes past nine. She could see Chris standing in front of his desk, jacket on, beaker of coffee clutched in one hand, cigarette dangling out of the corner of his mouth.

'Katherine! Jesus, I'm sorry, I didn't recognise you there for a moment.'

'Bad night last night?' she asked sympathetically.

'A real nightmare!'

Katherine's lips twisted in a bitter smile. She knew what a real nightmare was. She touched her breasts; they were still tender, though the bruising wasn't as bad as she thought it would be and the livid scrapes had faded to little more than faint red lines. How could a nightmare have that effect . . .? She deliberately pushed the thought away; she didn't want to think about it. 'What happened?' she asked.

'I had dinner with one of our authors who's in town,' Kamen continued. 'You know what it's like: he figures since we were paying for dinner, he was going for the best, and a lot of it! And could he drink! Surprised he can write at all with the amount he put away.' Katherine heard Kamen swallow hard, and guessed that the coffee would be very black and very strong. 'So what can I do for you, eh? Bet you're glad you're not working in this hellhole on a day like this, eh?'

'Absolutely.' Leaning forward, she looked through the slatted blinds into the garden below which was bathed in brilliant sunshine. The sky was completely cloudless, a pale, egg-shell blue, and the forecasters were unanimous in promising a record high.

'So what can I do for you?'

'Well, Chris,' Katherine began, unsure how the other editor was going to react. 'You know I've been asked to work on Robert Hunter's new book . . .'

'I suggested you for the job,' Kamen said.

'Oh. Why?'

'I thought he needed someone like you, to give him a really good shake-up.'

'But you know I don't read and I don't edit horror,' she continued.

'That's why I thought you'd be so good at it. You'd bring a completely new perspective to it.'

'Well,' Katherine said, 'it was very good of you to suggest me, and god knows, I need the money. But I'm having a few problems . . .'

'If there's anything I can do to help . . .' Kamen said.

Relieved, Katherine settled back in the chair. Getting Kamen's cooperation was the first hurdle. 'Have you got a few minutes now?'

'Sure. Go ahead.' She heard paper rustling and then a chair creaking.

'Talk to me about Hunter. What's he like . . . really like, I mean? Matthews gave me some bullshit about the bestselling author, a dedicated family man, but what's the truth?'

'The truth? The truth is he's a cold, calculating bastard, with one of the sickest imaginations I've ever come across.'

The vehemence in Kamen's voice stopped Katherine cold, bringing her upright in the chair.

'I've been with him almost from the start. I remember reading his first book, *The Possessed*, and being completely knocked out by it. It was brilliant. Over the years the books have gotten grimmer, the sex has become more explicit and perverted, the violence more graphic. And the sales have gone through the roof,' he added. 'Hunter is quite unique amongst horror writers I know, in that he professes not to read any other horror writer working in the field today. If you've seen his study, you'll realise that there are no fiction titles amongst all the books. He says that everything he reads is for research, and certainly a lot of the occult titbits in the text are spot on. He's a remarkable man.'

'I've met him. He seems quite nice.'

'Oh, he is. Don't get me wrong. He's always treated me with the utmost courtesy, but after a while I realised that it was nothing more than that: courtesy. The charm and the good manners are a front, something he does automatically. I'm convinced he doesn't give a shit about anyone . . . except maybe his wife and kids. He dotes on the two girls. But he seems to look down on everyone else; he was an academic for a very long time, maybe he considers us all his pupils.'

'Does he take editorial direction?' Katherine asked cautiously.

'Absolutely. Tell him what you want done and he'll do it with no fuss. He's very professional.'

'Talk to me about the books, Chris. How much sex and violence and tedious descriptions of occult ceremonies and paraphernalia should I leave in?'

'All of it. That's what the audience wants. They don't seem to mind wading through two or three pages of a black-mass ritual if they feel they're getting a taste of the real thing.'

'And is it real?'

'Absolutely. All his stuff is meticulously researched. He once told me he had actually attended occult ceremonies to get the details right. You probably didn't see it, but about a year ago, a black-magic coven was broken up because they were committing animal sacrifices. They had taken the rituals and invocations from one of Hunter's books, *Blood Passion* or *October Moon*, I don't remember which. But I do know the Image Press reprinted the book on the strength of the publicity.'

Katherine shifted the phone from one ear to the other. She had written down a list of questions before she had phoned Kamen. It was now time to ask the big one. 'Why didn't you want to edit the new book?'

There was a long silence at the other end of the line. Finally Kamen replied: 'I guess I just got tired of Hunter's work. And I got so used to his style and nuances that I began missing some fairly obvious mistakes.' Kamen hesitated a moment, before adding, 'Some of it is just so sickening, so bizarre. Shit – I was even dreaming about it.' He laughed shakily. 'It was time for me to move on; time for Hunter to move onto a more professional editor.'

Katherine was about to press him for further details, but sensed that she wasn't going to get anything else. 'I won't keep you, Chris. Thanks for all your help. I might ring you again, if that's all right.'

'No problem, Katherine. I hope you enjoy the book,' he added, and she didn't know whether he was joking or not.

Katherine worked on through the morning, promising herself a break at midday. Paradoxically, her terrifying nightmare, inspired, she knew, by Chapter Five in Hunter's book, had clarified her thoughts, and she was able to make several suggestions for reworking the female character's reaction to the demon. Although she'd been expecting to give herself to the demon, how did she actually feel about it?

Continuing, she moved through Chapters Six and Seven, and was almost pleased when she discovered a mistake in Chapter Seven where a minor character's eye colour had changed from brown to green. It was a simple mistake, but showed that Hunter's attention wasn't fully on the book, or that his notes weren't up to date. There were a couple of historical dates that she was dubious about, and the spelling of some of the Greek and Latin words used in the incantation needed to be checked – though she was sure Hunter would have spelled them correctly.

The first graphic murder took place in Chapter Nine.

Katherine read through the chapter quickly, skimming some of the descriptive passages . . . Bile flooded her throat at the shocking climax. Taking a deep breath, Katherine returned to the beginning of the chapter and read through it again, making notes.

Hunter's heroine, Magda, is a schoolteacher. Having failed to kill her lover in the previous chapter and desperate because the full moon is upon her, she lures one of her young male pupils back to her flat, seduces him and then kills him during lovemaking, sacrificing him to the demon, offering up his heart as a smoking sacrifice.

'I don't want to read this shit.'

It was only when she heard her voice echoing flatly in the quiet room that she realised she'd spoken aloud. Dropping the manuscript onto the floor, Katherine leaned back in the chair and stretched, working her neck from side to side. It was too nice a day to be reading about satanic sacrifices. She made a brief note on the text, marking where she'd finished, then saved her morning's work and turned off the computer. She'd come back to it later; right now, she'd do a little gardening, and simply soak up some sunshine . . . and try and get that taste out of her mouth.

Plucking her sunglasses off a shelf as she left the room, she wondered what dark visions Hunter was seeing on this summer's morning.

With the blinds pulled tightly closed, the window locked, the study was hot and stuffy, and the humming computer dried the air, tainting it with the tang of hot metal.

Robert Hunter sat hunched before the screen, slowly scrolling down the text of *The Earl of Hell*, trying to read it with a stranger's eyes, wondering how Katherine Norton would see it, wondering how she would react to it. Usually, he didn't give a damn, but *The Earl of Hell* was an important book for Hunter: it was his thirteenth . . . and he was determined it would be his last in the genre. Ten years ago, a combination of circumstances had forced him to become a writer. His first book, *The Possessed*, had been classified as a horror novel, and it was a label he had been unable to cast off. He had become trapped into a cycle of horror writing – a genre that fed off excess, a genre he had always detested. Once he'd completed this book, he could move onto something more worthwhile.

If he completed this book . . .

He had to complete it . . . because if he didn't, then he knew that there would never be another Robert Hunter book of any description.

Ten years ago. The time had passed so quickly . . .

Chapter Sixteen

IT was a nightmare.

Any moment now, he was going to wake up and discover that he was lying in his bed beside his wife of fifteen years in the small detached house which they got at a nominal rent from the college.

'Did you hear what I said, Bob?'

This was no dream, but it was still a nightmare. Robert Hunter looked away from the young blonde girl, suddenly – desperately – trying to remember her age. Fifteen? Dearest Jesus, but she'd better not be fifteen. Sixteen? Yes, he was sure she was sixteen. But was it legal to have sex with a sixteen year old? He thought so . . . he wasn't sure . . .

'Bob!' Emma Reynolds twisted in the passenger seat of the car, and caught his shoulder, forcing him to look at her. 'Bob, you're not listening to me.'

'I'm listening to you,' he said, feeling exhaustion wash over him in a long slow wave. 'I've heard every word you said. You're pregnant,' he added, proving that he had indeed been listening.

Emma Reynolds waited patiently, staring at the older man with her bright blue eyes, confident that he would come up with the answer. He watched as she brushed strands of blonde hair off her cheeks, and felt an incredible anger surge through him. He wanted to smash the trusting look off her face, close the wide blue eyes, shatter the bright, innocent smile. Gripping the steering wheel in a white-knuckled grip, he stared through the rain-spattered windscreen towards the grey sea.

'Are you sure?' he asked eventually.

Still watching his face intently, her eyes suddenly anxious – he wasn't reacting the way she thought he would – Emma nodded. 'I had a test. A proper test, not one of those do-it-yourself jobs. It came back positive this morning.'

Hunter nodded. He was weighing up the ramifications, both for himself and the girl. There weren't many options open to them. She was sixteen, he was thirty-six, married with two children. He was also one of Emma's teachers.

Beyond the dirty beach, grey sea met grey sky in an imperceptible line, merging their misery. It matched his mood exactly. When he glanced sidelong at Emma, he could see the fear in her eyes.

'You won't ask me to get rid of it,' she whispered, both hands going protectively to her flat stomach. Emma misinterpreted Robert's start of surprise for one of shock. He *had* been going to suggest an abortion. 'No, I knew you wouldn't,' she continued quickly. 'I couldn't.' She took his hand and rested it on her stomach. 'This child is precious to me . . . because it's part of us, Robert, this baby is a symbol of our love.'

A symbol of our love! The schoolteacher squeezed his eyes shut and bit the inside of his lip to prevent himself from saying something he was going to regret. The girl was physically advanced for her age, but she lacked maturity. That didn't stop you taking advantage of her, a cold voice whispered.

'You do love me, Bob?'

Reaching over, he squeezed her fingers. 'Of course I love you,' he said automatically, telling her the same lie he'd been using since they began their affair eight months previously.

Emma brought his hands to her lips, then pressed his fingers back onto her belly. 'I knew it would be all right, Bob. You told me you were going to leave Nicole when the time was right . . . well, I think the time is right.'

'How long are you gone?' he wondered.

'Four months.'

'Which means you're due early next year,' he said slowly.

'February,' she smiled.

Four months pregnant . . . which probably meant that she had conceived in June. That would have been around the time they'd spent the weekend together in London. She'd told her parents she was staying over with friends; he'd told Nicole he was doing some research in the British Library. At the last minute Nicole told him she'd managed to get a babysitter for the weekend, so she would be able to come down to London with him for the weekend. He'd been so besotted with Emma at that stage that he'd deliberately engineered an argument with his wife on the Friday evening, and left for London on his own the following morning.

God, that weekend in London!

They'd barely left their hotel room. He'd acted like a teenager who's just discovered sex, and Emma had been insatiable. She was his every erotic dream come true; the girl had been willing to try everything, to do anything to please him, and she'd even surprised him with a few tricks of her own . . . tricks that no self-respecting country schoolgirl should know.

Four months pregnant. He wondered how long before she'd start to show.

'Who knows about this?' he asked eventually.

Emma bit her bottom lip, and he knew the news was going to be bad. 'Just my mother,' she said softly.

'Your mother!' he whispered.

'She's known from the beginning that I've been up to something. She guessed that I was seeing someone, but she didn't know who; she thought it was one of the local lads in the village. When I started getting sick in the morning, she knew immediately that I was pregnant – even before I did. A couple of weeks ago, she asked me straight out if I was pregnant.'

'What did you say?' Hunter wondered.

'I told her I wasn't sure. But then she asked me if there was any possibility that I might be pregnant . . .' When Hunter said nothing, she was forced to continue. 'I told her that there was a possibility.'

Hunter swivelled around in the seat to face the girl. 'Why didn't you say something to me before this?'

'What was the point until I was sure? Besides, I didn't want to put any pressure on you.'

'Pressure? What sort of pressure?'

The young woman looked out at the grey sea, suddenly unwilling to face him. 'Well, you had talked about leaving Nicole when the time was right; I knew that once you discovered I was pregnant, you'd want to leave her before the baby arrived.'

'It's not as simple as that,' Hunter whispered.

'Why not?' Emma asked innocently.

'It takes time to sort things out,' he snapped. 'I can't just up and leave Nicole in the morning, can I?'

Emma bit her lip and shook her head. Her bright eyes magnified behind brimming tears.

'Look, say nothing about this to anyone else. You've

got to give me time to sort things out.' Hunter turned the key in the ignition and reversed out of the empty parking lot that faced onto the beach. During the summer the lot would be full, but at the wrong end of a wet September, it was empty. As he pulled onto the road, he glanced sidelong at Emma. 'Does anyone know I'm the father of the child?'

'No,' she said quickly – too quickly – and he knew she was lying.

Hunter dropped Emma off at the bottom of her road on the way home, and then drove the half mile to his own house, in a quiet cul-de-sac behind the college. As he reversed into the drive, he attempted to calm his nerves and school his face to an expressionless mask. He needed to get into the house without Nicole seeing him, because he knew that all she had to do was to look at him, and she'd know that something was wrong. It was impossible to have lived with someone for fifteen years and not develop a rapport with them. He'd reached the stage with Nicole where they could now finish sentences for one another, and know instinctively what the other was thinking. It had always been his secret fear that this same rapport would alert her to his affair with Emma.

The hall door opened as he climbed out of the car, and he immediately knew that something was wrong the moment he saw Nicole's face. He breathed in deeply; it was just his guilty conscience. When Emma's mother and father – and then the principal of the school – all appeared in the hallway, stepping out of the sitting room to stand in silent accusation behind his red-eyed wife, he knew just how much trouble he was in.

Chapter Seventeen

'I'M sorry I phoned so late yesterday,' Katherine Norton said, stepping past Emma Hunter into the hall, 'but I didn't want to arrive this morning without phoning first. I hope I didn't wake the girls.'

'No, no, you didn't,' Emma smiled easily. 'They'd been running around for the whole day and were absolutely exhausted last night. I don't think they'd have heard the phone if it had been in the room with them.'

Katherine followed Emma into the cool kitchen. She perched on a high stool while the younger woman crossed to the sink to fill the kettle. Emma was dressed much as she had been when Katherine had first met her on Tuesday morning, in a lemon-yellow leotard, which was startlingly vivid against her deeply tanned skin. She turned around and leaned back against the sink, folding her arms across her small chest. 'I hope you didn't waste all day yesterday working,' she smiled.

'I did a bit in the morning,' Katherine admitted, 'but, to be perfectly honest, it was so beautiful outside, I took the rest of the day off.'

'And I'll bet you felt guilty about it.'

'Oh yes . . . for about ten minutes.'

'Good for you!'

'I promised myself I'd do a little more work last night, but I felt completely drained – even though I'd done nothing all day – and I had a pounding headache . . .'

'Sounds like a touch of the sun to me.'

'I think so. I made myself a large glass of warm milk and went straight to bed. I slept right through.' Katherine paused and then asked, 'Was Robert working yesterday?'

'Like yourself, he only worked in the morning. Apparently you told him to stop working on the main body of the book and write some body chapters. Well, he flew through those, but it meant that he had nothing to do yesterday afternoon. He actually sat in the garden for the first time in ages. I suppose I have you to thank for that.'

As the kettle came to the boil with a shrill whistle, the kitchen door burst open and two young girls raced in. They stopped when they saw Katherine, staring at her with huge blue eyes. They were both pale-skinned and blonde, and bore a remarkable resemblance to their mother.

'This is Violet,' Emma said, putting her hand on the head of the older girl.

'I'm six,' the girl said solemnly.

'And I'm Rose and I'm four,' the young girl said immediately.

'My name is Katherine. And I've got two girls of my own, Elizabeth, but we call her Lizzie, and Jody.'

The girls stared at her for another few moments, then, deciding that she was no longer of interest, raced back out into the garden.

'They look just like you,' Katherine said.

'So everyone tells me,' Emma smiled.

'Do they take after their father, at all?'

104

'Oh, they've got his stubborn streak,' Emma smiled. 'You'll come to recognise it soon enough in the way he juts his chin. When you see him do that, you know you're on a loser.'

'I'll remember that.'

Emma made tea in the same pot she'd used two days before. Pouring herself a glass of grapefruit juice, she put it alongside the teapot on a tray and carried it out into the garden. The two women sat facing one another across the small wooden garden table. The children's voices sounded lost and distant in the early-morning silence. Emma poured tea. 'Is there much work to be done on the book?' she asked casually.

'A little; not much,' Katherine said, wondering how much of an input Emma had into her husband's writing. She knew some writers discussed every step of their books with their wives or lovers, while others were very secretive. 'Have you read it?'

Emma shook her head. 'I won't read it until it's published. I've read all of Bob's books,' she added slowly, 'though I can't say I've enjoyed them.' She sipped from her grapefruit juice. 'It's very difficult for me to reconcile the quiet and gentle man that I know with the writer of books which are so violent and pornographic.'

'Never confuse the writer and the writing,' Katherine smiled. 'I know a grandmother of sixty-five, living in northern Scotland, who writes incredibly pornographic novels for one of the cheap mass-market paperback houses. Then there's a retired inspector of taxes, now living in Ireland, who has just finished his fiftieth Western. He's never even been to America and doesn't own so much as a pair of cowboy boots.' Concentrating on the teacup to disguise her interest,

Katherine asked casually, 'What is it about Robert's writing which disturbs you?'

'You've read them,' Emma said quickly. 'Surely you can see what I'm talking about.'

'They're very bloody . . .' Katherine said. She realised that Emma had something on her mind.

'You haven't read all his books?' the younger woman asked.

Katherine shook her head.

Emma sat back in the wooden chair and pulled a pair of enormous sunglasses down over her eyes. They made her look like a schoolgirl. Picking up her grapefruit juice, she rolled the sweating glass between the palms of her hands, before sipping from it.

'Over the years, I've seen Bob's books change,' she said. 'They've become more and more violent and pornographic . . . it's always the women who come out as either the victims or the aggressors.'

'And this disturbs you?' Katherine asked.

'I . . . I wonder about it.'

'Over the past ten years the horror market has changed,' Katherine said. She was guessing now, but based her assumptions on her years spent in the publishing industry. 'The reader has become used to degrees of horror. A lot of readers now demand no-holds-barred, out-and-out horror: shock tactics. Books are being published as mainstream or as horror-genre novels that would never have seen print ten years ago. Robert is unique because he has the ability to move with the times. His books have become increasingly graphic to stay with the market.'

Emma leaned forward slightly. 'Do you think this writing has any effect on him?'

Katherine knew that this was the question Emma had been leading up to. 'I don't know. I shouldn't imagine so. I suppose that if Robert is putting down on paper some of his own bizarre fantasies or nightmares, he's actually exorcising those demons.'

'Making him a saner person?' Emma said quickly.

Katherine grinned. 'Well . . . I wouldn't be too sure about that. He is a writer. No writer is ever fully sane!'

'Do you believe I'm insane?' Robert Hunter asked as Katherine stepped into the long study.

She turned quickly. 'I beg your pardon?'

Hunter nodded towards the open window. 'I overheard your conversation with my wife,' he continued. 'I wasn't eavesdropping. Your voices simply carried on the still air.' The author sank back into his chair, and as always steepled his hands before his face. He was wearing a pair of baggy black jeans, a teeshirt advertising one of his own books – *October Moon* – no shoes and no socks. 'Do you think I'm insane, Mrs Norton?' he asked again. His colourless eyes were expressionless behind his glasses.

Katherine took a few moments to place her briefcase on the table, while she considered her answer. Sitting facing Hunter, she said, 'I think the point I was making to your wife was that writers of fiction spend so much of their lives living in worlds of their own creating, playing with the characters and situations they have created, that often the real world becomes far less interesting.' She smiled, attempting to lighten the mood. 'Ordinarily, we classify people who live in dream worlds as insane or eccentric . . . so I suppose by applying the same criterion, we could say that all writers are somewhat insane.'

Hunter stared at her for a few moments longer, his eyes wide and unblinking, then his thin lips curled into a smile and he suddenly threw back his head and laughed, a peculiarly soft laugh. 'By God, it's been a long time since I was called mad and then had it so convincingly proven to me. There's probably a very good book in there somewhere,' he added. 'Something about a writer who is unsure whether the world he's living in is in fact real or the product of his own imagination. Nightmare stuff.'

'I think it's been done,' Katherine said gently.

'Probably,' Hunter agreed. 'There are very few good ideas left out there.' He gestured towards the computer screen, which showed *The Earl of Hell* directory, with its listing of chapters. 'So, tell me . . .' he said, suddenly all business.

Opening her briefcase, Katherine pulled out the bundle of corrected manuscript and set it down on the table. She placed her small Compaq laptop computer beside it. 'Well,' she began, 'I think what you've written so far is excellent . . .'

'There's a "but" coming . . .' Hunter said with a grin, 'I can feel it.'

'I haven't had a chance to read all of it, of course, but I thought you might like to see what I've done so far. The opening chapter is very good; very strong. Very gory, too,' she added. 'However, we're immediately presented with the novel's major flaw: the main female character, Magda Boam. I found I simply couldn't visualise her. I feel she needs to be anchored more firmly in the reader's imagination . . . and if you do that I think the minor faults in the later chapters will vanish.' She shuffled through the sheaf of manuscript she had printed up. 'She's also not a particularly likeable character. I found it impossible to empathise with her. When she's in trouble, I found myself saying – so what?'

Hunter turned away from Katherine, his fingers

moving across the clicking keyboard. A series of differently coloured windows opened up on the screen. 'it's an interesting point,' he said. 'When I first conceived the novel, I decided that the heroine/villainness should be female, but when I actually sat down to write it, I decided to change the character to a male. I haven't written an evil male before. However, I was never very comfortable with the concept of a male killer – and it gives the conjurgation scene, when the demon is raised and demands sex in payment, a very different aspect indeed. So, I changed it back to female again.' He paused and then asked, 'What do you suggest?'

Caught off balance by the question, Katherine said, 'Well . . . what do you usually do when you're creating characters: make them up or base them on someone you know?'

Hunter grinned. 'All the victims are based on people I know or knew, friends, aquaintances, neighbours.' The grin turned feral. 'You never know, you might end up a victim in *The Earl of Hell*.'

'Thanks!' she said, feelingly.

Hunter opened Chapter Two and ran through it on screen. 'I don't want to have to start again from the beginning . . .'

'And we don't have the time,' Katherine said.

'So, I'll have to adapt the existing character.'

'Make her more sympathetic.'

'She kills people,' Hunter reminded her, 'she has sex with them, and then sacrifices them to the demon. Black-widow spider.'

'Make her two people in one,' Katherine suggested. 'You started with a male character; why not give her a split personality, a loving, gentle feminine side, and a brutal, masculine side?'

Hunter lifted his left hand and, holding it horizontally, tilted it slightly from side to side. 'Surely that's been done too often,' he said. 'But . . .' he added, and then fell silent.

Katherine waited, saying nothing, simply watching him.

Fully five minutes later, Hunter raised his head and grinned widely. He came out of his chair and strode down the long room, hands locked in front of him in an attitude almost of prayer. In that moment he looked so much like an academic that Katherine had to smile.

'Split personality's been done,' he said, 'and the public always find it just a little bit suspect, a cop-out. How about if we make our heroine sympathetic, but misguided, desperate, completely crushed by events that force her to take the extraordinary chance of going through with this conjurgation?'

Katherine nodded, allowing him to talk. She always found it fascinating to observe writers work, the sudden sparking of ideas, curious, sometimes bizarre and completely dissociated ideas flowing together to fashion a plot or create a character.

'But once she is possessed by the demon, he can work through her at particular times of the month – the full moon!'

'Is she aware that he is working through her?' Katherine asked.

'Yes . . . no!' Hunter immediately corrected himself. 'Dreams, maybe . . . nightmares?' He shook his head quickly. 'I'll work that out.' He turned to face her. 'What do you think?'

'It's a nice twist. I think it will work.'

Hunter slid into the leather chair and made a series of lightning-fast notes, the computer keys clicking softly. He stopped abruptly and swung around to face

Katherine. There was an expression on his face that bordered on respect. 'Thank you,' he said simply. 'Your suggestion is excellent. It gives me a whole new slant on the character. And having the demon kill his own victims is a nice touch.'

'It will also allow you to keep the feminine side of your character sympathetic. Perhaps you could consider a scene where she gradually becomes aware of the creature lurking in her unconscious and attempts to do battle with it.'

Hunter's fingers moved, recording the suggestion. 'It would make an interesting final chapter. Would she succeed?' he asked.

'This is a Robert Hunter novel,' Katherine replied. 'Of course she won't succeed!'

Hunter threw back his head and laughed drily. 'You know, I think I'm enjoying this, Katherine Norton!'

Katherine smiled. Picking up the manuscript she crossed the room to stand beside his chair. 'I've made a few minor corrections – principally tenses, spelling mistakes, minor inconsistencies. In Chapter Seven we have a character's eye-colouring changing from green to brown. I've sorted that out.'

Hunter took the pages and flicked through them quickly, stopping when he spotted a red editorial mark. 'There's nothing I can disagree with here,' he murmured.

'Read through it; it will give you a very good idea of how I operate. And I think it's important for you to be confident in my work.'

Hunter tapped the screen with his fingernails, the sound sharp and brittle. 'I'm already confident.' He passed across a floppy disk. 'These are the two chapters I wrote over the past two days. They're body chapters, self-contained, and can be slotted into the main body of the text at almost any point.'

'I suppose they're bloody, too,' Katherine said.

'Absolutely!' Hunter grinned.

Chapter Eighteen

KATHERINE slid between the sheets, the material cool against her hot and sticky flesh. She had been going to have a bath before she came to bed, but she had read the print-out from the disk Hunter had given her and caught the words 'naked body', 'bath' and 'bathroom', and decided that wasn't such a good idea.

Propping herself up in bed, she shuffled through the sheaf of paper, reluctant to read the chapter before attempting to sleep. The memory of her nightmare was still vivid, and although the bruising and scratches on her breasts and belly had faded to vague red blotches and lines, her skin still felt tender. But she knew she had to come back to Hunter with a comment tomorrow. She needed to keep up the pressure on him. He had four weeks to write twenty thousand words, while simultaneously working on the corrections of the earlier chapters. Bringing the book in on time was going to be very tight indeed.

She had planned to read the work he'd given her as soon as she returned from Eaton Square, but when she'd arrived home in the early afternoon, she discovered that Peter had gone out, leaving a note under the salt cellar on the kitchen table. *Job interview at 2.30. Kids with next door. Love P.*

By the time she'd collected the kids and managed

finally to drag herself away from Mrs Potter, the next-door neighbour, it had been close to four. The old woman's continuous chatter and high-pitched, squeaky voice had set her nerves on edge, and she found she couldn't settle. Making herself a cup of tea, she sat reading a magazine, allowing the articles on cooking, fashion and health – and a badly edited short story – to soothe her frayed nerves. When the clock pinged five, she started guiltily, realising that she'd have to begin preparing dinner, only vaguely conscious that Peter was late.

She held dinner until six-thirty, and by then the children were clamouring for food. She ate with them, not tasting the food, becoming more aware that Peter's job interview – why hadn't he said anything about it to her before now? – had been at half-past two; it was now going on for seven.

When he phoned at seven-thirty, she had worked herself up into a panic. She could hear the unmistakable sounds of a pub in the background.

'How did the interview go?'

'Good. Good.' She could tell by the hesitation that he was lying.

'Where was it for?'

'Coopers, the big accountancy firm. They phoned this morning.'

'I was expecting you home earlier,' she said evenly, knowing she had to keep a tight rein on her temper. She was all too aware of Peter's fragile ego.

'I met some friends from the old place. They were in Coopers sorting out a mutual account. They invited me out for a drink.'

'That's nice,' she said quietly. She wondered who the 'friends' were . . . and wondered why they hadn't bothered picking up the phone over the past few months. 'What time will you be home?' she asked, knowing that he was setting out to make a night of it.

'Ten. Tennish.'

'Did you bring your keys?'

There was a momentary silence, and then she heard keys rattle. 'Yes.'

'Try not to wake the children when you come in,' she said, and hung up. She could just imagine him staring at the phone with that lost-dog, bemused expression of his she found so infuriating.

She wasn't sure why she was quite so angry. It wasn't that she begrudged him the night out; far from it, it had been a long time since he'd taken himself down to the pub for the simple pleasure of a pint. It was just that, right now, she needed all the help she could get. And since Peter couldn't help with the editing of Hunter's manuscript, the most practical help he could give her was to keep the kids out of her way and help around the house. Instead, he was doing neither.

It was close to eight-thirty before she finally got the kids to bed; the two eldest, Lizzie and Mark were no problem, it was little Jody, the five year old, who wanted to stay up and watch TV. By the time Katherine had washed up the dishes – she really wanted to leave them for Peter, but knew she'd have to face them in the morning – it was after nine.

While the water heated for a bath, she sat at the kitchen table with a cup of tea and glanced quickly through Hunter's new work, steeling herself to face new atrocities.

That's when she decided not to take the bath.

At ten o'clock, Katherine slid between the sheets, plumped up the pillows, put on her glasses, and began to read . . .

DeeDee sat bolt upright in the bath in a cascade of floral-scented bubbles. Smoothing her shoulder-length, honey-blonde hair back off her face, she stood in the bath for a moment to allow the lukewarm water to drip off her shoulders and breasts. The feel of the water on her skin was deliciously cool. Although it was close to ten, the night was heavy and airless, and already she could feel the sweat beginning to bead her forehead. Thunder rumbled in the distance.

Catching hold of the edge of the bath, DeeDee stepped out onto the fluffy bath rug. She turned to face the long mirror on the back of the bathroom door. Its surface was misted over and she ran her hand across it, opening a little window onto the glass: long lines of liquid curled down to the floor. Putting her hands on her hips, DeeDee examined herself, turning her body from side to side, trying to see herself as others would see her.

She was sixteen, but looked a couple of years older, mainly because her breasts had begun to develop when she was twelve and hadn't stopped yet. Personally, she thought she looked top-heavy but the boys didn't seem to mind. Standing straight, head thrown back, she ran both hands down her body, across her full breasts, feeling her nipples hard and erect beneath her touch, across her flat belly and onto her thighs. She tilted her head from side to side, looking at her features: her eyes were pale, almost grey-blue; her forehead was high and broad, her nose straight, her teeth as perfect as money could make them. It was only her chin which let her down. She felt it was too small and had a deep, horizontal cleft.

DeeDee desperately wanted to become a model. She knew she had the body for it and with a little work, the

116

proper make-up and lighting, her face could be beautiful. There were plenty of girls modelling at fifteen and sixteen, but her parents had insisted that she complete her A-levels and probably a secretarial course – 'something to fall back on' – but by that time she'd be going on eighteen. And eighteen was practically ancient for a model. She cupped her heavy breasts. These would probably have started to sag by then.

She towelled her hair dry and pulled on a light satin bath robe. It stuck to her damp body and her nipples were prominent against the silky material. Opening the bathroom door, DeeDee stepped out onto the landing and listened. Her parents had gone out for the night, but she just wanted to make sure they hadn't returned for anything before parading half-naked around the house. 'Mom? Dad?' she called, though she was certain by then that she was alone in the house. If they'd been home, the TV in either the sitting room or the kitchen – or both – would have been blaring.

DeeDee raced down the stairs and turned on the porch light: the signal for Matt that she was alone in the house. Then, she hurried back upstairs and into her bedroom, throwing off the robe and sitting naked before the dressing table. Matt was due at ten-thirty and it was twenty-past already.

She ran a brush through her damp hair, pulling it back off her face, then catching it in a tight ponytail. It would be frizzy and wild in the morning, but she could wash it again. Make-up. Only the barest minimum, she wanted Matt to know that she had just stepped out of the bath. She stepped into a pair of white panties and pulled on the satin dressing gown again, belting it loosely, knowing it would gape open every time she moved. First she'd tease him unmercifully, then she'd do it with him. She'd let him kiss and touch her before this, allowed his hands to explore her breasts and nipples, even allowed him to slide his hand high on her thigh – but never too high. Tonight, though, she'd let him go all the way. She'd seen the way he'd been looking at Louise Cooke and Beth Ross; if she didn't give him something soon, she'd lose him. And there was no way she was going to lose him to either of those stuck-up bitches.

DeeDee was making her way down to the kitchen to put on the kettle when she heard the sound of breaking glass.

The sudden noise shocked her motionless. It had sounded close by, but muffled. Had it come from the house, or sheds, or maybe one of the neighbouring houses . . .?

A shard of glass tinkled onto the floor, and this time the sound was distinct. It had come from the sitting room.

DeeDee looked towards the room, which was at the bottom of the stairs on the right. Her heart was pumping, the movement so violent that she could feel the flesh trembling. Without turning around, she took a step back up the stairs.

Something – it sounded like a length of cloth – tore in the sitting room with a long ripping sound.

What was she going to do? Run back upstairs, or try to escape outside. There was a phone in her parents' bedroom . . . but the phone in the hall tinkled with each digit dialled. And maybe the burglar didn't know there was anyone in the house. She could lock herself in the bedroom, but everyone knew that valuables were kept in bedrooms; surely the burglar would search all the bedrooms . . . and if he found a locked door, he'd simply break it down. And God knows what he'd do if he found her. No. She would have to get out of the house. It would take seconds to run down the stairs, open the hall door and down the path. And as soon as she got into the street, she could start screaming.

But she'd have to pass the sitting-room door. And the sitting room was right beside the hall door. DeeDee suddenly wondered if her parents had turned the key in the sitting-room door before they left. The key was still in the lock. All she had to go was to turn it, and it would give her precious extra seconds to make her escape.

Rubbing her sweat-slick hands on her dressing gown, she took another step down. She was holding her breath, conscious of the satin dressing gown's loud rasp as she moved, the beating of her heart, the rush in her temples.

There were no sounds from the sitting room.

Maybe they'd left. Maybe they'd heard her – or seen the light on the porch – and been frightened away.

Maybe they were still there, crouching in the darkness. Waiting.

Three steps left. Turn the key in the sitting-room door. Two steps. Slip the chain, turn the Yale and out into the night. Last step. It shouldn't take more than a couple of seconds.

DeeDee's hand was trembling as she reached for the key in the door. She squeezed her fingers into a tight fist before she touched the key, then quickly snapped it around. The lock clicked solidly shut. The girl exhaled a great gusting sigh of relief. She was safe.

She was turning away from the door when the fist punched through the flimsy wood and wrapped iron-hard fingers around her throat.

'DeeDee . . . DeeDee?' What the fuck was keeping her? Matthew Elliot glanced around anxiously, half-expecting to find DeeDee's parents looming up out of the bushes. He leaned on the bell again, hearing its ridiculous two-tone chime deep in the house. He shifted nervously from foot to foot. 'Come on, come on.' What was keeping the bitch? He'd been standing across the road for the past hour waiting for the signal that the coast was clear, though he could see that the car was missing from the driveway. He guessed she was keeping him waiting just to tease him. She'd been teasing him for the past couple of months, though he had a good idea that she knew he was getting tired of her act.

He'd checked his watch when the light had come on and then deliberately waited ten minutes; let *her* think he wasn't coming!

Matthew leaned on the bell, stabbing it furiously. 'Come on. Come on,' he muttered. One more ring and then he was turning around and walking away.

The latch clicked and the door cracked open a fraction of an inch.

What was this: another game? 'For Jesus' sake, DeeDee,' Elliot swore, pushing open the door, glancing behind him to make sure the coast was clear. When he turned back to the hall, he was looking at a nightmare.

The ice-cold metal slid easily through the soft skin, the 440 razor-sharp steel parting tissue, muscles and finally bone, as it slicked through the ribcage to expose the fibrous lung tissue. The knife carved a huge X in the tissue and then another, to expose the heart cavity.

The metal was cold as it separated the muscle from its supporting network of sinew and arteries – ice cold.

Katherine Norton felt the metal trace its length along her leg, across her buttocks onto her stomach, its ice-cold touch burning her skin. She screamed herself awake as it nicked at her breast.

'Katherine, it's me, Katherine. It's me.' Peter Norton rolled out of bed to avoid his wife's flailing fists. Although her eyes were wide, her gaze was blank and unseeing. 'Katherine!'

Images from the nightmare shifted and settled, and Katherine Norton realised where she was. She was bathed in perspiration, her nightdress stuck to her skin, her hair plastered to her skull.

'You were having a nightmare,' Peter said unnecessarily.

Katherine nodded. She sat on the edge of the bed and breathed in great heaving gasps, running her fingers through her sticky hair. Peter came around and put his arms around her, but she winced away from his cold touch . . .

the metal slick and icy as it slid beneath the skin

. . . and rubbed at her flesh with her warm moist hands.

The blood hot and warm and salty as it spurted.

'What was it?' Peter asked.

'You've been drinking,' she said, not answering his question. She turned around to look at the clock. 'It's nearly midnight,' she said accusingly. She saw him open his mouth to make his excuses and suddenly didn't want to know. 'Tomorrow. We can talk about it in the morning.' Peeling off her nightdress, she wadded it up and tossed it on the floor, then slid back between the damp sheets.

Peter lifted the bundle of corrected manuscript off the floor. 'You were reading this before you went to bed, weren't you?' he asked. Without waiting for an answer, he said, 'It's this damn book giving you nightmares.' He looked at a page covered in Katherine's neat pencil annotation. 'Do you want to talk about it?' he asked. He turned back a couple of pages to read the lead-up to the atrocity. He wasn't particularly squeamish, but he felt the beer he'd drunk churn in his stomach as Hunter described in almost loving detail the brutal butchery. 'You know, if you talk out a nightmare, it won't recur,' he said eventually. He tapped the page. 'I mean, this is every woman's nightmare, isn't it: attacked in your own home . . .?'

Katherine rolled over and pulled the cover up over her head. This hadn't been a nightmare; it had been more, much more. This had been so vivid, so real. But what had really terrified her was that in the dream, she was not victim: she was the murderer.

Chapter Nineteen

MARGARET Haaren stood before the mangled body, hanging on the sitting-room door and realised that she felt nothing: no anger, no sorrow, no pain. She was numb inside. But as she looked at the mutilated remains of what had once been a pretty young woman, the inspector decided – calmly, coolly – that if she got to the murderer, he was not going to stand trial. There were some crimes, she believed, where there could only be one form of justice: the black-and-white biblical justice of the Old Testament, *an eye for an eye, a tooth for a tooth . . . and a life for a life*.

DeeDee had been crucified against the sitting-room door, huge spikes driven through her outstretched wrists, pinning them to the hall. Her legs had been crossed at the ankle and another spike driven through the bones deep into the wooden door beneath. The inspector wondered at the strength it would have taken to do that.

She squeezed her eyes shut, but the image remained. The girl was naked, though when the inspector had first arrived, she'd thought the body was wearing a ragged, bloody cloth around her loins. It took her a few moments to realise that she was looking at tatters of flesh that had been peeled away from the body. There was a great gaping wound in the centre of the chest, ash-white slivers of the shattered ribcage poking through the bloody meat.

Margaret Haaren opened her eyes, deliberately not looking at the corpse now, concentrating on the occult symbols that had been daubed onto the wall and door above the corpse. They had been written in the girl's blood.

'We're finished here,' Stuart Miller said, 'we should take her down.'

'Just a moment,' the inspector said. She turned around, seeing that the rest of the team – the police, forensics, technicians and coroner's people – had gathered in the hall and on the stairs. As she looked from face to face, the expressions numb or blank, their eyes angry or ill, Haaren realised that they all *expected* her to solve this crime. She turned back to the body. 'You've all seen this animal's work,' she said very softly, but in the absolute silence her voice was clearly audible. 'He's broken rhythm, he wasn't due to kill until the next full moon, but he's killed out of sync. Whatever bizarre rules were keeping him in check are broken now. He's going to kill again, very soon. And only we can stop him.' She pointed to the ragged lump of meat that had been a young woman. 'This was a sixteen-year-old girl. How many of you have children?' she asked, and then turned and walked from the house.

There was a huge crowd outside, a mixture of neighbours and press. A television crew was setting up, arc lamps throwing harsh light across the crowd. Flashguns began strobing when the reporters spotted the inspector and sergeant. Haaren didn't even look in their direction.

'What about the parents?' she asked, swallowing hard. There was a sour taste in her mouth: a mixture of

124

the stench of blood and faeces, the acrid odour of death.

'We're still trying to trace them,' Miller said quietly. 'We can't get much sense out of the boyfriend . . .'

'Hardly surprising.'

Miller shook his head. 'He walked into the hall and discovered the body. Neighbours heard him screaming and alerted the police.'

The inspector leaned on the roof of the Granada, fingers interlaced. She stared into the distance, trying to pretend that it was the wind blowing into her face that was making her eyes water. 'Where is he now?'

'Hospital, under sedation. So are the two neighbours who were the first to reach the house,' Miller added. 'Two big men . . . and they both fainted. One had a heart attack.' His face flickered in a brief, humourless smile. 'When the first patrol unit got here, they thought it was a massacre: two bodies lying in the garden, the boy collapsed on the steps – and then the . . . mess in the hall.'

'The heart is missing,' Haaren said, a statement, not a question.

'I think so. The nipples have been cut off.'

The inspector's fingers closed into a tight knot. 'So it's the same killer?'

'It looks that way.'

'Then why has the pattern changed?' She swung around to look at the sergeant. 'For the past six months our killer has been working to a lunar cycle. Why has he changed his cycle?' She jerked her head in the direction of the house. 'He's never slain a victim at home before. Even the style of mutilations has changed . . . much cruder, far more destructive and he seems to have been working in haste. Why did he choose this girl?' she wondered aloud.

Miller shook his head. 'He'd obviously been watching her. He knew she was alone in the house.'

Haaren moved around the car and pulled open the driver's door. 'Find out everything you can about the girl, especially the full catalogue of friends and relations.'

'Where are you going?' Miller asked.

'Hospital. I want to see if I can get anything out of the boy.'

Margaret Haaren stood at one end of the cold, white corridor and watched the couple standing pressed up against the glass window at the other end. The staff nurse told her they were the boy's parents; she had also told her that the boy had taken a seizure and gone into shock in the ambulance on the way to the hospital. Moments later his heart had arrested. Prompt action by the ambulance crew had saved his life, but it would be another couple of hours before the doctors could decide if there had been any brain damage.

The inspector walked slowly down the corridor, her flat-soled shoes clicking slightly on the gleaming lino, the noise thunderous in the breathless silence. The couple turned. Haaren took a deep breath. How many hospital corridors had she walked down in her twenty-five years as a police officer; how many red-eyed couples had she faced, grieving mothers and fathers, sons and daughters, husbands and wives? She held out her hand as she approached, forcing them to come forward, pulling them away from the window which looked into the intensive care unit.

'Mr and Mrs Elliot; I'm Inspector Margaret Haaren, Metropolitan Police. I'm in charge of this case.' The couple looked at her blankly and the inspector knew that they weren't really seeing her. 'I'd like to ask you a few questions, if I may, about your son and Deirdre.'

'DeeDee,' the woman said, her voice barely audible.

'I beg your pardon?'

'DeeDee,' the woman repeated, looking into the inspector's face, 'she always insisted that we call her DeeDee. She hated the name Deirdre.'

'Did you know her well, Mrs Elliot?'

'Not very,' the woman said. She was small and frail-looking, with white hair that contrasted sharply with her black eyebrows. Her eyes were red and swollen from crying. 'I told Matthew that she was bad news,' she said sharply. She paused and added in a softer tone, 'The girl was . . . advanced.'

'In what way, Mrs Elliot?'

'Advanced for her years. She might have been only sixteen, but she dressed and acted like an eighteen or nineteen year old.' She stopped, suddenly realising what she was saying. Both hands flew to her mouth, then covered her face and she collapsed against her husband, crying bitterly. 'I'm sorry,' she whispered. 'I shouldn't be talking like this about . . . about poor DeeDee.'

'My wife is upset, inspector,' Matthew Elliot Senior said, looking into Margaret Haaren's green eyes.

'I understand,' she said automatically.

'Do you, inspector?' the man asked sharply.

'More than you'll ever know,' Haaren said grimly. 'I'm looking for a little help now, something that will help me understand the girl . . . and possibly her killer. The same person who killed the girl is responsible for your son's condition.'

Matthew Elliot smiled apologetically. 'I know very little about the girl, inspector. She took up with Matt two or three months ago. I got the impression from Matt that she was something of a coup; a lot of the lads in school were chasing her. I think he was rather surprised that he won.' He turned and looked back down the corridor. 'Won and lost.'

'Did your son ever say anything about the girl being followed, old boyfriends, weird phone calls . . .'?

'He was seventeen, inspector. If he said hello to me in the morning and goodnight in the evening, I was lucky. Maybe you should ask the girl's parents.'

'We will, Mr Elliot,' Haaren said, looking into the man's face, 'when we find them.'

'They don't know yet?' he whispered.

The inspector shook her head. 'Anything you can tell me about the girl would be helpful, Mr Elliot. Do you know if she belonged to any clubs; did she have a job?'

Matthew Elliot shook his head, pushing a lock of lank, grey hair off his high forehead. 'I'm sorry, inspector. I only met the girl once.'

'She didn't have a job,' Mrs Elliot said suddenly, 'but she did a lot of babysitting. Matt told me she had quite a list of wealthy clients. He was so excited because he got to meet one of his heroes – a writer – a couple of days ago. DeeDee sits – sat – for them.'

The inspector's buzzer bleeped. 'Excuse me,' she said, hurrying to the nearest phone, unwilling to take the time to go down to her car in the underground carpark. After a delay with an inexperienced dispatcher, she was eventually put through to Stuart Miller. 'We've managed to get hold of the parents,' he said, his voice flat and expressionless.

'I'm on my way,' she said quickly.

'Stay where you are,' Miller said. 'The father's had a heart attack too. They're on the way to the hospital at the moment.

'Jesus,' she whispered. 'Our friend's notching up quite a score tonight.'

128

'You can say that again,' Miller said quietly, 'we've got another body.'

'Where?'

'Would you believe, almost next door to the present victim's house?'

'Is it the same killer?'

'Well . . . yes and no,' Miller admitted cautiously.

'I'm too tired for games, Stuart,' the inspector snapped.

'Yes, ma'am. We've got another body two doors down from the girl's home; the MO is the same, but the killer patently couldn't have carried out the second killing.'

'This isn't making a lot of sense . . .'

'We've got the killer,' the sergeant continued. 'A sixty-two-year-old grandmother who cut her husband's throat as he dozed in a chair waching TV. She then cut out his heart . . . and carved crude astrological symbols into his flesh. A neighbour called to tell her about the girl's killing and found her covered in blood.'

'Jesus!' Haaren breathed. 'Have you spoken to her?'

'Yes, ma'am. She said the devil made her do it.'

It was dawn by the time Margaret Haaren returned to her small apartment. Too tired to shower, she kicked off her shoes as she walked into the kitchen to boil the kettle for a cup of tea.

She felt drained, both physically and mentally, and a dull headache had settled in at the base of her skull which she knew from experience wasn't going to shift for days. She had spent the best part of three hours sitting with Mrs Rita Banks, DeeDee's mother, holding her hand, listening to her talk, about her husband – now lying alongside Matthew Elliot in intensive care – about DeeDee, but coming back again and again to the

129

question every victim's relatives and friends ask, 'Why?'

It was ordeal enough to tell a close relative that a loved one had died; it was doubly difficult when that death had not been natural, but when the death had been as violent and grotesque as DeeDee's and was then compounded by a further tragedy, the task became almost impossible.

Haaren had told Mrs Banks exactly what had happened, deciding that it was better that she hear it now, face to face, than read about it in the newspaper tomorrow. Although the authorities had managed to keep a lid on the previous killings, the inspector knew that there was no way they could keep this killing out of the papers. She could almost see the headlines now: 'Street of Horror – Carnage Street.' The only question Rita Banks kept asking was, 'Did she suffer?'

And the inspector was able to shake her head and truthfully answer, 'No.'

The woman had been in such a state of shock that she had answered all the questions the inspector had put to her. Much of the information Haaren dismissed as useless and because she'd been reluctant to write down the names and addresses of DeeDee's many boyfriends and babysitting clients in the mother's presence, the same questions would have to be asked again.

Haaren had finally left the bereaved woman in the care of a WPC and headed back to the scene of the murder. Although it was now well into the early hours, a time when the quiet suburban street should have been still and silent, a large crowd had gathered to watch the comings and goings of scores of police officers, white-coated technicians, and newspaper and camera crews who had set up to do 'on-the-scene' reports with the floodlit houses in the background. The inspector's arrival sent the press into a frenzy of activity as they shouted questions and attempted to snatch a hurried interview as she brushed past.

In many ways the inspector found the second murder even more disturbing than the first. The first crime was obviously the work of a sick and perverted mind, but here, a perfectly normal woman, sixty-two years of age, five-foot one-inch tall, just under seven stone, had taken a razor-sharp kitchen knife and eviscerated her husband of forty-one years, laid open the chest wall, sawing through ribs to gain access to the heart which she had then removed and laid, very neatly, on the chair beside him. Stuart Miller told the inspector that the woman had been constantly repeating, 'The devil made me do it . . . the devil made me do it.'

The kettle clicked off with a snap, jerking the inspector out of her light doze. Were the two cases connected, or was it nothing more than a bizarre coincidence? But surely it was the same bizarre coincidences, the terrible similarities, that proved that the cases had to be connected. What had tipped the woman over the edge? Miller had speculated that the woman had approached the Banks's house, seen the front door open, peered inside and been so shocked by the sight of the butchered body that she had snapped, gone back to her own home and sliced open her husband.

Haaren made tea and stood by the small kitchen window, staring across at a nearby block of apartments, her thoughts whirling with countless images. Miller's hypothesis was plausible . . . but she was coming to the conclusion that there was another, far more sinister explanation.

The police had investigated the occult angle of the killing right from the beginning. The occult symbols, which had first been daubed and later cut into the bodies of the dead women, and the lunar cycle had indicated a carefully thought-out ritual. But a ritual alone did not indicate an occult connection. The inspector knew that the vast majority of ritualistic killings were committed by people with no real interest in the occult.

The devil made me do it.

What made a perfectly ordinary woman kill and butcher her husband? Had something touched her fleetingly as she fled the scene of the first crime, had she seen or experienced something which had robbed her of her sanity?

There was something in the streets of London feeding off the flesh of young women, etching ancient symbols in to their skins. What was it? And was it human?

It was at times like this, in the still hours before dawn, that the memories returned, leaving the woman chilled to the bone. Two years ago she had witnessed a monster – a creature of legend – step from a slab of glass. In that instant all that she had believed, all she had been taught since childhood, disappeared.

Margaret Haaren knew that there were monsters walking this world . . . and only some of them looked like beasts.

Chapter Twenty

THE rich aroma of freshly brewed coffee brought her awake. Katherine Norton struggled to sit up in the rumpled bed. She felt wretched – exhausted after another night of unremitting terror where nightmare had flowed into nightmare in a series of bizarre and obscene images.

Her husband opened the bedroom door with his foot and stepped into the room carrying two large mugs of coffee.

'Strong and black,' he said with a wan smile. He too was feeling decidedly unwell, though his illness was due to a very late night and too much beer.

Katherine wrapped her hands around the mug and sipped gratefully at the coffee. She could feel it sear its way down her throat into her stomach. Closing her eyes, she lay back against the pillow.

Peter perched on the edge of the bed and watched her carefully as he sipped his own coffee. He had to speak, and might as well get it over with now . . .

'About last night,' he began.

Katherine's eyes opened. She frowned at him and he instantly regretted saying anything. 'What about last night?'

'I'm sorry I was so late,' he pressed on. 'I just didn't realise that the time was slipping by. I would have come home sooner,' he hurried on, 'but there was a problem with the Tube, something on the line . . .' He trailed off.

Katherine sipped the coffee, then closed her eyes. 'You took the car yesterday,' she said.

'Oh shit!' He *had* taken the car yesterday. He had parked it in the multi-storey carpark across from the accountants . . . and promptly forgotten about it. It was going to cost a fortune to get it out.

Katherine opened her eyes, her expression cold. 'Look, I really don't want to talk about this now. I feel like shit, and I just know if we continue this conversation then I'll say something I'll regret. Anyway,' she added, 'leaving the car behind was probably a good idea. You'd probably have killed yourself if you'd attempted to drive it home in the condition you were in last night.'

'Look, I'm sorry Katherine . . . it won't happen again, I promise . . .'

'Until the next time,' she finished. She twisted around to look at the alarm clock. 'Look, it's nearly nine. Why don't you get the kids up and fix them breakfast? Give me a few minutes to catch a nap; I didn't sleep too well last night.'

'I know, you were really restless. You were tossing and turning all night.' He tilted his head to show a livid spot on his right cheekbone. 'You caught me with a good right hand shortly after I got into bed.' He grinned. 'I don't know what you were dreaming about, but you put up a hell of a fight doing it.'

Katherine closed her eyes. 'I was dreaming about . . . I was dreaming about . . .'

She opened her eyes.

The coffee soured in her stomach, and she immediately threw back the covers and swung her legs

134

out of bed. It was a short hop to the bathroom, and she only just reached it before vomiting.

The bizarre double murder made all the headlines. Katherine lay back against the pillows and read through the newspapers with a growing sense of terror that caught at the base of her lungs, squeezing them tightly until she was panting, as if she had just climbed several flights of stairs.

She spread the *Daily Mirror* out on the bed and lifted Hunter's manuscript off the floor. Maybe she was imagining it; maybe she'd left the radio on last night and she'd caught a late-night news broadcast and it had somehow percolated into her dreams, and then she had dreamt that she had read about the killings in Hunter's book . . .

Crucified against the door, six-inch nails driven through the small bones in the wrists . . .

The newspaper report was only slightly less graphic.

'The girl was pinned to the wall by nails which had been driven through the wrists in the classic crucifixion posture.'

The ribs hacked open, the lungs hanging in shredded tissue, a gaping hole where the heart had once beaten . . .

'Police have refused to confirm reports that the victim's heart was missing.'

Katherine shook her head quickly, mouth forming a silent 'no'. She skipped the newspaper's somewhat restrained account of the killing, moving back up the page, scanning the short lines. She found what she was looking for above the grainy picture of the victim's house.

'Blonde and blue-eyed, Dierdre Banks (16) . . .'

Katherine pushed the paper aside, then carefully picked her way through Hunter's manuscript, trying to remember where she had come across the reference . . .

Denise Quinlan looked older than her sixteen years. With her blonde hair bobbed and styled, and her bright blue eyes hidden behind expensive sunglasses, she could have easily passed for nineteen . . .'

'Oh Christ!' Katherine hissed. Hunter had described the murder almost exactly; he'd even managed to get the dead girl's initial correct. She felt ice-water trickle down her spine. It was a bizarre coincidence, nothing more, just a coincidence..

The *Daily Telegraph* contained a fuller report on the double murder. It didn't dwell on the gruesome details, but contented itself simply with reporting the facts. It suggested that both murders were somehow connected, though by the end of the article, the reporter had to admit that he had nothing to substantiate the assertion.

It was the last line that caught Katherine's attention. As the women who had killed her husband was led away by police, the *Telegraph* reporter had caught her mumbled words on a tape recorder he had thrust into her face. 'The devil made me do it. The devil made me do it.'

Katherine swallowed hard. It was a line worthy of one of Hunter's books.

Robert Hunter folded away the newspapers and sat back into his leather chair, his elbows on the arm rests, hands before his face, index fingers pressing against his lips. Cold red light from the computer screen washed over his features, turning his eyes into tiny mirrors which reflected the white words on the red background. From the distance it looked as if his face had been washed in blood.

Denise Quinlan looked older than her sixteen years. With her blonde hair bobbed and styled, and her bright blue eyes . . .

Sixteen, blonde and blue-eyed. Denise. DeeDee. Deirdre.

What had he done this time?

Hunter allowed his eyes to flicker across the screen. His fingers automatically moved over the keyboard, changing 'blonde' to 'dark-haired', 'blue eyes' to 'brown', 'sixteen' to 'eighteen', 'Denise' to 'Anne'. He saved his changes, the disk light flickering, the hard disk whirring, consigning sixteen-year-old, blonde, blue-eyed Denise to an electronic death, giving birth to eighteen-year-old, dark-haired, brown-eyed Anne.

His fingers were trembling slightly as he lifted them off the keyboard. What *had* he done? Had he killed her? He closed both hands into tight fists. He didn't think so but, God help him, he didn't know any more.

He heard the front-door bell chime, and then, moments later, the intercom crackled. 'It's Katherine, Bob. Will I send her up?'

Hunter thumbed the send button. 'Of course. Of course.' It was only when he released the button that he realised that Katherine Norton had a copy of the manuscript with the original description of the victim. He wondered if she had noticed the similarities, and then he nodded fiercely. Of course she'd notice. She was an editor; she was trained to notice details.

Chapter Twenty-One

AS soon as he opened the door and saw the look in her eyes, Robert Hunter knew that she had seen the newspaper reports and made the connection with his text. A lot would depend on how he handled the next few minutes.

'You look tired, Katherine,' he said, standing back to allow her in.

'I didn't sleep too well last night,' she said quietly.

Hunter pushed the door closed and followed Katherine across the room. He could tell by her posture that she was nervous; her shoulders were taut, the indentations of her rigid spine clearly visible through her light summer dress, and when she turned to look at him, the wariness flared in her eyes, tension lines tightened around her lips. She sat in one of the high-backed wooden chairs before a long table and opened her briefcase, unwilling to meet his eyes. Hunter sat facing her in the hanging wicker chair, watching with his pale, colourless eyes as she attempted to disguise her nervousness beneath a veneer of efficiency.

Pulling out the laptop, Katherine set it up on the table before her, popped open the lid to reveal the screen and keys, and thumbed the switch which brought it alive.

'I take it you've finished the manuscript,' Hunter said suddenly.

'I've done as much work as I can for the moment,' Katherine said quietly, concentrating on the small screen.

'What do you think?' Hunter asked.

Katherine looked up, and found herself caught by the writer's fixed expression.

'It's very . . . powerful,' she said after a momentary hesitation.

Hunter began to laugh, the motion setting the hanging chair swinging from side to side. 'Powerful. Powerful.' He shook his head and the laughter suddenly turned bitter. 'Now if that isn't the most useless description of a book I've ever heard. It tells me exactly nothing. It doesn't tell me if the book is good or bad, if the storyline is cohesive, if the characters are three-dimensional, if the internal consistency is correct. "Powerful" is not exactly an editorial comment. "Powerful" is a word used by a reviewer.'

'I think you know exactly what I mean when I say it's powerful, Bob. The book is good. The storyline is cohesive, the characters are three-dimensional and the internal consistency is more or less correct. But then, you're a professional writer, Bob, I would expect nothing less.'

Hunter leaned forward. 'So tell me what's wrong with it!' he demanded.

'It's . . . it's . . .'

'It's what?' he demanded.

'It's giving me nightmares,' she said, surprising herself with the revelation.

'Bravo! I'm delighted.' Hunter clapped his hands together. 'I consider that a compliment.'

'I suppose it is one,' Katherine said.

'I've made a very good living over the years supplying people with the material for their nightmares.'

'Do you ever have nightmares, Mr Hunter?'

'None at all. All my nightmares are down on paper.' Without pausing, he said, 'And what did you dream about last night?'

'I dreamt about a young woman crucified against a door.' Hunter nodded. 'A blonde-haired, blue-eyed young woman,' she continued, watching him intently now.

Hunter's smile remained fixed.

Katherine realised she had gone too far to turn back. 'Last night a young woman was killed not two miles from here. She was murdered in precisely the same way one of the victims in your new book is slain. Her physical description matched that of the young woman in your book, even down to her initials.'

'So what are you saying?' Hunter said evenly. Katherine stopped. What exactly was she saying? Was she accusing Hunter? 'Are you suggesting that I murdered the poor girl?' the writer continued. His face betrayed nothing; his eyes were cold and empty.

'No, no, of course not.'

'What then?'

Katherine looked at him blankly. What exactly was she accusing him of? 'I was just . . . remarking on the coincidence,' she finished lamely.

Hunter came quickly to his feet, turned his back on the editor and strode down the length of the room to stand before the long window that looked down over the front of the house.

'It is a remarkable coincidence,' he said eventually. 'Shall I tell you something even more remarkable, Katherine? The young woman who was murdered last night, Dierdre Banks, was our babysitter.' He turned and stood with his back to the window. With the light on his back, his face was in shadow and she could no longer see his expression. 'And shall I tell you something else? It wasn't a coincidence.'

Katherine felt her breath catch at the back of her throat. 'What do you mean, "It wasn't a coincidence"?'

'Do you believe in psychic ability, Katherine?'

Caught off balance by the question, Katherine could only shrug. 'Yes . . . no. I don't know. I've never really thought about it.'

'You mean you've never edited a book on the subject?' he asked, teeth flashing in a quick smile.

'Never,' she smiled, relieved that some ice was breaking. If Hunter had gone back to the Image Press with the story that she had practically accused their star author of committing a murder, then she would never have worked for the publishing company again. And the publishing trade was small; if the story had got out – as it surely would – she would have never worked again. Period.

'I have been writing for ten years, Katherine. In that time I've become aware that I possess a certain . . . talent.' He shrugged. 'Occasionally what I write comes to pass.' He stopped, and then continued, hurriedly. 'That sounds dramatic, doesn't it? Perhaps you don't believe me.' Hunter came back down the long room, his carpet slippers hissing off the smooth floor boards. 'I made the discovery when I was writing *Blood Passion* my third book. One of the final scenes in the book is where the heroine falls through a plate-glass window, completely severing her head. As I was writing it, I could see it happening, I could visualise the girl in great detail, right down to the mole on her right cheek.

'And then it happened.'

'A schoolgirl – fifteen, sixteen maybe – in a shopping-centre in the centre of Leeds slipped and fell against a plate-glass window. By some extraordinary fluke, she struck it at a weak point and it shattered in around her, propelling her through the window and down into the mall two floors below. She was dead long before she hit the ground though, because the glass had sheered off her head.' Katherine swallowed hard. 'It took me six months to recover; I couldn't write. I had *seen* that accident, seen it with absolute and complete clarity. But I thought it was nothing more than another figment of my imagination. Some people who read the incident in *Blood Passion* wrote to me, thinking I got the idea for the incident from the accident in Leeds. But I'd written my text a week before the accident occurred.'

'You're saying you saw the accident before it happened?'

Hunter nodded. 'That's what I'm saying.' He sank into the chair before the computer, the leather creaking and sighing around him. 'Over the years, I've come to the conclusion that I possess a highly sensitive psychic ability. It doesn't work all the time, of course, so that's not to say that every killing in my books is mirrored in real life. It tends to happen when I'm very tired or deep in my books, and of course, the latest research into psychic phenomena has shown that it's at times like these that the conscious brain is at its lowest ebb and the unconscious highly active. Also, research has shown that psychic abilities tend to be concentrated in that portion of the brain which controls the unconscious.'

Katherine shook her head quickly. 'You must excuse me if all of this seems . . .'

'Bizarre?' Hunter suggested. 'Outrageous, nonsensical, stupid?' He nodded. 'It's all of those things, and more. But it also happens to be true.' He nodded

142

towards the manuscript. 'How else could I have written about DeeDee's murder?' He stopped suddenly. He was watching Katherine's reflection in the computer screen. 'Unless, of course, I killed her myself,' he murmured.

'No, no, I'm sure I never thought that,' Katherine said hurriedly.

'Admit it. It's what I would have thought if I'd been in your position. A bloody murder is described in detail in an unpublished book, of which there are only two copies, and since you know that you didn't commit the murder, it can therefore only be . . .' He trailed off.

Katherine looked at the manuscript, thoughts whirling, trying to make sense of what the writer was telling her.

'And do you know what is the most terrifying aspect of my peculiar gift?' Hunter continued. Without waiting for an answer, he hurried on. 'I never know which bloody events are going to happen. Maybe one in every book, sometimes two, occasionally three will take place – the rest exist only in my imagination.' He tapped the side of his head, his thin lips twisting into a wry smile. 'I thought when I crucified someone against a door I'd be safe enough. I thought something like that could only exist in my imagination. I was wrong.'

Katherine felt the small hairs on the back of her neck stand on end. Hunter's revelation was far more chilling than anything she'd read in his books. To be able to look upon a brutal death, like a television viewer tuning into a channel . . .

Licking dry lips, she asked, 'Does it always happen to someone around you?'

'Usually. The girl in Leeds was a next-door neighbour. The girl last night was our babysitter.

143

We've lost a cook to a bus accident, numerous neighbours ... and of course, our first baby was stillborn.'

'Oh,' Katherine breathed. 'I'm terribly sorry.'

But Hunter continued as if he hadn't heard her. 'I had written a piece about a child sacrificed in a black mass. I described in loving detail the tiny coffin being lowered into the cold, wet soil. A couple of weeks later, Emma gave birth to our first child. Two days later, I was standing by an open grave watching a tiny white coffin disappearing into the earth.' He spun around to face his computer screen, fingers idly tapping the keyboard, then swung back to Katherine. 'Of course, I didn't realise the significance of what I was seeing then. I do now. And sometimes I can't help but wonder, do I merely report trouble or, by reporting it, do I activate it? You were wondering if I was guilty of murder ... well, perhaps I am!'

Chapter Twenty-Two

ALL the major newspapers carried similar headlines . . .

BUTCHER STRIKES AGAIN

A savage killer struck again in a quiet London suburb. Fifteen-year-old Deirdre Banks was crucified in her own hallway and her naked body then daubed with occult symbols . . .

BLACK-MAGIC BUTCHER

Police are refusing to confirm that parts of the girl's body are missing, taken by the killer. Sources close to the investigation, however, have revealed that the police have not ruled out the possibility that the killer may be indulging in cannibalism . . .

OCCULT KILLER

Scotland Yard has confirmed that Inspector Margaret Haaren (43) is leading the investigation and that an early arrest is expected. However, they have refused to confirm reports that this case is related to six similar killings across the Midlands and the Home Counties and have dismissed suggestions that this killing was part of an occult ritual.

HORROR-SCOPE KILLINGS

This reporter can exclusively reveal that the investigation into the death of Deirdre Banks is the seventh in a series of increasingly brutal and bizarre killings that have baffled police across Britain. So far all the victims have been young women and the killings have all the hallmarks of a black-magic ritual. The occult and astrological symbols carved into the bodies have caused the killings to be dubbed the Horror-Scope Murders. Inspector Margaret Haaren who is heading up the investigation was unavailable for comment. It is significant that the inspector, who made her reputation in solving two occult-related murder cases, has been given the task of bringing the offender to book.

Chapter Twenty-Three

WITH the morning newspapers scattered in disordered sheets on the floor around her feet, Margaret Haaren sat at the kitchen table in her small apartment and watched the lunchtime news from the BBC on the portable television.

Like the newspapers, the reports had concentrated on the murders. While a pleasant-faced young woman recited the toned-down catalogue of horrors – the full version would come later on the nine o'clock news – the picture showed the dead girl's home. There was an estate agent's sign on the house next door. The inspector smiled grimly; any chance of selling it had gone right down the toilet. She squirmed in embarrassment when she spotted herself emerging from the crime scene, the harsh glare of the camera lights washing over her. She looked old and tired, she decided, her forehead gleaming with a sheen of sweat. Her brusque 'No comment at this time' sounded arrogant and insensitive.

A tight-lipped male reporter gave a terse commentary as Deirdre Banks's body was carried from the house and there was a brief, floodlit glimpse of the interior of the hall before the door was pulled shut. The glimpse had been enough to show the bloodstreaked walls and the occult symbols which had now dried to flaking brown patches.

Back in the studio, a panel of experts spoke briefly on the rise of occult-related crime in the British Isles in the last ten years. The inspector listened intently until she determined that they were all talking rubbish; she stabbed down on the remote control, turning the TV off. In the long silence that followed, she stared through the grimy window – she would clean it soon – at the washed-out blue sky, and wondered about her next move.

The investigation had always been difficult. Leads were few, there were no clues to the killer and no obvious connections between the victims: they were from different ethnic groups, different social classes, and ranged in age from Deirdre, the youngest at sixteen, to one of the earliest victims who had been in her forties. But however difficult the investigation had been to date, it was nothing compared to how difficult it was going to get now with the press breathing down their necks.

Summer was traditionally the silly season for the newspapers; a story like this – with sex, torture, death and the occult – was a gift to the tabloids. Increased press activity would mean that her superiors would be putting the pressure on for a result. Folding her hands onto the table, she laid her head down on them, allowing her eyes to blink closed. She had finally got to bed around six, but had managed nothing more than a light doze, and had started awake more than once, images of the latest atrocity dancing behind her eyelids. She was drifting into a light doze when the phone rang, jerking her fully awake. She raised her head, listening as the answering machine cut in, her brief 'Leave a message after the tone' sounding curt.

'Ma'am, it's Stuart, if you're there . . .'

The inspector snatched the phone off the wall and the answering machine clicked off.

'Stuart!'

'I'm sorry for ringing you at home . . .'

'What's wrong?'

'I've got something for you, ma'am . . .' he began.

She could hear raised voices and muted shouts in the background. 'What's happening down there, Stuart?' she interrupted.

'Oh, its a real three-ringed circus here at the moment. We've got press everywhere, both home and international, radio, and TV – I wouldn't be at all surprised to find a sports reporter here too. At least half a dozen pressure groups – including a witches' group, would you believe? – are demonstrating in the street outside. The station is crawling with brass, and every nutcase in the city has come out of the woodwork to testify that he or she did it.'

'I'm sorry I asked.'

'Well, this much I can handle, I think. However, what I do have for you is a letter which gives details about the meanings of the occult symbols. It was addressed to you personally and hand-delivered about an hour ago. The letter-writer also says that the killer may be giving us a clue to his identity in the symbols, and offers to decipher them for us.'

The inspector took a deep breath. This could be the break they were looking for . . . or it could be just another crank . . . or it might be the killer, playing a macabre game of hide-and-seek with the police. It had happened before. 'I don't suppose we have a signature on the letter, do we?' she asked.

'We do,' Miller said. 'It's signed Father Michael Carroll, S.J. And I've got an address where he'll be this morning.'

'A priest?' Haaren asked. 'What's an S.J.?'

'A Jesuit priest.'

'What's the difference, Stuart? I'm not a Catholic.'

'I went to a Jesuit school in Jamaica, and they were tough bastards. Pardon my language, ma'am. Jesuits are a breed apart. Anyone can become a priest, but becoming a Jesuit is a lot more difficult. They're sort of an elite amongst the priesthood.'

'And this Jesuit says he can help us? What would a priest know about occult symbols?'

'Can't answer that one, ma'am, but Jesuits tend to be scholars and intellectuals. He might be able to help.'

'What's his address?'

'Westminster Cathedral,' Miller said, and then added quickly, 'that's the Catholic one, not the Abbey.'

'I know that,' Haaren said, though she had actually been thinking of Westminster Abbey, and wondering what a Catholic priest would be doing there.

'What do you want to do?' Miller asked.

'I think I'll go and talk to this priest. Can't hurt, anyway.'

Margaret Haaren got out of the cab in Francis Street and looked across at the grotesquely ornate frontage of Westminster Cathedral. Although she'd lived in London for most of her adult life, she had never visited the place before ... nor had she visited any of the other tourist sights either, so it wasn't just prejudice. As she hurried across the open plaza in front of the cathedral, she found the overall effect of red and white brick, the enormous cupola and the towering campanile overpowering, almost oppressive. Haaren stopped just inside the door and looked at the list of priests and chaplains connected to the parish. There was no Michael Carroll listed.

The interior of the vast cathedral – and it was enormous – was a shock to the inspector. She rarely went to church now, and she had never stood inside a Catholic church. She had been expecting something like the spartan elegance of her own C of E chapel, but the opulent lushness took her by surprise. She breathed deeply, tasting an odour that brought back vivid memories from her childhood: candlewax and incense.

The inspector turned to the left. A service was in progress. As she made her way up the left-hand aisle, she spotted a young man in a long white surplice. 'Excuse me . . .' she said too loudly. Heads turned to look at her. Lowering her voice, she tried again, 'Excuse me.'

'How may I help you?' the young man asked, his colouring and accent betraying his French origins.

'I am looking for a Father Michael Carroll,' Haaren said.

The young man frowned. 'There is no priest here of that name,' he answered.

'A Jesuit,' she added.

The French cleric shook his head again. 'I will enquire for you,' he said. 'Will you follow me?' Without waiting for a reply, he turned away, crossed the bottom of the cathedral, pausing to genuflect before the altar, and headed up the right aisle. He didn't turn to see if the woman was following him.

They passed small side chapels, some set in behind closed metal grilles, others open. In most, there was someone sitting in the pews before the miniature altars.

'How long is the cathedral?' the inspector asked, panting as she attempted to keep up with the younger man's silent and effortless glide.

151

'The cathedral is three hundred and forty-two feet long and one hundred and forty-nine feet wide,' he said, without looking around, obviously answering a question he had been asked a hundred times before. 'Wait here,' he said brusquely, 'I will go into the sacristy to make your enquiry. The name of the priest again . . .?'

'Carroll. Father Michael Carroll, S.J.'

'Thank you.'

The inspector slid into a wooden chair to wait as the young cleric vanished behind an enormous pillar.

'Margaret Haaren? Inspector Margaret Haaren?'

The inspector surged to her feet, almost upsetting the flimsy wooden chair, vaguely disappointed that she hadn't been aware of the person slipping into the seat beside her. She was looking down at a tall, elegant man in his fifties, with fine, white hair that flowed to his shoulders. He was dressed in clerical black with a Roman collar. Coming smoothly to his feet, long-fingered hand outstretched, he smiled. 'I am Michael Carroll.' He allowed a copy of the *Sun* to fold open. 'Your picture does not do you justice.'

The inspector shook the priest's hand. His flesh was cold and dry. 'I thought you were associated with the church here.'

'No, inspector . . .' he began, and stopped as the young French cleric materialised out of the gloom.

'I'm afraid there is no Father Carroll . . .' he began.

'I've found him, thank you,' the inspector said quickly. 'I'm sorry to have put you to so much trouble.'

'It was no trouble,' the young man said. He bowed to the older priest. 'Father.'

'Peace be with you, my son.'

When the young man disappeared down the length of the church, Haaren turned back to the priest. He

152

indicated a chair. 'Let us sit.'

The inspector came around to sit beside the priest. Now that she was closer, she could see that he was older than she had first imagined – late fifties, early sixties – and the deep black bags beneath his blue eyes, which were magnified by thick-lensed glasses, made him look even older.

'You said you could help our investigation, Father Carroll,' the inspector said quickly.

'Indulge me for a moment,' the priest said. 'Why did you respond?' he asked. 'Why did you come here? I imagine you got several communications like mine.'

'Dozens,' the inspector corrected him. 'I came because I was curious. We haven't had a communication from a priest before, and that was certainly unusual. And of course, the fact that you didn't confess to the crime yourself was different. Most of our letter-writers end up by confessing.'

'The urge to confess is very strong in most human beings,' the priest said, and the inspector caught a hint of an accent.

'You're Irish, father?'

'Your ear is good, inspector. I was born and raised in Wicklow, to the south of Dublin, though I haven't set foot in my native country for thirty and more years.' Glancing sidelong, he said, 'Surely it was more than curiosity that brought you here?'

'Just curiosity,' she said.

'But any one of those dozens of letters you received could have roused your curiosity. I think the real reason you came here was because I mentioned the symbols,' he continued.

Haaren looked at him in surprise. 'You're right. You were the only person who mentioned the symbols.'

'The symbols are the key,' the priest said simply.

'From the very beginning I've felt that the answer lay in the symbols. I felt that our killer was telling us something.'

Carroll nodded. He brushed strands of his white hair back onto his head. 'I only caught a glimpse of the symbols on the news last night,' he said slowly. He opened his newspaper to show an artist's reconstruction of the scene inside the hall. From the amount of detail it was obvious that the artist had actually been inside the hall or was working from a very good photograph. Probably one of the photographers had slipped the constable on the door a few bob for a quick peek inside. The papers couldn't use the shots, so had provided an artist's 'Impression'. A side panel showed four crudely drawn symbols. The sub-headline read 'Killer's code'.

'How close are these to the real thing?' the priest asked, resting his long fingers on the newspaper paper.

Haaren turned the newspaper to the light. 'Close enough,' she said. 'I have photographs and detailed drawings of each inscription,' she added.

'Which you will show me if I can give you something useful in return,' Carroll smiled.

'Do you always know what people are thinking?' the inspector asked, 'Or is this a special Jesuitical skill?'

'I have always been a student of human nature, inspector. But it is true that we Jesuits are trained to think, to analyse.'

'I am not a Catholic, father, but my sergeant tells me that your order is something of an elite amongst the priesthood.'

'Oh, I wouldn't say that, inspector. Modesty and humility must dictate that I deny the accusation.'

'Is false modesty not also a sin?'

'*Touché*!'

Haaren leaned forward and tapped the newspaper. 'Tell me what you know about these symbols.'

The priest ran one of his long-nailed index fingers down the illustrations, stopping at the last ornate circle. 'The first two mean nothing, they are crude hieroglyphics; possibly the originals would reveal something. But this: this is the sigil of the Beast.' He stood up suddenly. 'Come, Inspector Haaren. We are about to have a conversation that is particularly unsuited to this hallowed place.'

The inspector remained in the chair. 'I'm not in the humour for riddles or dramatics,' Haaren said tiredly. 'And I'm not moving until you tell me something more than that.'

Michael Carroll leaned forward, straight arms resting on the back of the chair, his face inches from the inspector's. His breath was warm on her face. 'Your killer is sacrificing his victims to one of the Earls of Hell.'

Chapter Twenty-Four

MARGARET Haaren was relieved to step out into the sunshine. The inspector wasn't sure if it was because she was now standing outside the oppressive cathedral building, or simply because she could finally accept what she had known almost from the beginning.

From the moment she had seen the symbols gouged into the flesh of the first victim, she had suspected an occult connection. She had even voiced her suspicions at one of the early meetings, but her opinion had been met with a less than enthusiastic response. The force treated occult-related crimes with a great deal of scepticism, and so far had been particularly unsuccessful in tracking down any one of the numerous satanic cults which made the Sunday papers so regularly.

When Haaren had been tracking Jonathan Frazer, the serial killer, and during the vagrant killings, she had come face to face with the true horror of the occult. It had very nearly cost her her life. As she had spilled her lifeblood onto an enormous mirror, she had watched as a beast – a clawed and cloven-hoofed nightmare – stepped through the glass and butchered a room full of people. The peculiar aura of evil she had experienced then had washed over her again as she had stood before the mutilated body of the first victim.

Carroll strode along silently by her side, hands clasped behind his back, head thrust forward, pale eyes squinting in the harsh morning light. 'I find your attitude interesting, inspector,' the priest said quietly. 'You did not mock nor doubt. You accepted my most outrageous statement at face value.'

'I've been a police officer for most of my adult life, Father Carroll. You don't need to tell me about the existence of evil.'

'I'm not talking about men and women who operate outside the law, inspector. I'm talking about a primal force that is older than the human race.'

Haaren caught the priest by the arm, forcing him to stop and look at her. 'If you know me, you know I was involved in two occult cases. Most of the details that got into the papers were incorrect or simply fabrications ... and they didn't even begin to approach the truth. Do you want to know what happened then, do you want me to tell you how a creature that had no existence outside a nightmare stepped through a slab of solid glass and devoured a congregation of devil-worshippers?' Her voice fell to a ragged whisper. 'I know what you're talking about!'

Carroll was watching the woman closely, obviously weighing her every word. 'Initially, I thought it was going to be difficult to talk to you, inspector, but I find my task has been made surprisingly easy.'

'Why – because I believe you?'

'Precisely. Not many people believe in demons . . .'

They turned to the left into the narrow sidestreets that run alongside and behind the cathedral. One half of the almost deserted street was in shadow, and unconsciously, the inspector crossed the narrow road to walk in the sunshine.

'Any help you could give us, father, would be most

welcome. This killer will slaughter again and again unless we stop him. The crimes are becoming more frequent and more violent. You spoke about sacrifices ... months ago, when I saw the first body, I knew immediately that it had been sacrificed. And sacrificed for a reason, not as part of some sham, quasi-occult ritual. How can you help us track this killer?'

The white-haired priest shook his head briskly. 'I will need to see the symbols on the bodies first. However, I am almost certain that your killer is sacrificing his victims to one of the Earls of Hell. When I see the symbols, I will get a better idea which one.'

'How would that help?'

'The demons of hell are graded into a strict hierarchy. Different groups and ranks have the ability to grant various powers and desires. Perhaps if we knew to whom the killer is sacrificing, that might give us a clue to his identity.'

'You keep saying "he", father – is that just a figure of speech or do you suspect that the killer is indeed male?'

'No, not at all. I'm merely extrapolating from the evidence at hand. All the victims have been female, and the killing and type of mutilations required great strength. I think it is unlikely that the killer is a woman – but if it is, then you'll find she is a woman of particularly masculine qualities.'

The inspector nodded. 'Our psychological profiles indicated that it was a male.'

They had come round to the back of the church, stepping from the narrow streets into bright and blinding sunshine. The inspector stopped, rubbing her eyes, patting her pockets for her sunglasses. Without a word the priest reached forward and lifted them off the top of her head.

'Can I ask you a personal and possibly arrogant question, Father Carroll?'

'You can ask,' the priest said softly. 'I may not answer, though,' he added.

'Why are you doing this? What do you get out of it?'

The priest didn't immediately answer. When he looked back at the inspector, he said simply, 'Tea!' Haaren looked at him blankly. 'I need some tea,' he said with a smile.

The inspector repeated the question when they had settled into a long, narrow booth in a small café off the Vauxhall Bridge Road.

'I see nothing surprising with my offer of help,' Father Michael Carroll said, nudging the salt cellar around the formica-topped table. 'Any person of conscience would offer to help.'

'I'm not sure I agree with you, father. There must be people out there who know something – people of conscience, as you call them. But they're not coming forward for reasons of their own.'

'Fear,' the priest said. 'Fear of knowing the truth. Fear of not knowing the truth. Too often the fear of knowing is too much.'

'Ignorance is bliss?'

'Precisely.'

'You still haven't answered my question,' the inspector reminded him.

Carroll rested his elbows on the table before him, the tips of his fingers poised beneath his nose in an attitude of prayer. 'I have travelled across the world, usually into those places where the Catholic Church is still struggling for a foothold. I have taught and preached in Africa, South America, Eastern Asia and the furthest reaches of the Soviet Union with varying degrees of success. I have seen both good and evil in these places . . . though more of evil, I fear.'

He stopped as a young waitress in a dirty apron appeared. The inspector ordered tea for two.

'Evil interests me, inspector.' He smiled. 'Ah, now I think you have just added me to your list of suspects.'

'You're very perceptive, father,' Haaren said quietly.

'Evil interests me, inspector,' the priest repeated, 'because it is the yardstick by which we measure good. How can we say that this and this is good, if we are not able to judge it against evil?'

'I'm not sure I see the analogy, father, nor am I sure I can see how it relates to the case in hand.'

'Inspector, we Jesuits are trained to be coldly rational. If I can prove the existence of a Satan, a devil, an Earl of Hell . . . then I have also proven the existence of God.'

The waitress returned with the large metal teapot, cup and saucers on a scratched metal tray. The inspector dropped two pound coins on the tray and waved away the change. She was undecided whether the strange priest was genuine or just another nut. All her instincts were warning her that something was awry, that the priest was only telling her what he wanted her to know – or what he thought she wanted to hear. She poured weak tea, wondering if she was wasting her time, and deciding that if the priest was simply giving her the run-around, then – Catholic priest or not – she'd run him in for obstruction.

'You don't trust me, inspector,' Carroll said, sipping his tea. He drank it black with no sugar. 'Nor should you – you know nothing about me . . . yet. But I am presuming that you will check up on me before you take me into your confidence.'

'You're quick to presume things, father,' the inspector said.

'I'm simply telling you what I'd do if I were in your shoes.'

'OK,' the inspector sighed, 'you're trying to prove the existence of God by establishing the existence of the devil. Is it not a little strange for a priest, of all people, to be looking for the answer to this question?'

'We are all human, inspector. We all know doubt. Have you never questioned yourself, your motives, your reasons for living?'

'I'm not sure. I suppose there are times . . .'

Carroll nodded quickly. 'Precisely. The human race has advanced because mankind has constantly questioned his condition.' He paused and added softly. 'I have been a priest for forty of my sixty-five years. It is only in the last ten that I have begun to doubt my faith, my belief in God . . . even the very existence of a god. You cannot even begin to imagine what it is like to discover that you now doubt everything you once held precious. Like Thomas who doubted the risen Lord, I need to see this demon.'

'So if you discover that this killer is sacrificing his victims to the devil, then you can start believing in God again?' the inspector asked, unable to keep the sarcasm from her voice.

'Yes,' Carroll replied.

Haaren shook her head and looked away. She wanted to believe that this priest could help her – she was desperate enough to take any help – but she was beginning to suspect his motives. 'Give me something practical, father,' she suggested.

'You have investigated the occult organisations,' the priest said suddenly.

'No,' Haaren said, surprising him – surprising them both, wondering why she hadn't thought of it.

'I'm not talking about witches, wiccians or New

Agers,' the priest said softly, his blue eyes watching her. 'You should direct your attention towards the devil-worshippers, those who practise sacrifices and pay homage to evil.'

'These people tend not to advertise, father.'

'I know,' Carroll said, sliding a folded sheet of paper across the table. 'This is a list of the thirteen – naturally – major coven-leaders in the London area. You may be surprised at some of the names. Now, I am not for a moment suggesting that these people are involved, but possibly someone in one of the covens, is the man you're looking for.' He tapped the paper with a long-nailed finger. 'You're looking for a fanatic; every religion has its zealots.'

The inspector unfolded the paper, and read the names to herself. Half were familiar. 'I hardly think these people will be willing to co-operate.'

'Point out to them how difficult you could make their lives. Whisper the magical word "publicity".' The priest smiled. 'They'll talk to you then.' He glanced at his watch and stood up. 'Check me out, inspector. I will contact you again tomorrow afternoon.'

'Let's hope there hasn't been another killing in the meantime.'

The priest's eyes grew distant as he shook his head. 'Not yet. But soon. That is the danger of feeding the evil ones,' he said absently. 'They grow to enjoy the taste of human flesh.'

The inspector added sugar to her tea to take the foul taste from her mouth.

Chapter Twenty-Five

ROBERT Hunter looked down onto the square and watched Katherine Norton walk away from the house. He wondered what she must be thinking now; had he convinced her? She had come to the house suspecting him of being a murderer – and she had gone away believing that he was afflicted with a terrifying psychic gift. Whatever she thought, he knew she'd be back tomorrow.

And tomorrow she would have questions.

He hoped he'd have the answers.

The look of pain in Hunter's eyes stayed with her on the Tube on the way home. When she had stepped into the room earlier that morning, she realised she was terrified of him, and even when he'd started to tell her about his psychic gift, she hadn't quite believed him. But there was no way he would have been able to disguise the pain in his eyes. That was genuine enough.

She wondered what it must be like to live with a gift – a curse? – like that, to know that the written word could all too easily turn into reality, never knowing which fictional horror would become actual tragedy.

On the seat opposite her, a young man was reading the back page of the *Sun*. The two-inch headline on the front page was facing her: 'HORROR-SCOPE KILL-INGS . . . ' She knew what the headline was referring to: the killer who carved occult and astrological symbols in the bodies of his victims, just like a scene from one of Hunter's books . . .

Katherine felt herself drawn up short. It *was* a scene from one of Hunter's books. In *Zodiac*, Hunter's last book, the killer cut symbols into the bodies of his victims. Katherine pressed her hand to her chest, feeling her heart beat against her breastbone.

Was it possible that the killer was emulating the acts in Hunter's books? Surely not. *Zodiac* was just out in the UK, and the murders had been going on for longer than that . . . but had the book been available in any other edition: a foreign edition, an American edition, a hardback?

Katherine had a ghastly image of a deranged fan reading Hunter's books and then enacting some of the violent scenes. Or was the writer somehow tapping into the killer's unconscious? She shook her head suddenly, startling the woman sitting beside her: which came first, Hunter's book, or the killer's deeds? Was it Hunter's dark imagination which fired the killer, or the killer's bloodlust which found a spark in Hunter's unconscious? How else explain Hunter's knowledge of the murders unless he himself was doing the killing . . . and *that* was patently impossible.

Where did she draw the line between the fantasy and the reality?

Chapter Twenty-Six

STUART Miller looked up as the inspector made her way through the crowded police station. 'How did your meeting with the priest go?' he asked, falling into step beside her.

'I'm not sure,' Margaret Haaren said. 'I can't make up my mind if he's genuine, or just a plausible nut. I think he's genuine. He's offered to help: he believes the bodies are being sacrificed in an occult ceremony.'

'You said that from the beginning.'

The inspector nodded. 'He believes that the symbols cut into the bodies and painted onto the walls may give us some clue to the identity of the killer. However, he needs access to the pictures of the scenes before he can give us any further details.'

The sergeant raised his eyebrows. 'You sure he doesn't just get his jollies looking at butchered bodies?'

'Could be. Check him out for me, though. He'll be in touch tomorrow.' She passed him the folded sheet of paper. 'He's also suggested we investigate the people on this list: he claims they are the top coven-leaders in the country.'

'I hate this fucking black-magic shit,' Miller muttered.

'Get me as much information as you can on each person on the list – and Stuart,' the inspector added, 'be very, very discreet. You and I will handle this aspect of the case personally.' Stepping into her office, the inspector closed the door behind her.

Puzzled, Miller opened the page and ran his eyes down the list of names . . . and then he knew why the inspector wanted absolute discretion. Some of these names were public . . . and one was a police officer – a detective chief inspector. Miller shook his head; this was going to get shitty. Personally he didn't give a damn if the chief inspector was Church of England or Church of Satan . . . but the chief inspector was going to be really pissed off when he discovered that his little secret was out. Miller reckoned he could count his remaining days as a sergeant on the fingers of two hands.

Miller tapped on the door and opened it before the inspector called out. 'Sorry for disturbing you, ma'am, but I thought you'd want to know about this.'

Haaren pushed aside the forensics report and the glossy ten-by-eight colour photographs of the young woman's brutalised body. She'd been trying to figure out how much time the killer had spent working his butchery upon the young woman. The pathologist suggested at least two or more hours, but the evidence to hand suggested only a fraction of that time. And how had the killer managed to escape when he would have been bathed in blood?

She stretched, and rubbed stiff neck muscles. 'What have you got, Stuart?'

'A call from a woman who claims she may have some information about the Horror-Scope Killings.'

Haaren grimaced at the use of the name; but the killings had been christened by the press, and the tag would stick. 'What makes this call so different?' She nudged a pile of yellow slips, notes of phonecalls. 'Every nut in London and the Home Counties has been on giving us "valuable information".'

Miller glanced at the note in his hand before sliding it across the desk. 'This was no anonymous tip; this woman left her name and phone number, which is unusual enough. She claims that she thinks she knows what is inspiring the killer to kill . . .'

'Voices from God?'

'She claims the killer is slicing off his victims' nipples,' Miller added with a grim smile.

Haaren straightened. 'That detail wasn't released to the press.'

'It wasn't. I checked. There's been no mention of it anywhere.'

The inspector turned the slip of paper around, looking at the name and address. 'Katherine Norton . . .' She looked up at her sergeant. 'Do we know her?'

'I ran her through the computers. She doesn't have a record under that name. Nor is she listed as one of our cranks. I took the liberty of phoning her, telling her we'd be over,' he added as the inspector rose to her feet, pulling her jacket off the back of the chair.

'Two offers of help in one day. Maybe the gods have decided to smile on us.' Haaren breathed. 'God knows, we need it.' She pulled open the door and spotted the braided cap of the chief inspector at the far end of the corridor. 'Quick. He'll spend the next hour looking over the reports and asking for suggestions.' Catching Miller by the arm, she hustled him out of the room, and down the corridor towards the emergency exit.

'I've checked into that priest, too,' Miller said as they hurried out into the underground carpark. 'He's genuine enough. And get this: Father Michael Carroll is a recognised authority on the occult – the real occult, not the fortune-telling rubbish. He's written a couple of popular books, an enormous two-volume history and maybe a hundred articles on the subject. Some of his occult books landed him in hot water with the Church and he is currently between parishes.'

'What does that mean: between parishes?'

'I suppose it's the equivalent of a police officer taking enforced leave of absence.'

'So he's a renegade?' The inspector jerked open the door of the dusty Granada.

Miller slid into the driver's seat and pulled down the sun visor to retrieve the keys. 'He's that all right. Bit of a personality, too, in his own right. A couple of years ago, he did the radio and TV chat-show circuit discussing the occult. There was quite a controversy when he admitted that, in the course of his research, he'd attended a black mass. His religious order came down on him, and he disappeared for a while.' Miller eased the car out through the throng of reporters gathered in front of the station. One spotted the battered blue car and pointed. A small group raced off after the car, cameras flashing.

'Lose them, Stuart. If this Norton woman has anything genuine to offer, I don't want her scared off by this mob.'

Miller turned out into Marylebone Road, flicked on the siren and cut through the early-evening traffic. Haaren settled back into the cracked plastic seat, her eyes drifting over the blank faces of people heading home from work. It was Friday evening; the weekend started here. She supposed some of them would be going out later, the cinema, maybe down to the pub or out for a meal. Ordinary people, ordinary lives: she envied them. She couldn't remember the last time she'd had a weekend off, when she'd been able to relax without waiting for the phone to ring. They passed a bus queue, heads turning to follow the car as it sped past, siren wailing. The woman wondered what it would be like to be able to leave a job at the end of a day and forget about it.

It was at times like these that she was glad she hadn't got a family. Police work, even at the best of times, put an unnatural strain on any relationship. And, as one moved up the ranks and shouldered more and more responsibility, that strain increased. It took a very special kind of partner to be able to take that pressure, even just to understand. That was why officers tended to socialise with fellow officers, who understood the pressures and were able to make allowances. Her father had been a police officer, but in a small country town where his children got to see him every day, and crime was neither as prevalent nor as violent. Times – and crimes – had changed, and even if she had had children, she wasn't sure if she'd have recommended that they join the force.

'Your kids ever talk about joining the force?' she asked abruptly.

Miller glanced sidelong at the inspector. 'No, Stu's talking about a career in graphic arts, Jade wants to be a nurse.'

'How old are they now?'

'Stu will be thirteen next birthday. He's going to be a big lad, taller than me, I'd say. Jade is almost seventeen, and a real beauty. You don't feel the time slipping away.'

'No, you don't.' She would be forty-four next birthday; she was resigned now to never having children. She brought her thoughts back to the present. 'Arrange to meet the priest tomorrow.

Somewhere very private. If the press got wind of this, they'd have a field day.'

Miller grinned, showing strong white teeth. ' "The Policewoman and the Occult Priest",' he suggested.

Haaren laughed. 'They wouldn't be so kind. It would be along the lines of "desperate police officers . . ." '

'Baffled,' Miller supplied.

' "Baffled police officers have consulted the noted occult priest . . ." '. She shook her head quickly. 'Neither you nor I would survive the scandal.'

Miller nodded. He hit the brake and horn simultaneously, swearing as a motorcycle courier darted out in front of him. The cyclist gave him the finger as he roared off. The number plate was thickly coated in mud, making it impossible to read. 'You know one of the names on that list was Detective Chief Inspector Maddox,' he continued.

'I know that,' Haaren said.

'He's going to be upset when he discovers that we know his little secret.'

'I know that too.'

'He's very powerful,' Stuart added, glancing at the inspector. 'Tipped as the next Chief Constable.'

The inspector remained silent.

'Even if we do bring this investigation to a successful conclusion without involving him in any way, the fact that we know his secret could really piss him off. You could find yourself walking a beat in outer suburbia, or driving a desk in the traffic division.'

'On the other hand, Stuart,' Haaren said with a wry smile, 'the very fact that we know his secret might just make him respect us. After all, it's not a secret he'd want the press to get hold of.'

'You wouldn't . . . ' Miller began.

170

'And I thought you knew me, Stuart,' Haaren said reproachfully.

Miller thought about it for a moment, before he nodded. 'I want to be standing beside you when you talk to him,' he said eventually. 'I want to see the look on his face when you lay that on him.'

'He'll be upset.'

It took an hour, through ever-thickening Friday evening traffic, to reach Katherine Norton's address on the outskirts of the city. Miller missed the turning and they eventually ended up cruising slowly through an up-market housing development checking the house numbers. Curtains twitched as they passed. 'This is a neighbourhood-watch area,' Miller grinned. 'They're probably reaching for the phone now, calling the local station reporting two suspicious characters checking the houses.'

The inspector tapped her side window. 'This way . . .'

Miller turned left into a quiet sidestreet. Haaren noticed that there were no 'For Sale' signs in the gardens. They had become such a feature of the landscape of the last few years that their absence seemed odd. She couldn't remember the last time she had seen a street without at least one sign.

'How do you want to handle this woman, ma'am?'

'Gently, gently,' the inspector said. 'We don't want to spook her, just in case she really does know something. I'll hold her in conversation, you can look around, use the loo, get a drink of water. You never know, maybe it's a husband, boyfriend or neighbour.'

Miller tilted his head. 'Number forty-three is . . . here.'

'Drive past; we'll approach on foot,' the inspector

muttered. She twisted in her seat to look back at the house. 'No car in the driveway, but oil on the path and a kid's bike lying on the grass. Married woman with at least one kid, hubby at work.' She glanced at her wristwatch. 'Five o'clock. Hubby's probably on the way home.'

Miller pulled in to the kerb and turned off the engine. Reaching under the seat, he pulled out a truncheon and stuck it into his waistband. 'Well, you never know – it might be the husband,' he grinned.

'I said we deserved a little luck – not a bloody miracle.'

Twenty-Seven

SHE had phoned the police on impulse – an impulse she now regretted. If word of what she had done ever got out, she'd find herself a laughing stock . . . and her career prospects weren't going to be enhanced either. Thinking back over her suspicions, she realised just how foolish they must sound. With any luck, the police would have marked her down as a nut and dismissed her phonecall as the ramblings of a nut. The officer she'd spoken to had said they'd send someone around to talk to her, but he probably said that to all their callers; she was sure they must get loads of calls from people claiming to have important information.

And what would happen if they did send someone around to take a statement? She had visions of a police car parked outside the door; she could just imagine what the neighbours would say. And what would Peter say if he came back and discovered a police car . . . ?

Katherine was standing in the kitchen, scraping carrots, when the doorbell rang, startling her. She glanced up at the wall-clock as she hurried from the kitchen into the sitting room, pausing to look out onto the street, relieved to find no police car outside. It wasn't them. There were two shapes outlined against the speckled glass of the hall door; one looked black and male, the other white and female. Neither was wearing uniform. Jehovah's Witnesses, probably.

Wiping her hands on her apron, Katherine opened the door, smiling automatically. She recognised the woman and the smile faded.

'I'm Detective Inspector Margaret Haaren, and this is Sergeant Stuart Miller.'

'I've seen your face on the news and in the papers,' Katherine said, opening the door wider and stepping back to allow them into the hall.

'No one ever remembers my face,' Miller said ruefully, as he stepped past.

Katherine indicated the open sitting-room door. 'Please . . .' she gestured. 'I was expecting a police car,' she added, following them into the room.

'We didn't want to cause you any embarrassment, Mrs Norton,' Margaret Haaren said easily, taking in her surroundings as she turned back to look at the woman, noting the booklined alcoves on both sides of the fireplace, the ornamental picture frames with photographs of three babies, a girl in a Guide's uniform, a snapshot of the entire family standing before Niagara Falls.

'You have a lovely home,' Stuart said.

'Thank you. Please, sit down,' Katherine said nervously. 'Can I offer you something to drink? The kettle is on.'

'Tea would be lovely,' Stuart said, 'if it's not too much trouble.'

'It's no trouble at all.'

The inspector followed Katherine out into the kitchen, leaving Stuart alone in the sitting room. 'Thank you for contacting us,' she said, leaning against the door, folding her arms across her chest.

Katherine plugged in the kettle and turned to face the inspector. 'Look, I'm not sure if I really know anything. I mean, I've thought about it again . . . and it sounds so . . .'

'Stupid?' Haaren asked. She shook her head. 'You wouldn't believe some of the stories I've listened to in my time. And a surprising number of those "stupid" stories have given us the clue we've needed to crack a case. A neighbour reporting a strange smell led us to a multiple murderer; a librarian reporting an overdue book from a regular customer lead to the apprehension of a rapist; the report of a child's toy in the window of a childless couple enabled us to arrest a child snatcher.' She smiled, trying to put the young woman at her ease. 'And no matter what you tell us here, it won't go any further. Your name won't be used in any reports or leaked to the press. At the moment, only Sergeant Miller and myself know your identity.'

'Thank you,' Katherine whispered, then visibly jumped as the kettle came to the boil with a squeal. 'You must excuse me, I've never done anything like this before.'

'I know,' Haaren said. 'Some people make it a habit to phone the police with exclusive leads and tips. Usually if that doesn't work, they'll then either accuse someone they know, or admit to the crime themselves. We keep a file on all of them. One of the first things we did was to check the files: the very fact that you weren't on it encouraged me to come and see you personally.'

Katherine filled the teapot, placed three mismatched cups, milk, sugar and a plate of biscuits on the tray. The inspector held open the door to the sitting room as she carried the tray through. Stuart Miller was standing with his hands clasped behind his back, staring out through at the street. He turned as the two women came into the room, caught the inspector's eye

175

and shook his head slightly. There was no one else in the house.

'Are they your children?' Miller asked, nodding to the young boy and girl arguing over the bike on the lawn.

'That's Mark and Jody.' Pulling back the curtain, Katherine tapped on the window. The children looked startled and dropped the bike. 'Stop that, right now. Go and find Lizzie; tell her dinner's in half an hour. I'm glad the holidays are nearly over,' she said, turning away from the window. 'They've really been getting on each other's nerves – mine too – in the last couple of days.'

'It's the weather,' Miller said sympathetically. 'My own pair are a bit older, but they still fight like cat and dog.'

Haaren and Miller sat at opposite ends of the settee, facing Katherine. She poured tea, offered around the plate of biscuits, and then waited, suddenly unsure.

'I was the officer you spoke to on the phone, Mrs Norton,' Miller began, forcing Katherine to look at him. The inspector watched her closely. Too many years watching people squirm had made her an expert in body language, and she knew instinctively when people were lying.

'You said that you had some information about the Horror-Scope Killings. You said you thought you knew what was inspiring the killer . . .' Katherine nodded. 'Would you like to elaborate a little on that?'

'And please,' Haaren interrupted, 'take your time and spare us no details, no matter how small or inconsequential.'

Katherine put down her cup and looked from Haaren to Miller, finally fixing on the West Indian sergeant as the most sympathetic. Although her lips were curled in a smile, Haaren's face was forbidding. 'I suppose there's little enough to tell. I'm a freelance editor, non-fiction mainly, but I also do fiction. I used to work full-time for a publishing house called Image Press, but I gave that up when the children came along. However, I always did bits and pieces to keep my hand in.' She lifted her cup and saucer, and sipped some tea; the inspector noted that the tremble had gone from her fingers. 'My husband lost his job a little while ago. He was an accountant and the firm went into liquidation, so I took on extra work with Image, just to tide us over, give us some cash.' Miller nodded understandingly. 'Earlier this week I was called into Image and asked to assist an author with a manuscript he was having difficulty with.'

'What sort of difficulty?' the inspector asked.

'The book was late and the publishing company had paid out quite a lot of money for it. My brief was to visit his home, take away what he'd written so far and edit it. I was also to edit as he wrote, in order to get the book into print as quickly as possible.'

'I understand. Does that happen often?'

'Not terribly often,' Katherine admitted. 'The author's name is Robert Hunter; he's a horror writer,' she added, 'though perhaps you don't read horror.'

'We see enough of it in our everyday work,' Haaren remarked.

'Hunter is a retired academic, a quiet man, married with two young children. He writes some of the most powerful horror in print today – some of it quite stomach-churning.' Katherine sipped some more tea. 'I was with him this morning. On the way back home in the Tube, I saw someone reading the newspaper. It was the headline that caught my attention, and then I remembered . . .' She stood up and crossed to the bookshelves, lifting a fat hardback book. She held it up so that Haaren and Miller could see the garish cover of a zodiacal wheel dripping blood.

'This book has been available in the States for a couple of weeks, but it's just been published over here,' she said, flicking through it. 'It's about a serial killer who slays according to the phases of the moon. There's nothing unusual about that, serial killers are very popular now – at least in fiction.'

'In real life, too,' the inspector muttered.

'What struck a chord in my memory was that the killer in this book carved astrological symbols into the flesh of his victims.

Haaren and Miller straightened.

'Let me read you a piece . . .' Katherine said. 'This is from about half-way through the book; it's a scene where the killer is working on one of his victims . . .'

> *With infinite precision, he pressed the blade of the razor into the woman's breasts. The skin parted silently, the wound opening up like a flower blossoming. She had been dead for three days now, so there was no blood, only a pale, viscous fluid.*
>
> *With quick, deft strokes, he began to carve the signs of the zodiac into the blue-white skin. When he was finished, he pressed his lips to the wounds, breathing into them, whispering the myriad names of God into the cuts, bringing the magical zodiacal signs to life.*
>
> *When he could feel the corpse trembling with magical life, he completed the ritual and bit off the nipples, and added them to the others . . .'*

Katherine finished, closed the book and handed it to the inspector. 'So, I began wondering,' she said, shakily, 'if the killer was a reader of horror fiction, and was, in some way, acting out the fantasy he read on the page.' She looked from Miller to Haaren. 'I mean, you hear about it with videos all the time: kids who have been influenced by watching too much sex or violence on video, going out and committing crimes.'

'May I keep this book, Mrs Norton?' Haaren asked.

'Yes, yes of course. Has anything I've said been of any use . . .?'

The inspector relaxed. 'It has been excellent. You may have given us the clue to cracking this case, Mrs Norton. And if you have, you can take some comfort from the fact that you will have saved countless young women from similar terrible deaths.' She stood up and Miller came to his feet with her.

'If you talk to Robert Hunter,' Katherine said, rising also, 'I'd prefer if you kept my name out of it. My publishers probably wouldn't look too kindly on it if I involved one of their authors in a murder investigation. And I can't afford to lose this job,' she added.

'Rest assured; we won't mention your name,' the inspector said.

'Mind you – that sort of publicity wouldn't do the sales of the book any harm,' Miller remarked.

'Probably not,' Katherine agreed.

Squealing children's voices made them turn to the window. A tall, grey-haired man was struggling up the driveway, a child hanging out of either arm, another on his back.

'It's Peter, my husband. He was at a job interview,' Katherine said, knowing instinctively by the set of his shoulders that he hadn't got the job.

'We'll be off, Mrs Norton,' Haaren said. 'We may need to talk to you again, if that's all right.'

'Yes, of course.'

'We'll phone beforehand, of course.'

Peter Norton had his key in his hand when the door opened and he found himself faced by a black man. Before he could say anything, a large masculine-looking woman appeared behind him. She shook hands with Katherine, nodded to him, and then the curious couple went down the path without a backward glance. Peter stood on the doorstep and watched them climb into a nondescript blue Granada parked down the street.

'That was the police,' Katherine whispered as she kissed Peter on the cheek. 'There's nothing wrong,' she said, seeing his eyes flare in alarm. 'I'll tell you later.' She watched the car drive away, and wondered, once again, if she'd done the right thing.

Margaret Haaren flicked through the book, stopping at some of the particularly gory pieces – and there seemed to be a remarkable number of them.

Miller concentrated on manoeuvring his way through the traffic, not speaking, giving the inspector time to think. She swore twice as she read passages from the book, then finally closed it with a snap.

'What have I always said is the first rule of police work?' she asked.

'Look for the simple solution,' Miller replied immediately.

'Mrs Norton suspected a horror fan, perhaps tipped over the edge by the images in this writer's book.' The inspector turned the book over in her hands. 'I've read a couple of passages. The woman was right: it's sick stuff. Not only do we have the killer cutting off pieces of bodies; we also have him carving astrological symbols into the flesh, tearing out the hearts, cutting off the nipples, the ears, the tongue . . . and keeping pieces to eat later on.'

'That's our killer all right,' Miller said simply.

'I think we should be looking at the man who wrote this.' The inspector turned the book over to look at the title. 'Robert Hunter: the Master of Terror.'

Chapter Twenty-Eight

'**YOU** did what! Jesus Christ – are you out of your fucking mind?' Peter Norton stared at his wife, unable to believe what she had just told him.

Katherine stepped back, frightened by her husband's sudden anger.

'I don't believe it! I don't fucking believe it!' He roughly pushed his plate away from him, scattering kernels of corn across the table.

'Language,' Katherine said sharply. The children were watching television in the sitting room. She gathered up the plates and piled them into the dishwasher, trying to ignore Peter's glare. 'I've told you what I said to them, and all they said to me – there's nothing more to it than that. Inspector Haaren gave me her word that my name wouldn't be mentioned.

'And you believed her!' Peter spat.

'Yes!' Katherine snapped. 'Yes, I believed her.'

'And what happens if the case goes to court – and you're called as a witness? What then? You'll have your name in every rag in the country. Every fucking psycho is going to come looking for you. We'll have to move out . . .'

'Oh, for Christ's sake, Peter. I'm the one who deals with fiction – not you! I simply told the police about the connection I'd made between Hunter's books and the killings. That's all. I couldn't tell them anything else – because I knew nothing else. I just don't see what all the fuss is about.'

'Maybe you're being deliberately stupid!' Peter shouted. 'What do you think the first thing the police do when they get a call from someone like you?' Before she could answer, he hurried on. 'They investigate the family. They look into your background, my background!'

Katherine attempted a laugh. 'Well, I've got nothing to hide – have you?' As soon as she said it, she saw the wariness in Peter's eyes and realised she'd struck close to home. 'Yes, you have,' she said.

Peter jumped to his feet, the sudden movement knocking the chair backwards.

'You're a stupid bitch!' he snarled. He stormed out of the kitchen, slamming the door behind him with such vehemence that one of the glass side-panels cracked.

Lizzie poked her head out of the sitting room. 'Mum . . .?'

'Everything's all right. Watch TV,' Katherine called back as she ran out of the room. She heard the bedroom door slam, mattress springs creak as her husband dropped heavily onto it. She hesitated outside the bedroom door, her hand on the handle, then took a deep breath and pushed it open. When she stepped into the room, she turned the key in the door, locking it.

Peter was lying flat out on the bed, his forearms thrown across his eyes, his chest heaving.

'Tell me what's wrong,' Katherine said, crossing to the window, leaning back against the sill, folding her arms across her breasts. Something *was* terribly wrong.

'There's nothing wrong,' Peter said coldly.

'I know there is. I suppose I've known that there was

182

something wrong for a very long time. Only I was afraid to admit it. It's time you told me.'

In the long silence, the buzz of the television from the room below was clearly audible.

When he showed no sign of speaking, Katherine pressed on. 'You're afraid of a police investigation; you're afraid that it'll show up something. I think you'd better tell me. I have a right to know.'

'There's nothing.'

'If you'd trusted me enough to tell me before this, I'd never have called the police, and we wouldn't be in this situation. Tell me!' she demanded.

'OK. OK. I *am* vulnerable to a police investigation,' he said, reddening.

'Vulnerable? In what way?'

'Before I left the job . . . when I knew the writing was on the wall . . . I . . . I transferred some money from a client's account to an account I'd set up in a dummy company's name.' Katherine stared at him in horror. 'It was spur of the moment. Well, not really spur of the moment. The money came from dozens of sources, bits and pieces of clients' earnings that either hadn't been claimed or had been forgotten about, the tail ends of suspension accounts, earnings from special-interest accounts . . .'

'How much?' Katherine asked.

'I invented this new company, registered in the Isle of Man, and transferred all the money into it through a series of credit transfers and direct debits . . .'

'How much, for Christ's sake?'

'Thirty-eight thousand pounds.' He sat up. 'I did it for us, for the children . . . as an insurance policy.'

'You're a lying bastard, Peter Norton. You did it for yourself. Why have you never mentioned this money before? Why did you allow me to go back to work, why did I have to scrimp and save every penny, working all hours, while you had that tucked away? What were you going to do – walk away one day with your little nest egg?' She felt the anger stream out of her, leaving her drained and cold. 'How could you?' he asked.

'I did it for us,' he repeated. 'I was going to use it to set up in business.'

'There's more, isn't there?' Katherine said. 'Tell me.'

Peter stared straight ahead, unable to look her in the eye. 'One of the reasons I wasn't offered a job in the new firm – and probably the reason I'm not being offered a job elsewhere – is because some people suspect what I've done. They can't prove it – they haven't got the resources,' he added hastily.

'But the police have,' Katherine finished. 'If the police look into our background, they might start asking questions about you – and then this would come out.'

'I'd go to jail, Katherine,' Peter said.

Katherine looked up, her eyes swimming with tears. 'Do you know something – right now I couldn't give a damn. I thought you loved me.'

'I do.'

Katherine shook her head. 'If you did you wouldn't have done something like this. You've been living a lie for the past three months. I just wonder if you'd ever have told me about this money if you hadn't been forced to.'

'I would, I swear . . .'

'Don't . . .' Katherine said tiredly. 'Don't promise me anything else. I'd find it difficult to believe you. What are we going to do?' she asked aloud.

'If you hadn't called in the police . . .' he began.

Katherine stepped forward and struck him hard across the face, the force of the blow rocking his head

184

to one side. The imprint of her fingers stood out lividly on his flesh.

'Don't you try and blame this on me, you bastard! This is all your doing. You brought it on yourself.' She was about to add more, but knew it would be something she'd never be able to back away from. As she stepped past the end of the bed, Peter reached for her, but she slapped his hand away. Knowing he would attempt to follow her, she locked herself in her study. When the knock came to her door a few moments later, she ignored it.

'Katherine . . . Katherine . . .'

Katherine switched on the radio-cassette, snapped a cassette into the player, plugged in her earphones and turned up the volume. The thunderous opening of Mahler's Resurrection Symphony startled her. When she raised the volume slightly higher, she couldn't even hear Peter's voice or rapping on the door.

The music matched her mood, her anger, disappointment – and her sense of impending doom. And now she was forced to ask herself: what other secrets was he hiding?

Katherine moved Hunter's manuscript around on her desk, aligning the edges of the pages. Spotting a typo, she picked up a pencil and automatically corrected it. The lead snapped and she suddenly flung the pencil across the room. Her hands were trembling and she pressed them down flat onto the manuscript.

If she hadn't gone to the police . . .

If she hadn't read Hunter's book . . .

If she hadn't met the writer . . .

If Peter hadn't lost his job, forcing her to go back to work . . .

Too many 'Ifs'. And while Hunter might be responsible for many things, he couldn't be held accountable for her husband's being a thief.

The very word stopped her dead.

Peter was a thief, and if the police investigated, they would almost certainly discover that he had stolen money, and the courts were now taking a very dim view of white-collar crime. He would go to jail.

And what would she do for money then?

Katherine allowed her forehead to drop down onto the manuscript. If the word got out that she had spoken to the police about Hunter, she would lose her job at Image Press . . . She had no other way of earning a living if Peter was in jail. What were they going to do; how would she feed and clothe the children? And what about the legal fees: would they lose the house too?

Her fingers closed, tightening into claws, crumbling the top sheet into a ragged ball. When she realised what she was doing, she smoothed the page straight. All she could do now was to try and complete the book as quickly as possible, and get the money due to her.

As she straightened the manuscript, she suddenly wondered why she hadn't told the police about the explicit details of the most recent murders. Was it because it might implicate Hunter?

So much had happened today, she'd barely had time to think about Hunter's extraordinary story about a psychic gift. And now she wondered if she believed him.

Chapter Twenty-Nine

KATHERINE stirred as Peter slid naked into bed beside her. She twisted her head – though she didn't recall moving – and kissed him lightly on the lips before turning away. She felt him settle in against her, wrapping an arm around her waist, sliding one arm around her neck to cup her breast. Her buttocks settled onto his lap and she felt him hardening beneath her.

'I've been waiting for you,' she whispered, lifting her leg, pressing herself onto him. She reached down, pulling him in closer, grinding her buttocks into his lap.

Peter began moving gently, his whole body shifting, drawing her into a gentle, effortless rhythm, which built to a convulsive orgasm.

Katherine Norton cried out, turning to catch her husband's lips . . . discovering it was Robert Hunter grinning over her shoulder . . . then the face dissolving, shifting, the angles and planes altering to that of a beast.

Razor-tipped claws dug into her breasts, slicing the soft tissue, cutting through muscle and bone, snapping ribs as they tore into her lungs, destroying the flesh, reaching for her heart and then squeezing, squeezing, squeezing: the muscle exploding audibly.

And all the while the beast was driving itself deeper

into her body, its enormous, ice-cold member tearing through her, piercing her delicate inner flesh, rupturing organs.

Katherine awoke.

She had fallen asleep across the table, her head resting on Hunter's manuscript. Her entire upper body was numb, and her every breath hurt. That and the pressure on her kidneys had awoken her.

Hunter had a lot to answer for, she decided.

Chapter Thirty

MARGARET Haaren lay back on the bed, wrapped in a ragged dressing gown, an enormous towel wrapped around her head. She'd taken a long, leisurely shower when she returned to her apartment, first turning the nozzle up to a needle spray to cleanse the city grime from her pores and set her flesh tingling, then reducing it to a soft mist to help ease her taut muscles.

Although she hadn't been hungry, she'd forced herself to eat a bowl of soup, while watching the late-evening news. The double murder was still headlines, and now the networks were exploring the occult connection, with all the stations trotting out so-called experts to explain the significance of the symbols scrawled on the wall.

A Labour MP had attempted to raise the case in Parliament, but had been ruled out of order. But she knew then that whatever heat had come down from upstairs so far was nothing like the inferno that would descend on her tomorrow. To her acute embarrassment there was a five-minute potted biography of *'the officer leading the investigation, Inspector Margaret Haaren . . .'* She felt she was portrayed as a hard-bitten dyke. More importantly – and dangerously, too – it placed her very much as the officer whom the public would now associate with the case. Her past successes would be forgotten; she was the one who would get the blame if there was another killing. As she turned off the television, she smiled bitterly: a scapegoat was being prepared.

It was close to midnight before she climbed into bed. Her hairdryer had burnt out – again – and she didn't want to lie down with wet hair, so she picked up Hunter's book and turned it over in her large hands.

Zodiac. A zodiacal wheel of astrological symbols, dripping blood.

What sort of man wrote horror novels for a living? What sort of person read them? Lying back against the headboard, she opened the book and started to read.

She had intended to skim through it, looking for pieces that might be useful, but the brutal slaying on the very first page drew her in. Although she'd never read a horror novel before, she had to admit that the writing was very powerful, the imagery vivid and disturbing, the story quite frightening in places. She stopped twice to make notes of page numbers. Katherine Norton's impression that the text contained similarities to the murders had been correct, but Haaren knew instinctively that these were more than coincidences: in the two cases she'd noted, the text perfectly matched the murderers.

Someone was using the book as a blueprint for murder.

A sudden thought made her close the book. Was the killer, even now, reading this book and planning the next murder?

She'd been going to turn off the light, but she pressed on with the book, reading up to the point where a young woman, working in a bookshop, was picked up by a customer who then murdered her. The chapter following the killing was brief, devoted to the killer ceremoniously eating a piece of the girl's heart.

Haaren swallowed hard. If the killer was following the text, then there was no doubt that he was also indulging in cannibalism.

The next killing took place a few pages later, four days after the previous one. Haaren sat up and swung her legs out of the bed, shaking the towel off her frizzy hair as she read the text closely, looking for any clues to the killer's identity, or the location. This murder was a double event, a teenage couple parked in a quiet suburban street, slaughtered as they made love, their cries of passion turning to screams as a bayonet impaled them both, pinning them together. Haaren closed the book on her knees, her forearms resting on the cover, hands clasped together.

What was she going to do now?

There was no doubt in her mind that the killings were directly related to the text. The killer was using the book as a springboard for his diseased imagination, making fact out of fiction. The book was an incredibly important piece of evidence ... and yet she wasn't sure how she was going to use it. If the killer kept to schedule, however, she had less than two days to prevent another murder.

Dropping the book onto the floor, she pulled off the dresing gown and slid naked between the cool sheets. Locking her hands behind her head, she stared upwards, reflected light from the street outside casting long shadows across the ceiling.

She had never been able to figure out the seemingly random – yet rigidly defined – pattern. But now that she knew that killer was playing to a script, pieces began to fall into place. The book was the link, the thread that bound the murders together. She suddenly wondered how this fitted in with Father Michael

Carroll's assertion that the killings were part of an occult ceremony. The occult lore in the books was very detailed and read as if the author knew exactly what he was talking about. She'd show Carroll the book tomorrow and get his reaction.

She also needed to talk to Robert Hunter.

Chapter Thirty-One

'BREAKFAST is served.' Stuart Miller shook a paper bag in Margaret Haaren's face as he stepped into her apartment.

'You'll give the neighbours something to talk about,' she yawned.

'What – a black man visiting you at six-thirty in the morning?'

'No . . . any man visiting me!' She padded into the kitchen, slippers slapping on the floor. 'I know it can't be bad news,' she said, filling the kettle, 'otherwise you'd have been on the phone, and wouldn't have brought breakfast. Tell me it's good news.'

Miller leaned in the doorway, arms folded across his broad chest. 'It might be the break we're looking for,' he grinned. 'But first, tell me: did you find anything in Hunter's book?'

Haaren turned from the sink, dragging her fingers through her short hair. Her face was still puffy from sleep, her eyes gritty and the remnants of a nightmare echoed somewhere at the back of her skull. 'Hunter's book,' she said very softly, shaking her head with the memory. 'I've read about half-way through it and I've no doubt that our killer is using it as the blueprint for murder. It contains detailed descriptions of the killings and mutilations. The ages of the victims in the text matches almost exactly the ages of our victims, and the descriptions too are more or less identical.'

'That's unbelievable.'

'It gets better,' she smiled grimly. 'If I'm reading the text right, the next killing is a double-header, a courting couple, killed in their car as they make love in an unnamed London suburban sidestreet,' she finished. She filled the teapot.

'And when does this happen?'

'Two days, three maybe. I'm not sure. We need to talk to Hunter this morning.'

'We certainly do,' Miller said, with a broad grin. He reached into his jacket pocket and pulled out a folded brown envelope. Opening it, he extracted a ten-by-eight glossy photograph of a young girl. 'Deirdre Banks, more commonly known as DeeDee, the girl who was killed on Thursday . . . she was Hunter's babysitter.'

Margaret Haaren poured scalding tea over her hand.

They drove around Eaton Square twice before they discovered the house. The inspector, sitting in the passenger seat, spotted the numeral as they drove past. 'That's it.'

Miller drove on, looking for a parking space, finally discovering an opening beween a Bentley and a Ferarri. The Ferarri had a bright yellow clamp on its front wheel. 'This heap of junk is going to stick out like a sore thumb here.'

'We can claim it's retro chic,' Haaren remarked, swivelling around in the seat to look back at the house. 'Now, I wonder how we should play this.'

'Very cautiously. He's no fool,' Miller said.

'What have you found out about him?'

'He's forty-six years old; his wife Emma is twenty-six. She's his second wife. Bit of a scandal there. She was originally one of his pupils when he was a teacher; they had an affair, she became pregnant, he lost his job, wife divorced him. They have two daughters, aged six and four. He supports himself solely by his writing. He's one of the top horror writers in the world, right up there with Stephen King, earning astronomical advances. Eleven years ago, he had lost everything – house, wife, car, job – but he's built it all up again from scratch. He owns this house.'

'Owns it? It must be worth a million!'

'Double that, probably.' Miller glanced at the notes again. 'He has no record, an excellent credit rating, belongs to no clubs or organisations.'

'OK. Let's take it gently. We're investigating the mystery of the young girl's death, looking into her background.' She glanced at the sergeant. 'Any word on the boyfriend?'

'Nothing yet. However, we did discover he is a great horror reader. His bedroom is wall-to-wall paperbacks, most of them horror and – you'll like this – he's a special fan of Hunter's. He has practically everything he's written,' he added.

Haaren glanced at him sharply. 'You're not suggesting that he . . .'

'No, not at all. He couldn't have. I'm simply mentioning it.'

The inspector pushed open the door and stepped out onto the empty pavement, feeling the heat of the stones burning its way up through her shoes.

By the time Miller caught up with her, she was standing at the foot of the steps leading up to Hunter's house, looking at the grotesque lion's head door knocker.

'Mr Hunter has his image to live up to,' she remarked, looking around for a bell. Finding none, she gripped the knocker and rapped hard. She could hear the sound echoing along the hall.

'Rather unusual to have no bell,' Miller murmured.

'I'd imagine it discourages casual visitors.'

There was a scratching sound behind the door and the inspector resisted the temptation to press her face up against the fish-eye viewing lens set into the centre of the lion's mouth.

'I wonder what we look like,' Miller muttered. 'Jehovah's Witnesses, encyclopaedia salesmen . . .'

The door opened suddenly. 'You look like police to me.'

'Robert Hunter?' Haaren turned the question into a statement, looking up at the figure standing in the door.

'I am Robert Hunter.'

'I'm Inspector Margaret Haaren; this is Sergeant Stuart Miller. We would like to speak to you.'

Hunter stood back, allowing them both into the hall. 'I suppose I should ask for a warrant or something like that,' he said, smiling to take the sting out of his words.

'We don't need a warrant, Mr Hunter. We're not going to search your house.'

'It's done in all the best television shows.' Hunter pushed open a door and stepped into a sombre, book-lined library. The blinds were closed to protect the book bindings from the sun and the room smelt of old leather, paper and polish.

'Please sit,' Hunter said, sinking into a chair before the empty grate. 'I would offer you tea, but my wife is out at the moment, and I'm afraid I'm not terribly domestic.'

Haaren sat in the high-backed leather chair facing Hunter, while Miller moved slowly around the room, admiring the books. The author wasn't what the inspector was expecting. With his closely cropped hair, check cotton shirt and faded denims, he looked like an ageing hippie. 'How did you know we were police officers when you opened the door?' she asked.

'You're investigating DeeDee's murder,' Hunter said, sitting back into the chair, circular glasses burning briefly gold with reflected sunlight. 'I knew it was only a matter of time before the police called. I assumed you would interview everyone DeeDee babysat for.' He shook his head. 'What a terrible business. Appalling. My wife is over visiting Mrs Banks at the moment,' he added.

'It's a terrible tragedy,' the inspector agreed.

'If there is anything I can do to help,' he continued.

'This is a magnificent library,' Miller said suddenly. 'I envy you. I've always wanted a library like this. Is this where you do your research?'

Hunter laughed lightly. 'No, Sergeant . . .' he paused.

'Miller.'

'No, Sergeant Miller.' With his elbows on the arms of the chair, Hunter spread his hands. 'This is all for show. I've looked at the books on a couple of occasions, but to tell the truth, I bought the library as a job lot from a London dealer who specialises in putting together collections for people like me. Whenever I'm interviewed, it is always in this room. The photographs usually impress.'

'You're very frank,' Haaren said.

'When your whole life is a lie – as mine is, inspector – you discover that truth is a very important commodity.'

'I'm not sure I understand,' the inspector smiled, unsure if he was teasing her or not.

'Inspector Haaren, I write for a living. I create

grotesque fantasies, which are nothing more than lies – one-hundred-thousand-word lies. And to maintain that lie, I create a fictional biography about myself. I will tell fans and interviewers exactly what they want to hear: more lies, lies heaped upon lies . . . but only because the truth is far less interesting. If anyone else had asked me about this room, I would have said "yes, absolutely, this is where I do my research". And when the magazine article appeared, there would be a shot of my exclusive and extraordinary library of occult and magical texts. However, if you look closely at the books, you'll find that they are simply nice bindings covering bad novels, religious treatises and bound runs of journals. Even the people who interview me in this room never bother to look at the books: they simply see what they want to see.' He smiled again. 'I believe that is true of people in all walks of life. Now,' he continued briskly, 'how can I help you?'

'Perhaps you would tell us what you know of Deirdre – DeeDee – Banks,' Haaren said. Behind Hunter, Miller silently flipped open his notebook.

Hunter shrugged. 'I know very little, inspector. She was a nice young woman, sixteen years old, I think. She came wih excellent references. She babysat my two young daughters every Tuesday night, when my wife and I go out to a local restaurant.' He shrugged again. 'I don't know why we do it on a Tuesday – simply because we can, I suppose. DeeDee would also sit in on the children if Emma – my wife – and I were going out to a function.'

'When was the last time you saw her?'

'Last Tuesday night. That would be the ninth. Two days later she was dead,' he added.

'Was she alone when you saw her?' Miller asked.

Still looking at the inspector, Hunter answered. 'No,

she had brought along a boyfriend who wanted a book signed. I don't remember his name.'

'Matthew Elliot. And was this one of your books, Mr Hunter?'

'Robert. Call me Robert. Yes, inspector. This was one of my books – I try not to sign other authors' books. This was an early one . . . *October Moon*, I think. A werewolf novel.'

'Was Matthew a fan?'

'Definitely. He said he'd read everything.'

'And DeeDee – was she a fan too?'

'No, not at all. As far as I can remember, she'd only read two of my books, and only then because she was working for me and because her boyfriend was a fan. I don't think she liked them.'

'Did you have much communication with her, Mr Hunter?'

'No. Very little. My wife takes care of that end of things.'

'Did DeeDee ever confide in you?'

'I'm not sure I understand you, inspector.'

'Did she ever talk about her home life, family, friends, things like that?'

He shook his head. 'I didn't have that much contact with the girl. I'm sorry I cannot be of more help. But my wife will be back soon – she may have something to add. Maybe DeeDee talked to her . . . but if she did then Emma certainly said nothing to me.'

'We would certainly like to talk to her,' the inspector said. She glanced at her watch and stood up. 'Thank you for your time, Mr Hunter. I appreciate how busy you must be. I've always thought that writing must be such a demanding occupation.'

'You're certainly in the minority, then. Most people think the books simply appear out of the word processor with hardly any intervention by the writer.'

'I'm looking forward to your next book,' she said casually. 'I'm reading *Zodiac* at the moment.' Haaren was watching Hunter closely, but he showed no expression. 'Perhaps if we meet again, I could bring it along and ask you to sign it for me.'

'I would be delighted, Inspector Haaren. I'm delighted to have such a distinguished fan.'

The inspector paused with her hand on the handle of the door. 'Do you get much fan mail, Mr Hunter?'

'Quite a bit,' he said surprised.

'Any . . . weird letters amongst them?'

'They're all weird,' he laughed.

'What about crazy?'

'Some.' He attempted a smile. 'It depends how you define crazy.'

The inspector turned to face him, her arms folded across her chest. 'How do *you* define "crazy", Mr Hunter? After all, I've read pieces from *Zodiac* which I'd consider crazy.'

'I detect a note of disapproval in your voice, inspector.'

'Absolutely not. The people who write to you: how do your images influence or inspire them?'

'I'm quite sure the images in my book do nothing to inspire them. I get letters from serious academics about the historical details in my books; practising cults will contact me looking for further references to the source material I use, a few crazy people will write asking where they can join a coven.' Without hesitating, he continued smoothly. 'I'm not a fool, inspector: all of this is leading up to something. If you care to share it with me, perhaps we can both stop wasting one another's time.'

'As you wish, Mr Hunter,' Haaren said. 'We believe

that the motive for the killings, or at least the method of killing, may have been taken from one or more of your books.'

'That's absurd, inspector!'

'It's not. There are certain aspects of the killings which have not been revealed to the press, the nature of the injuries inflicted on the victims, for example. However, they match the mutilations in *Zodiac*. We believe that someone is using your books as a blueprint for murder and mutilation.'

'That is an outrageous accusation, inspector,' Hunter said icily. 'I think you should leave now . . . and if you wish to speak to me again, please phone for an appointment.' He brushed past Haaren and pulled open the hall door. 'Good day, inspector. Sergeant.'

'I think we upset him,' Miller whispered as he followed the inspector down the steps.

'I wonder why?'

Chapter Thirty-Two

PARTING the closed blinds with thumb and forefinger, Robert Hunter watched the police inspector and the sergeant drive away in a battered blue car, and wondered . . .

How much did they know?

Did they know anything?

He could feel a pulse throbbing in his throat, and he smiled at his sudden nervousness. A visit from the police would make even the most innocent person anxious, but it was only natural that they would interview everyone associated with the murdered girl. As he climbed the stairs to his study he wondered why he had been interviewed by the inspector. Was it because he was a writer of explicit horror . . .? The inspector had made a common error: she had confused the writer with the writing, possibly believing that because he wrote about sex and murder he was capable of the crimes himself. However, he was sure she didn't think he was responsible for the actual murders – she was too intelligent for that. But she did believe that the killer was using his books as murder manuals. It was like a scene from a bad novel.

The irony of the situation struck him as he sat at his desk. 'Life imitating art, or art inspiring life?' he murmured staring at the screen. He picked up the keyboard when the idea came and he immediately reached for the phone. He was laughing so hard that it took him two attempts to dial the number.

Chapter Thirty-Three

FATHER Michael Carroll leaned forward and tapped the photographs on the long pew beside him. 'No, I simply do not believe it.' He swivelled the glossy ten-by-eight photograph around with his fingertips so that it faced Margaret Haaren. The inspector glanced up and down the length of the cathedral to ensure that there was no one close enough to overhear their conversation, before looking down at the picture. It showed details of the glyphs carved into the flesh of one of the first victims, Maddy Riggs.

'These are precise occult symbols, Inspector Haaren, sigils invoking various demons, imps and some of the lesser Earls of Hell. They are taken from the Legermation of Solomon.' The white-haired priest looked up, his blue eyes catching and holding the inspector's gaze. 'Individually, they mean little or nothing, only as powerful as the faith of the user. However, taken together, they signify the dedication of the victim to Lucifuge Rofocale, one of the Earls of Hell.'

'Lucifer?' the inspector whispered, unwilling to mention the name in the cathedral.

'No,' Carroll shook his head. 'Not Lucifer. Lucifuge Rofocale, the Great Imp. One of the most popular of the medieval demons, though barely known nowadays.' He touched a particular grouping of circular symbols. 'These are interesting when read together, and shed some light on your killer,' the priest continued. 'These signify that the killer was not only dedicating the victim body and soul – and the soul is important in such transactions – to the Great Imp, but that it was being done in part payment of a debt.' Carroll smiled coldly. 'Yes, inspector: payment of a debt. Some time ago, a number of years, maybe seven, maybe ten, someone did a deal with the devil . . . or should I say, *a* devil. Now, payment has fallen due. And there are some debts that can be paid without money. Like all the best deals with the devil, payment is made in flesh and souls, usually, though not always, the flesh and immortal soul of the person who has done the deal. The killer is repaying his debt with the flesh and souls of the innocent.' The priest smiled quickly, showing strong teeth. 'It doesn't matter if there ever was a deal with the devil – the killer believes there was. However, to return to your earlier question: do I believe that the symbols and ritual could have been gleaned from a book? The answer is most definitely no. There is too much knowledge here – real knowledge.' He sat back into the pew, facing the high altar and glanced sidelong at the inspector. 'Tell me why you asked the question in the first place?'

Haaren folded her arms and looked up the length of the cathedral. All around, tourists moved singly and in groups, videos whirring, cameras clicking, their hushed voices broken by an occasional stifled laugh. Ordinary people, ordinary lives . . . and yet, barely a dozen feet from them, she was sitting beside a white-haired priest, looking at a batch of photographs of foully abused women, and calmly discussing a medieval demon.

'You can trust me,' Carroll added softly.

'I have trusted you,' she reminded him. 'We were given a tip, which led us to a horror novel, a piece of popular trash, I thought. But when I read the novel, I discovered that portions of it matched the killings in almost exact detail.' The priest's face remained expressionless. 'So naturally, we assumed that the killer was using the books as some sort of blueprint for murder: reading the books and then mimicking the crimes.'

'It is an interesting theory,' the priest murmured.

'It became even more interesting when we learned that the last victim was the novel writer's babysitter.'

'You visited the writer, of course?'

The inspector pushed across a jiffy bag. Carroll took it and pulled out the copy of *Zodiac*. When he saw the writer's name, he pushed it back into the bag again.

'A little bedtime reading. I would appreciate your comments.' She tapped the bag. 'Yes, we visited the man. He is perfectly pleasant. A retired academic, a full-time writer, he lives quietly in Belgravia with his wife and two young children. He seemed amused to think that someone could be using his books in such a manner. He claimed it was an absurd accusation.'

'It is. Don't get me wrong, inspector. You may be correct in your assumption: someone may be reading the books, but if so then this is no casual reader. This type of ritual murder, this ritual of appeasement, where another soul is offered in place of the intended victims, is incredibly complex, subject to rigid rules and guidelines.'

The inspector smiled. 'You make it sound like a loan form, with foreclosures and penalties . . .' She stopped, when she saw the expression on the priest's face.

'Don't you see, inspector,' he whispered, 'that's precisely what it is. Someone out there is paying back a debt, completing a bargain he made with a demon. Now you may choose not to believe in demons – though I know you have had experience of such – but that does not really matter. What does matter is that the killer believes it.' He tapped the photographs. 'And the killer is well-versed in occult mythology and ritual. And that is not something you get out of a book – especially not a piece of pulp fiction! That sort of knowledge takes training, sometimes years of training. I don't want to tell you your job, inspector, but I would suggest that you're not looking for a crazed youth, but rather an older, mature, emotionless and highly intelligent killer.'

'Will he kill again?'

'Absolutely. He has to pay off his debt . . . and this is the sort of debt where the interest is very high.'

'And what happens if he fails to pay off the debt.'

'Then the demon collects!'

'I didn't know you worked Saturdays.' Robert Hunter stood back and allowed Katherine Norton to step into the hall.

'I wanted to get this back to you as quickly as possible,' Katherine said, suddenly nervous in the man's presence. She passed across an A4-sized manuscript box.

'Come up to my office,' Hunter said, turning away, leaving her holding the manuscript, forcing her to follow him up the stairs. 'What did you think?'

'It's good – very good,' Katherine admitted. 'That piece where the heroine belives she's being made love to by her husband and it turns out to be the demon . . .' She paused. 'Tell me, do you ever have nightmares, Robert?'

'Very rarely. Usually, I put my nightmares down on

paper – and then give them to someone else.' He stopped outside the door of his study and dug into his pockets for the key. 'Everyone is barred from this room,' he explained. Turning the key, he pushed open the door and allowed Katherine to precede him into the room.

'The house is very quiet,' she said.

'Emma and the children are out.' He stretched out his hand, the sudden movement startling Katherine, who involuntarily stepped back. 'The manuscript,' Hunter said, very quietly.

'I'm very sorry. I had a late night and when I did sleep, your demons walked through my dreams.'

'I wish I had it in my heart to apologise, but I have to say that I consider it a compliment.'

'I think I meant it as one.'

Hunter returned to his desk and opened the box. 'If you have a few moments, I'll read through this.'

'Of course.'

The writer glanced sidelong at her, face washed in the red glow from the computer screen. 'Look, why don't you go down and make yourself a cup of tea or coffee? I'll have whatever you're having. By the time you've made it, I'll be finished here.'

Katherine nodded. She was half-way down the stairs before she stopped, suddenly appalled at the extraordinary arrogance of the man ... and equally annoyed because she had done what he'd asked without a second thought. She was a highly skilled freelance editor – not some skivvy. She had a good mind to go back in there and tell him exactly what she thought of him ... but she wouldn't, of course. She needed the job and, besides, she also needed a cup of tea herself.

The pages of the manuscript were scattered on the

floor when she returned carrying a small tray with an enormous teapot, two thick-bodied mugs, and matching milk jug and sugar bowl. Hunter was staring intently at his computer screen, fingers moving slowly across the keys, moving the cursor up and down, locating words, deleting some, changing others.

'I don't object to any of your changes,' he said without turning round. 'Initially, I couldn't see why you deleted those two sentences on the last page, but when I read through the text without them, I realised that you were perfectly correct: it strengthens that final scene considerably.' He turned to face Katherine, a smile on his thin lips. 'I think I'll have to insist that you're my editor from now on.'

'Oh, I'll imagine you'll move back to your old editor after this,' Katherine said lightly.

'Having worked with you, though, I can see that you are better than Chris. He'd worked with me for so long, he was inclined to indulge some of my idiosyncrasies. As I became more successful, he became almost reluctant to edit me.'

'That's not uncommon,' Katherine said. 'When a writer is very successful, many of them come to believe that every word they write is graven in stone. It takes a particularly brave editor to go up against them.'

'And you're such an editor, I suspect.' Hunter's smile was genuine.

'I want to make your book as good as I can.'

'Good.' He turned back to his computer and tapped keys. The laser printer on the small table beside the desk started up, spitting out sheets of paper. 'This is the new material. I'll give it to you on disk, of course, but I thought you'd find it easier to read this way.'

'Thank you . . .'

Without turning around, Hunter added, 'And

perhaps you'd like to tell me the real reason you came here today. This could very easily have waited until Monday.' Katherine looked up guiltily. She was glad the writer wasn't looking at her . . . until she realised he could see her reflection in his computer screen. 'There is another reason, isn't there?' he asked.

'Do you read minds?'

'Only sometimes,' he said, and she wasn't sure if he was joking or not.

Cradling her cup in both hands, staring deep into the murky liquid, she spoke slowly and distinctly, having rehearsed every word.

'I think I've done something incredibly stupid. I'm not sure why I did it. No, that's not true,' she added immediately, 'I do know why I did it. I was going home on the Tube and I saw someone reading the newspaper reports of these latest terrible killings . . .' Hunter's expression never altered, but suddenly Margaret Haaren's visit made a lot more sense. He should have known that police inspectors didn't read horror; they saw enough of it in their daily lives. 'The pieces I'd been reading in your books were so similar to the killings that I knew they had to be connected.'

'So you contacted the police,' Hunter stated flatly, 'and told them about *Zodiac*.'

She looked up quickly. 'How do you know?' And then answered her own question. 'They've been here!'

'A few hours ago. They didn't mention your name,' he added. 'Do you want to tell me what you told them?' he asked.

Katherine nodded. 'I suppose I wasn't thinking clearly. I read about the young girl who was killed and I suddenly felt for her mother. I wondered what it would be like if my own daughter was killed and someone knew something that might help the police, and I knew I'd want them to go to the police and tell them, even if it didn't seem to make sense, and . . .' She stopped. 'I don't suppose *I'm* making much sense, am I?'

'No,' Hunter said, 'you're not.'

She looked directly at the writer. 'I phoned the police, told them I had some information about the killings. A woman police inspector and a black plainclothes man came to the house . . .'

'Inspector Margaret Haaren and Sergeant Stuart Miller.'

'That's them. I told them what I knew, pointed out the correlations between the killings and *Zodiac*, and that was that. It's fairly obvious that the killer is using *Zodiac* as some sort of reference.'

'That's what the police said. Did you mention anything about the new book?' he asked casually. Katherine shook her head. 'Well then, no harm done, eh?'

'When Peter, my husband, came in, and I told him what I'd done, he was livid. He made me realise just how stupid I'd been. I didn't want to get you into trouble. I decided I'd better tell you . . . so that's why I came here this morning . . .' she finished lamely.

'No harm done,' Hunter repeated. 'They came, they spoke to me, they went away. I'd nothing to say which could help them.'

Katherine put the cup down on the saucer and looked into Hunter's colourless eyes. 'If Image Press got to hear of it . . .' she began.

'I phoned them this morning.' Katherine looked at him blankly. 'Oh, I didn't mention your name, of course. I didn't know you were involved in it then, and as far as I'm concerned you're still not involved in it. But I told them what had happened.'

211

'And?' Katherine prompted.

'They were delighted!'

'Delighted?'

'Of course,' Hunter grinned. 'Can you think of better advertising for the books? You've done me an enormous favour; they predict that sales will go through the roof.'

'Time. You promised me more time.'

Payment is due.

'But I've already paid something on account.'

Not enough.

'You want more?'

I want more.

'How much more?'

More. Much more. Otherwise, I will be forced to call in your debt and collect now.

'But you promised me more time. You cannot go back on your word.'

Why not?

'I'll give you more. I promise.'

I do not want your promises. I know what they are worth.

Chapter Thirty-Four

THE devil made her do it.

She could think clearly when the drugs wore off. Only for a little while, though, because once she started to think about the events of . . . how long ago? It felt like a lifetime, but she knew it couldn't have been more than a day or two. What day was today . . . Friday, Saturday, Sunday? It didn't matter, because time had stopped when she had taken the knife and . . . and . . . and . . .

Gemma Windwood deliberately forced herself to think about something else. If she dwelt on the killing again, then the images would come, and she would start screaming and the nurse would sedate her again.

She was sixty-two years old, with three grown-up children – all married now, thank God – and four beautiful grandchildren. She went to church every Sunday, was a member of the Women's Institute, helped out with the old folks' home . . . and she had taken a knife and cut her husband's throat from ear to ear before ripping out his heart.

The scream bubbled up from deep in her stomach, swelling her chest, threatening to burst from her throat. Swallowing hard, she concentrated on the hospital ceiling. There were cobwebs in the corners. She'd never had cobwebs in her home; it was always spotless. She was forever dusting and cleaning; it used to drive poor Charlie mad. And how was she going to get that blood off the carpet and floor? When she'd cut his throat it had sprayed all over the place; some of it even spattered onto the ceiling . . .

Gemma Windwood swallowed hard again and watched the cobwebs sway in an unfelt breeze.

The devil made her do it.

If she'd been able to bless herself, she would have, but the restraints kept her hands and feet close to the metal bars set into the side of the bed. She didn't know why she was tied down, but she had a vague memory of throwing herself against the walls, pounding her head off the padding. She could almost dismiss it as a dream, except for the bruises on her face . . .

The devil made her do it.

Somehow she knew what had happened. Perhaps she had subconsciously picked up on the nurses' conversations as they had cared for her, or maybe overheard the police talking as they had led her from the house. The girl next door, young DeeDee Banks, had been murdered – *sacrificed* – at about the same time as she was lifting the knife off the draining board, slivers of carrots and onions still clinging to the blade, and walked into the sitting room, where Charlie's bald head was just visible above the top of the easy chair. The young woman had been pinned – *crucified* – up against the wall in the hallway. She knew the devil had fed off her heart, her breasts . . .

Gemma Windwood shuddered. Such words – *sacrificed, crucified* – were alien to her vocabulary. The images that haunted her dreams – of the young girl splayed against the wall, while the creature worked over her, razor-sharp knives glittering, sparkling until their metal turned red – these weren't her thoughts.

215

The devil made me do it.

A devil.

'Mrs Windwood? And how are we today, Mrs Windwood? My, but you're looking brighter.' It was the Scottish nurse. There were three nurses: an English nurse, an Irish nurse and a Scottish nurse . . .

'I see you've a little smile for us today, Mrs Windwood. That's very good.'

. . . and she knew there was a joke about that, but she'd never been very good at jokes. All the nurses treated her like a child. How are we today, Mrs Windwood? Take your medicine, Mrs Windwood. I think you should eat this, Mrs Windwood. Would you like to use the toilet, Mrs Windwood?

'You have a visitor today.' The nurse was busy with the pillows, plumping them up, raising her higher on the bed, pulling the sheets up to her chest, hiding the straps that tied down her arms and legs. The nurse turned away and spoke to the stocky, masculine woman standing in the doorway. There was a black man standing behind her. Gemma Windwood didn't know them, but she was curious enough to listen to the conversation between the nurse and the strange couple. She smiled again; the nurses didn't think she was aware, but she heard everything, she saw all that went on around her.

'I'm not sure if you'll get much response. She's been very withdrawn since she was brought in. Initially, she was very distressed and tried to injure herself, so we've taken the precaution of strapping her down.'

'Is she eating?' the woman asked.

'No. We'll have to begin intravenous feeding soon if it keeps up.'

'Is she aware?'

'We're not sure. You can see her today; she seems

216

quite bright and alert, but we're not sure how much is sinking in.'

'Fine. Thank you, nurse. If we need anything, we'll call.'

'Please don't stay too long – and try not to upset her.'

The woman approached the bed. She had kindly eyes – bright green – but her face was lined and heavy as if she'd seen much pain. Gemma Windwood had always been sensitive; her intuition had always been strong, and she sensed now that this woman genuinely wanted to help – not provide the professional, solicitous help of the nurses – but help with a genuine sympathy. She attempted a smile, but it didn't feel right on her face and she knew it had come out as a snarling grimace.

'My name is Margaret Haaren. I'm a detective inspector with the Metropolitan Police, and I'd like to ask you a few questions.'

A police woman. Neither Gemma nor Charlie nor any of the children had ever been in trouble with the law. The police had never stood inside the house before until . . . until . . .

She swallowed hard.

The policewoman wanted to help and she wanted to help the policewoman.

The woman reached out and brushed a strand of hair off the side of her face. Her fingers were hard, callused, but the touch was gentle. 'I'm not sure if you can hear me, but I want you to know that I don't believe you were responsible for your husband's death.'

The devil made me do it.

'I want to try and help you. I want to stop the person who's doing these killings before he kills again, before he makes people like you kill again.'

The devil made me do it.

'Maybe you saw what happened next door. Maybe

you were looking out of your window and you saw something, someone covered in blood, maybe . . .

The devil made me do it.

The devil.

'The devil made me do it.'

Gemma Windwood turned to look at Inspector Margaret Haaren. She was absurdly pleased that her voice was steady as she repeated the sentence. 'The devil made me do it.'

The policewoman glanced over at the black man. He had pulled out a notebook and was taking notes as if what she had said was important. And it was important.

'The devil made me do it.'

'Did you see this devil?' the inspector asked.

'Felt him.' Gemma nodded fiercely. 'A man with a demon inside. A demon with the form of a man. He killed the girl, then crucified her against the door as a sacrifice to the demon inside him. Then he opened her and fed off the heart. The demon is partial to the choicest cuts of meat.'

'How do you know this?' the policewoman asked softly.

'Oh, I've always known things like that. I know when people lie, by the look in their eyes, the tremor in their voices. I know when people are ill, when the phone is going to ring, or when a letter is going to arrive. I knew about my sister's letter from Melbourne days before it arrived. I've always known things like that. Charlie says I'm psychic, but it's just intuition. Woman's intuition.'

The inspector nodded seriously, listening to every word she said. Gemma didn't think she had ever spoken to anyone as important as the inspector. 'Would you be able to describe the man? The man wearing the form of the beast.'

'An ordinary man. Such an ordinary man – except for

his eyes. His eyes. His eyes are empty. The beast looks through those eyes. He is a hunter.' She nodded fiercely. 'A hunter.'

'Why . . . how did he make you do the things you did.'

The things she did? Taking the knife and leaning over the back of the chair, the movement waking Charlie, making him raise his head, looking up blearily, exposing his throat . . .

'The beast in the man. The beast, the devil, reached out and touched my soul, and it was hungry, so hungry. The man had sacrificed the girl to it, but it was still terribly hungry. It wanted more. Another soul . . . dearest God, another soul.' Gemma stopped, thinking about it, suddenly realising what she'd done. She had taken a knife and cut her husband's throat, then carved on his flesh and all the while she had been dedicating his life to a demon . . .

'Lucifuge Rofocale.'

The name of the beast.

The policewoman was looking at her now, her bright, grass-green eyes wide with sudden terror.

There was a sound in the room. A curious, high-pitched, vibrating sound. Then there was a taste in her mouth, copper and metal and salt meat.

It took her a few moments before she realised that she was screaming and that she had screamed her throat raw and bloody.

Chapter Thirty-Five

THE MURDER MANUALS

Police officers investigating the Horror-Scope Killings today questioned bestselling author Robert Hunter (46). Police believe that the killer may be using Hunter's latest novel *Zodiac* as a murder manual. Striking similarities have been noticed between Hunter's book and the modus operandi of the killer.

BLUEPRINT FOR MURDER

Bestselling author Robert Hunter today denied that there was any connection between his novels and the recent spate of occult-related killings that have gripped the city. However, an eminent psychologist is quoted as saying that there is every possibility that the graphic content of Hunter's books could adversely influence someone suffering from a mental illness.

INTRODUCTION OF CENSORSHIP

Calls for the reintroduction of censorship received unexpected support today with the report that bestselling horror author Robert Hunter's books have been used by the killer as blueprints for murder. Bookshops report a run on all of Hunter's titles, including his earlier works. Tony Matthews of Image Press, Hunter's publishers, angrily denied that the reports are merely a publicity ploy to increase sales of Hunter's next book, *Tarot*, due out shortly.

Inspector Margaret Haaren, who is heading the investigation, confirms that Robert Hunter was visited by the police, but simply as part of the ongoing investigation into the murder of Deirdre Banks. Deirdre, the latest victim of the Horror-Scope Killings, was a trusted and reliable babysitter, and regularly cared for the writer's two small children. Inspector Haaren denies any suggestion that Hunter's books are connected with the murders.

BESTSELLER LIST

1. (-) *October Moon*, Robert Hunter, Image Press
2. (-) *Blood Passion*, Robert Hunter, Image Press
3. (5) *Zodiac*, Robert Hunter, Image Press

Chapter Thirty-Six

KATHERINE Norton awoke, her nightdress plastered to her body, the remnants of the same terrifying nightmare – where her husband changed into Hunter, then into a demon – still vivid. There was a chill deep in the pit of her stomach and when she pressed a hand to her groin, she discovered the flesh was tender and bruised.

All across the city, church bells were tolling Sunday morning.

She'd been making love in the back seat of a car with her boyfriend. It had been a long time ago . . . an old car, a Morris Minor, and the boy . . . the boy had been named Paul . . . Paul Something-or-other. She'd been sixteen; she knew that clearly. At the precise moment Paul clumsily, painfully penetrated her, the creature had risen behind the car and drove a metal-tipped fist through the glass, except that it wasn't a fist, it was a hand holding a blade, and it wasn't Paul who was penetrating her flesh, it was the blade, sliding coldly and smoothly into her. She would hear it ringing, booming off her bones . . .

Margaret Haaren awoke as the church bells tolled Sunday morning across the city. *Zodiac* was lying open across her chest. With a cry of revulsion, the woman flung it across the room.

*

'So, publishers work Sunday mornings too, do they.'
Robert Hunter said, leaning back in his chair, cradling
the phone between chin and shoulder. He pushed up
his glasses and pinched the bridge of his nose. He'd
been staring at the computer screen for the past two
hours and his eyes felt sore.

'I'm at home,' Tony Matthews replied.

'To what do I owe the pleasure of this call?'

'Have you seen the ads in the papers?'

'I've seen them.'

'What do you think?'

'I think you've spent a lot of money; you're
obviously expecting a bestseller.'

'We are. Take my word for it, with this sort of
publicity, you're going to be number one on the
bestseller lists next week. I've taken ads out in all the
Sundays.'

Hunter nudged the untidy tumble of newspapers at
his feet. He'd unfolded the *Mail* to the ad for *Zodiac*.
' "Discover the mind of a murderer," ' he read. ' "Is
this the blueprint for murder?" Very subtle,' he added.

'I wrote it myself,' Matthews said proudly, his voice
crackling on the other end of the phone.

'I'm surprised it was published.'

'I've got three of the big Sundays clamouring for
serial rights to *Tarot*. We're talking big bucks here.'

'That's good,' Hunter said absently. He scrolled
down through the text on the screen, barely paying
attention to the publisher.

'We've had a lot of requests for interviews, some TV
and radio, a lot of magazines and newspapers. What
do you think?'

'I'll do one or two of the high-profile ones, but that's

223

all: I really don't have the time at the moment. Not if you want me to finish this book, that is,' he added, giving the publisher the opening he was waiting for.

'How's it coming along? How are you getting along with Katherine?' Matthews said immediately.

'It's coming along,' Hunter said slowly, 'and I'm getting along fine with Katherine. She's a good editor.'

'Good. Great.' Matthews paused and added, 'I know we've spoken about this before, Bob, but what about the next book? After *The Earl of Hell* . . .'

'I haven't made up my mind about it yet.' Hunter paused. 'I rather like the idea of finishing with thirteen novels, don't you? It seems a fitting number.'

'You're a young man, Bob. What are you going to do with the rest of your life? You get better with every book you write. All this media interest is going to make you into a big celebrity, and sales are going to go into orbit. First thing Monday morning, I'm going to call in the sales and production people, and we'll talk about reissuing your entire backlist with new and uniform covers. What do you think?'

'I think you're trying to bribe me to do another book. I haven't said I wouldn't. Let me finish this one first.'

'OK. OK. I won't pressure you. But don't forget, Bob, if the police do come around again, phone me first. I want to be there with a lawyer . . . and a photographer.' He laughed wheezily. 'What's that saying about every cloud having a silver lining. . .?'

'We're talking about women being brutally murdered,' Hunter said. 'You make it sound as if it was some cheap publicity stunt dreamt up by your sales people.'

'No, Bob, don't take me up wrong . . .' Matthews began, but Hunter slammed down the phone.

The writer sat back into his chair and smiled. He

could imagine the look of consternation on Matthews's face. He had insulted his bestselling, hottest-property author. Tony would brood about it for a couple of hours, then send around an enormous bouquet of flowers, chocolates and champagne – for Emma, of course – and when he was sure they had arrived, he would phone to apologise.

Only this time Hunter wouldn't take his call; he'd leave it on the answering machine. Let him sweat for a few days.

Hunter pulled the keyboard onto his lap, then stopped, fingers lying still over the keys. Events were beginning to move with a momentum all their own. He was losing control – and that frightened him.

Returning the keyboard to the table, he stood up and stretched. He was buzzing with nervous energy, his head filled to bursting with conflicting ideas and emotions. Taking deep breaths he walked slowly from one end of the long room to the other, hands locked behind his back, head thrust forward, unconsciously mimicking the posture he'd first used in the classroom more than twenty-five years ago. Control. He needed to remain in control. Writing gave him the ultimate control. The writer was God, shaping the imagined world and all the characters that populated it. He'd been in control yesterday when the police had called. When he'd picked up the phone and called Tony Matthews, he'd been acting upon a decision he arrived at based upon the known facts. He had gauged Matthews's reaction to his call, and judged the public reaction accordingly. He was still in control there.

The fact that the police had been alerted to the similarities in his books and the killings unnerved him.

The fact that he'd overlooked the possibility of Katherine Norton spotting the connection between the latest killings and the material in the new book also unsettled him. And he was curious why she hadn't mentioned this damning piece of evidence to the police.

He had known that the police would interview him in connection with DeeDee's death; that was only natural. It was unfortunate, however, that they should be aware of the substance of his book. He didn't want to attract their interest, not just now, now when he was so close to completing *The Earl of Hell*. Another reason for phoning Matthews – knowing he'd go to the press with the story – was to put some pressure on Inspector Margaret Haaren, make her look foolish, drive her away from him. He hoped he'd judged her correctly.

Control. He needed to keep everything under control for a little while longer – until he had finished the book.

Stalking back to his desk, he slumped into the chair, looking blankly at the words on the screen, white text glowing on a red background. He found he could read the individual words, but couldn't make anything out of the sentence. Lifting his left hand to his face, he bit into the ball of flesh at the base of his thumb, the sudden lancing pain clearing his thoughts, bringing tears to his eyes. When he'd wiped his eyes clear, he found he could make sense of the words again.

He was back in control.

As he lifted the keyboard onto his lap, he remembered the last time he'd felt so confused. Ten years – no, closer to eleven – just before he'd married Emma, right around the time he'd discovered she was pregnant . . .

Chapter Thirty-Seven

HE had lost control. He had allowed himself to be seduced by the charms of an overdeveloped sixteen year old.

The scandal had made the Sunday papers for a single day – but the five hundred words of coverage had cost him his marriage of fifteen years to a woman he dearly loved, the job he had gone into the day he had left college and every penny of his meagre savings. Friends and colleagues ignored him, even his own family ostracised him. Shunned by the local community, he had fled to the anonymity of London with Emma.

And for what: one weekend of passion. It had turned out to be one expensive weekend.

Six months from the day Emma Reynolds had told him she was pregnant, Robert Hunter was living with her in a seedy bedsit in Camden Town, just another mismatched couple with their own private tragedy. The tiny room was packed with dozens of boxes of books, three suitcases of clothes, and two pathetic plastic bags filled with baby clothes and toys. They wouldn't be used now. The baby had been stillborn.

And Hunter blamed himself for the death of the child.

He had been unable to find work. His qualifications

– a BA, an MA and a PhD in Metaphysics – should have qualified him for work in any school or college. But, despite dozens of interviews and several promises, no jobs materialised. Initially, he convinced himself that the job had gone to someone with more teaching experience or better qualifications – but in his heart and soul he knew that no one was willing to employ a teacher who'd had an affair with one of his own pupils. He managed to find employment briefly in a succession of badly paid jobs – bookshop assistant, record-store assistant, *maître d'* in a small French restaurant – but his uncertain temper and arrogance lost him the positions just as quickly.

To bring in a little money, Emma worked in a series of menial jobs – waitress in a cheap, all-night café, usherette in a Soho cinema, stacking shelves in a supermarket – often going straight on from one job to the other, arriving back to the flat completely exhausted. When her pregnancy became obvious, she'd been let go and then found it impossible to get work.

Too many hours spent on her feet, poor food and horrible living conditions took their inevitable toll on Emma's health. First, her feet swelled until she was unable to wear shoes, then her weight doubled and her limbs bloated. Although they realised that something was seriously wrong, they'd put off going to the doctor for as long as possible. When Hunter finally realised that the slender young woman he'd once known had changed almost beyond recognition, he'd called the doctor. He'd immediately admitted her to hospital with toxaemia – blood poisoning.

Hunter had sat with her every day in the antiseptic hospital ward. He had visited the library and consulted a medical dictionary; he knew just how serious

Emma's condition was. But when she asked him if the baby was going to be all right, he'd lied, telling her that it was going to be fine. He was unwilling to cause her any more pain and he realised then that while he would never love the young woman, he had developed a strong affection for her. And every time she raised her enormous blue eyes and looked at him, there was no denying the depth of her feelings.

Unable to read in the last weeks of her pregnancy – her swollen fingers made turning the pages of a book difficult and it was an effort even to raise her head – Hunter had read out loud to her. Emma loved fiction, she loved listening to him read in his educated voice, then talking about the characters, analysing them, forcing her to see them as real people.

He had finished reading *The Adventures of Tom Sawyer* one Friday evening – he always remembered the day – in the week before Christmas when she had raised her head and looked at him. 'You should write, Bob. You know so much about it, I'm sure you'd be a great writer.'

She said it casually, almost jokingly, but even as he was shaking his head, laughingly dismissing the idea, it was sinking in, blossoming, growing, and he suddenly found himself nodding unconsciously.

Emma misinterpreted his silence as doubt. Reaching out, she squeezed his hand. 'You could do it. You know so much. I'm sure you'd make a great writer.'

'Maybe I would. Maybe I will.'

'You could make us rich,' Emma had laughed.

He reached out and stroked the back of her swollen hands. 'Do you know, I've always wanted to write – ever since I was a boy. I grew up reading Biggles and Just William and Dan Dare.'

Emma nodded; the names meant nothing to her, but

she was happy because Bob was smiling and he hadn't smiled in a long time.

'When I was teaching,' he continued, 'I often toyed with the idea of writing a book of essays, or perhaps a textbook.'

Emma shook her head quickly. 'There's no money in textbooks.'

He nodded. 'I agree. If I'm going to write, it'll have to be something that will make us some quick money. What sells?' He wondered, glancing around the hospital ward, realising that there was a book on the locker beside every bed. 'What do people read?' He looked down at Emma. 'What do people of your generation read?'

She shrugged, blankets tumbling off her shoulders and swollen breasts. He covered her up again, tucking her in like a child. 'Most girls read romantic stuff, Mills and Boons, fat blockbusters, historical romances; boys tend to read science fiction, fantasy and horror. What would you like to write?'

'I don't know. I've never thought about it.'

'Our teachers were always telling us to write out of our own experiences,' Emma continued. 'So you should write about what you know. And you know so much, Bob.'

'Not really,' he confessed. 'I've spent all my life teaching.'

'And studying. You know so much about history and folklore, for example. Maybe you could use some of that as an idea for a book.'

Hunter nodded. Maybe he would.

The following day he had called in on every bookshop within walking distance. Working carefully, methodically, he had gone through the Bestseller and Just Published sections, carefully analysing the types of books which were selling.

Oxford Street was bright with Christmas lights as he walked to the hospital; he was barely aware of them. He had come to the conclusion that by far the greatest number of sales were in genre fiction: science fiction, fantasy, romantic fiction and horror. Naturally the bestselling big-name authors sold, but he imagined that their sales' potential was limited, whereas genre fiction continued to sell. Fantasy appealed to him; he knew enough history to be able to give his fantasy an air of verisimilitude, but the sheer size of most of the fantasy novels put him off. Five hundred, even six hundred pages were not unusual. He needed something slender that he could write quickly.

Horror was the next obvious choice. The books seemed to be slender enough, sixty, seventy, eighty thousand words, and many of them had an historical background. From his quick perusal, they all seemed to be written to one formula: plenty of sex, lots of bodies and either a disembodied force or creature, a possessed or insane human or mutated insects to wreck the havoc. Many of them were badly written. Hunter knew he could do better than that. He would write about real horror. Real horror was an emotion – despair, desperation, loss – these were the real horrors.

However, all thoughts of writing were driven from his head as he'd entered the hospital ward and discovered that Emma's bed was empty. She had gone into labour.

It was only later, much later, as he had sat in the recovery room, holding Emma's limp hand, numb with the news that his son had been stillborn, that the idea returned to Hunter and he nodded fiercely.

Now he could write; he knew now what horror was.

Chapter Thirty-Eight

'THE writer interests me.'

Father Michael Carroll slid the copy of *Zodiac* across the pew to Margaret Haaren. He glanced sidelong at the inspector, his expression lost in the gloom of the cathedral. 'His knowledge of the occult is extremely detailed, and he writes about the killings and mutilations with – if you'll pardon the expression – real feeling.'

'We called on him yesterday,' Haaren murmured. 'He wasn't entirely helpful, but I don't think he's the murderer. We're looking into his background at the moment.' She tucked the book she'd lent Father Carroll under her arm. 'What did you think?'

The priest shuddered visibly. 'It gave me nightmares,' he said. He shook his head. 'And yet I cannot say why it did that. I've experienced many horrors, both spiritual and physical, and they never affected me in this way. It is so soulless. This is not horror fiction; I read the classic horror stories, and they were genuinely frightening, they were the sort of stories which made you want to look over your shoulder. But this ... this is writing without morality, without conscience, cold and clinical. The only passion I found in the book occurred during the murders, then the writing came alive. You could almost feel that this was the part that he was really interested in. Perhaps the writer is not your murderer – but he could be.'

'Everyone is a potential murderer,' Haaren said drily. 'When I put it to him that someone was using his book as a blueprint for murder, he dismissed the idea as absurd.'

'Why are you refusing to face the obvious, inspector?' Carroll said suddenly. His bitter expression made the woman turn in the pew to look at him. In the gloomy half-light, she could see the priest was glaring at her. 'Do you believe in coincidence, inspector?' he demanded.

'Absolutely not!' she said emphatically.

'In the past you have experienced some of the forces that exist beyond the senses of men. They are not all evil.' He reached out and touched the book. 'Was it coincidence that this book came into your hands? Was it coincidence that the woman working on it remarked upon the similarities between it and the killings? Was it coincidence that the latest victim was the writer's babysitter?' He shook his head. 'The book is the key. The writer is involved. I'm not sure how or why, or even if he is aware of his own involvement. But he is involved,' he insisted.

'In what way? Is there any possibility that his involvement is innocent?'

The priest took a moment to consider. 'Unlikely. He writes about the occult ceremonies and practices in a way that suggests that he is intimately familiar with them. His knowledge of the black mass in Chapter Seven, for example, suggests that he had attended one.'

'I read somewhere that you attended one of these ceremonies once,' Haaren said.

Father Carroll crossed himself. 'That was a long time

ago, inspector. I was young and foolish, and I made myself believe that it was in the cause of research. But yes, I attended one, I know what goes on. I know that to attend is to partake. If the writer has been to a black mass, then he has indulged in an orgy of absolute depravity.'

The inspector shook her head. 'I thought things like black masses were just sensational Sunday newspaper stories, sex-orgies under another name.'

'The majority, yes. But there are a few – a very few – which are the real thing. Sex is part of the genuine black mass, but it is not the sole reason for being there, unlike an orgy. In the black mass, sex is simply the prelude and the postscript to the ceremony itself, a ceremony designed to worship evil as a force, to pay homage to a god devoted to evil.' He tilted his chin towards the enormous crucifix hanging above the ornate altar. 'If you believe in God, you must believe in the devil – one cannot exist without the other; we define good because we recognise evil. This book, this *Zodiac*, is a hymn to evil.' He stopped and then nodded slowly. 'Yes, I think that is what disturbed me about it. Its morality and thinking are so corrupt, so debased. At the very least,' he added, 'Hunter is a satanist. But he knows much more about the killings than he's telling. From the descriptions of the murders in the book, it's almost as if he's seen them.'

'You think he's involved?'

'I know he is!'

Margaret Haaren shook her head. A headache was beginning to throb and her eyes felt heavy. 'Let's assume for a moment that Hunter is the murderer – and there's no evidence to suggest that he is, I should add, but let's suppose that he is. We won't ask why he's doing it – his reasons will be bizarre enough – but what I do want to know is: why is he writing about it?'

The priest's smile was bleak. 'Vanity,' he said simply. 'Vanity. The ultimate sin.'

Father Michael Carroll remained in the cathedral long after the inspector had left. Although his lips formed the old familiar phrases of prayers and his fingers worked steadily through the smoothly polished rosary beads, his mind wasn't on the ritual. He was thinking of murder.

Murder he could understand. He had been a missionary in most of the world's trouble spots. He knew the myriad reasons why men murdered: revenge, greed, sometimes love. For most men the act of murder was enough, satisfying whatever primal need had driven them. But what sort of man killed . . . and then dedicated the act to a god? The priest shuddered. He knew the type: the fanatic.

Coming slowly to his feet, the priest slid out of the pew and genuflected before the altar, before turning to walk back down the aisle to the dark doors. He stopped when he came in line with the last pew, turned to face the altar, genuflected again and crossed himself.

Every race, every creed had its fanatics, from those who burned and tortured in the name of the Holy Inquisition to the cultists who committed suicide in the name of their religion. For the fanatic, the act of believing was reason enough. The act of believing was his reason for living.

Stepping out into the late-afternoon sunshine, the priest turned to look at a stream of tourists alighting from a coach, heading towards the cathedral. He searched their faces, watching their eyes, but there was no *light* there, the fierce, burning light of fanaticism: the same light he saw every time he looked in a mirror.

Was Hunter a fanatic?

'No,' he said aloud. A close reading of the text of *Zodiac* had revealed a man in tight control of his emotions. It showed in the careful sentence structure, the meticulous plotting and attention to detail. However, it was the scenes of bloody butchery which revealed the writer's true character. He revelled in the descriptions of the killings, lingering ghoulishly over the mutilations. But how much of this was Hunter and how much was dictated by a market that had become increasingly jaded, demanding more and more excess? He needed to know.

Glancing at his watch, Father Michael Carroll set off to find a bookshop open on a Sunday. He had some reading to do.

The police station was relatively quiet for a Sunday afternoon. Margaret Haaren discovered Stuart Miller sitting before a computer terminal, slowly going through a list of names and addresses. In a wine-coloured Waterstone's bag on the floor, she could see the garish covers of Hunter's books.

Dragging up a chair, she sat beside the sergeant. 'What have you got?'

'Nothing.' He sat back in the ancient swivel chair, ignoring its squealed protest. 'This is the database we've compiled of similar murders committed in the past twenty-four months. We've liaised with the Scottish and Welsh constabularies, and also with the French and Irish police, just in case our killer likes to take a little holiday now and then.' His fingers moved fumblingly on the keyboard, scrolling the screen upwards to some highlighted data. 'The seven definite cases we're investigating bear a remarkable similarity to a scattering of cases across the South of England and the Home Counties. I think our killer practised his technique.' He tapped the screen with the splintered end of a pencil. 'Here's a murder in Camden Town eighteen months ago: a black prostitute killed in a crucified position. Three months later, in Dover, a female vagrant was found hanging in a derelict building: her nipples had been cut off. A month later in King's Cross, we've a single mother who picked up a few bob working the streets, found dead in a crucified position with nails driven through her wrists and ankles.' Miller shrugged. 'Individually, there is no connection, except that all the victims were women . . . but looked at again in the light of the current batch of killings . . .'

Haaren nodded. 'You're right – our killer was practising.'

Miller tapped a key and a new list of names came up on the screen. 'I've marked a dozen deaths – excluding the latest seven. They may or may not be connected, but I'll lay money on it that they are.'

'Father Carroll is convinced that Hunter is somehow involved in the killings – or, at the very least, knows more than he's saying. Draw up a list of the dates of these killings, then try and alibi Hunter.'

'I've done a bit of digging into Hunter's background, checking addresses, running down the names and addresses of all his known associates. Except there aren't any,' he added. 'The man is a loner. He belongs to no societies or clubs, has subscriptions to a dozen different magazines – *National Geographic, Reader's Digest, Time*, a couple of computer magazines. He rarely gives interviews, though he does attend some of the science-fiction conventions.'

'But he's a horror writer; what would he be doing at a science-fiction convention? I thought they were all *Star Trek* stuff.'

Miller grinned. 'You should speak to my Stu. He's a science-fiction fanatic, but he hates *Star Trek*. I went with him to a convention in Bournemouth six months ago. I'd intended dropping him at the hotel where the convention was taking place, but I ended up staying the day. It was madness, but I enjoyed it. There were a lot of writers there – science fiction, fantasy and horror writers. Stu came away with a load of autographs.'

'See if you can tie in the dates of any of the conventions with the murders,' Haaren said immediately. 'It would certainly be significant if we could make a connection there . . . especially if Hunter was at the convention.' She looked at the screen again. She could see her reflection overlaid on the list of dead women. 'Hunter is the best lead we've got at the moment,' she said.

'There's absolutely no evidence against him,' Miller reminded her.

'I know. Except that he has described the killings in detail.'

'It won't stand up in court.'

'I know,' she sighed. 'And yet . . . and yet . . .'

'You feel he's good for it,' Miller finished.

'I do, Stuart,' the inspector said very slowly. 'I do. Carroll reminded me today that too many bits just fell together . . .'

'You'll be suggesting now that something *out there* is pointing you in the right direction.' Miller suggested, careful to keep any trace of sarcasm from his voice.

Margaret Haaren looked at him, her broad face expressionless.

Chapter Thirty-Nine

'DO you want to talk about it?'

Katherine Norton looked up suddenly, her eyes wide and evasive with guilt. 'I beg your pardon?'

'There is something amiss,' Robert Hunter said gently. 'I know it's none of my business, but if I can help in any way . . .'

'I'm sorry,' Katherine shook her head. 'I didn't realise it was affecting my work . . .'

Hunter shook his head. 'It doesn't show up in your work – which is excellent, as usual, by the way – but I can see that you are troubled this morning. Are you still worrying about the incident with the police? Please, don't let it trouble you. And don't worry, no one at Image knows anything about it.'

Katherine smiled gratefully. 'Thank you. No, it's not that, it's . . . it's family. A few problems,' she admitted.

'If I can help at all,' Hunter repeated. He pulled off his wire-frame glasses. 'I know all about families,' he added, sitting back into his chair. 'None of mine has spoken to me for years.' He shook his head. 'Not since I married Emma, in fact.'

Katherine smiled. 'I know all about that. My own family kicked up such a fuss when I announced that I was marrying Peter.'

'Are you married long?' Swivelling around in the

chair, Hunter fixed her with his pale grey eyes. He forced his lips into a friendly smile.

'We've been married ten years . . .'

'Emma tells me you've three children.'

'Two girls and a boy.'

'We nearly had three,' Hunter said, 'but the first child was stillborn.'

'Yes, I'm sorry.'

'No one else knows.'

'I'll tell no one,' Katherine said immediately.

'I know that. I'd prefer if you didn't mention it to Emma, either.'

'Of course.'

Hunter leaned forward, elbows on his knees. 'We all have our secrets, our hidden troubles, our buried woes. Sometimes it helps to have someone to share them with.' He paused and added, 'Why don't you tell me what's troubling you?' Katherine started to shake her head. 'I need an editor with a clear head,' Hunter continued. 'You're not much use to me if you're distracted.'

Katherine attempted a smile, not sure if he was threatening her or not. 'Family problems,' she repeated. To fill the long silence which followed, she added, 'My husband Peter has been unemployed for the past six months. That's put me under a lot of pressure. He's at home all the time and we tend to get under one another's feet.'

'What did he work at?'

'He was an accountant.'

'And he can't find work?'

'No.'

'Did his company go bankrupt?'

'No, it was taken over by one of the big multinationals and he was let go.'

'I'm surprised they didn't keep him on. And I would have thought that if he was half-way good enough, he'd have absolutely no problem getting a job.'

'He's done a load of interviews, but he's had no success so far,' Katherine said defensively.

'There must be another reason, then,' Hunter said. He interpreted the look in Katherine's eyes. 'He must have done something in his previous job which precludes him from finding another position. Something illegal? If he was an accountant, then I'll wager it had to do with misappropriation or misuse of clients' funds.' He saw tears start in Katherine's eyes. 'Oh, there's no need to look so shocked, and of course it is none of my business . . .'

'How did you know?' she whispered.

'I'm particularly sensitive to reading moods. And I'm no fool either. Plus I know all about making a mistake in a job which ruins your prospects in the same field.' He opened a drawer beneath his desk and pulled out a box of tissues. Carrying them across to the editor, he placed them down on the table in front of her. She tugged one out and dabbed at her eyes.

Hunter sank into the hanging wicker chair, setting it swinging gently to and fro. 'Shall I tell you about a teacher who had an affair with one of his students? He was thirty-five, happily married with two children. She was sixteen. That teacher's marriage broke up, he lost his home and all contact with his children. His family never spoke to him again. He was forced to move from the town where he'd grown up. And the teacher never worked as a teacher again, either.' His lips curled in a cruel smile.

Katherine stared at him, saying nothing, wondering why he was telling her this.

'One Christmas, his sixteen-year-old pregnant

girlfriend gave birth to a dead boy, and the teacher was faced with the realisation that he had royally fucked up his life. Everything good he had ever known had been destroyed, lost because of a single sin. With a girlfriend in hospital, bills mounting at every turn, no money and no possibility of a job, he did the only thing left to him, the only job he didn't have to do an interview for: he became a writer. For several reasons, and I suppose his frame of mind would have had a lot to do with it, his first novel was a horror novel. About a man who was possessed by a demon. Except, of course, the twist at the end of the book revealed that he had given himself to the demon in return for certain favours, so he wasn't the innocent victim we all thought, he was actually the villain of the piece. The book was an enormous success,' he added.

Katherine watched him closely, unwilling to speak.

'I'm merely telling you this to illustrate the point that perhaps your husband should be looking for a career in a field other than that which he was trained for. You never know, he might make a success of it.' He stood up suddenly and pointed to the manuscript in front of Katherine. 'Now, I think we should get back to work.'

The carriage was empty. Katherine sank into the long seat beside the door with a sigh of relief. She was drenched in sweat. She'd had to run to catch the Tube and was breathless, heart beating fast, throat burning. She could taste the city on her tongue. The weather reports were warning that air quality was dangerously poor, and hospitals had reported an increase in respiratory-related admissions. She patted a handkerchief to her forehead; it came away black with grease and soot. If she ever got enough money she was going to leave London, and go and live by the coast where the air was clear.

Katherine stopped, mouth twisting into a bitter smile. She had the money – or rather, Peter had the money . . . except that it wasn't his. She still hadn't decided what she was going to do about that.

Shaking her head, she pulled open a brown paper bag and pulled out a battered, second-hand copy of *The Possessed*, Robert Hunter's first book. She stared at the front cover: it showed a large antiquarian book, the pages covered in curling glyphs, the edges of the paper blackened with flame, a taloned claw appearing over the edge of the ancient volume. She wondered why Hunter had spoken to her about the book, and about himself. Why had he told her how he had started to write. . .? Was he merely relating the plot of the novel?

With Hunter it was sometimes difficult to tell where fact stopped and fiction began.

Folding open the book, she began to read.

The game had reached a very delicate stage.

He had piqued Katherine Norton's curiosity, and now he was left wondering how interested she'd be. That fact that she had already taken her suspicions to the police could well be a bonus: she wouldn't be so likely to go to them again.

Because time was running out – in so many ways . . . it meant that he was forced to move far faster than he wanted to. Katherine was the key now; he needed to bind her to him. By giving her bits of himself, he was creating an intimate, almost conspiratorial, bond between them. Another day or two at the most and he'd be able to make his move.

Robert Hunter looked at his reflection in the blank computer screen. Almost of their own volition, his fingers moved across the clicking keyboard, accessing an innocuous-looking file. To a casual observer it would appear to be a spreadsheet, lines of figures dribbling off the edge of the screen. However, when he moved to the end of the file, the text changed to a series of times and dates, making up a crude balance sheet.

Hunter consulted the calender over his desk. His book would be finished in another week or ten days Katherine would be gone, and he wouldn't see her again. He needed to move now. It was risky . . . but Katherine was still his best bet. He had ten days left; by then he needed to have everything in place.

Chapter Forty

SHE was climbing into bed when a sliver of blue jutting out from amongst the white pages caught her attention. Margaret Haaren reached over to the bedside locker and flipped open the copy of *Zodiac* the priest had returned to her. The bookmark was a scrap torn from the end of an airmail envelope, the '. . .rroll' of Carroll still visible on the edge of the paper. Opening the book, she tilted it towards the light, wondering why the priest had marked the page . . .

'Pull in here.'

Gerry Cameron glanced sidelong at his passenger, blinking in surprise.

'You heard me,' Sonja Hamilton whispered huskily. 'Pull in here . . . under the trees.'

The young man eased the car in close to the kerb, allowing the red Mazda 323 to glide to a halt in the pool of deep shadow directly beneath the trees that lined the road of the small suburban estate. He was turning towards the girl when she suddenly leaned forward, both hands high on his thigh and kissed him on the mouth, her breath musky with an acrid mixture of alcohol and cigarettes.

Sonja slid across the seat, her right hand moving up to cup the back of his head, her other hand inching closer to his groin. 'I saw you watching those other girls this evening,' she murmured, her tongue tracing a line across his suddenly dry lips.

'There's no harm in looking,' Gerry mumbled. His heart was hammering in his chest and he was having difficulty breathing. He couldn't believe this was happening. ''Sides, they couldn't compare to you.'

'You were watching that tart in the white dress,' Sonja breathed. She brushed her lips along his jawbone, her tongue moist against the flesh, then tilted her head to nip at his earlobe. She suddenly caught his hand and placed it on her left breast. 'You were watching her breasts. I'll bet you like big breasts.'

Gerry squeezed the flesh gently. He could feel her nipple beginning to swell, budding through the soft fabric of her cotton shirt. Before he could answer, Sonja kissed him again, her tongue darting into his mouth, her hand locking into his groin, squeezing almost painfully.

Gerry Cameron had known Sonja Hamilton for the best part of three months. They had met through mutual college friends, and although they'd gone on numerous dates together, they'd always parted with nothing more than a kiss. But Gerry had known that tonight was going to be different. From the moment Sonja had caught him looking at some of the other young women on the dance floor, she had acted so possessively, holding him, touching him, making it plain to everyone that she was his . . . or he was hers.

The girl twisted open the top three buttons on his shirt and slid her hand in across his chest. 'Do you know why I like you, Gerry?' she mumbled, her voice moist against his chin.

'No,' he began, but it came out as a hoarse whisper. 'No. Why?'

'How long have we been going out together?' she asked. 'Eight weeks. . .?'

'Closer to twelve.'

'Twelve?' She sounded genuinely surprised. 'Is it that long? But do you know why I like you?' she repeated. 'It's because you're the first boy I've gone out with who hasn't tried to get me into bed with him. I respect you for that,' she continued.

Gerry slid his right hand down her body, across her flat stomach and onto her thighs.

'Tell me, Gerry, have you ever made it with a girl before?'

He started to nod his head, but then changed his mind. 'No, never. I mean, I've kissed, of course, but . . .' His voice trailed away.

'How old are you?' She moved her mouth down the column of his throat and across his chest.

'Eighteen . . . nearly nineteen.' He swallowed hard. He could feel her mouth just above his left nipple, where his heart was pounding so hard that his skin was pulsing softly against her lips.

'Nineteen.' Sonja sounded astonished. 'A nineteen-year-old virgin. I lost my virginity when I was sixteen on the floor of the kitchen at home.' She suddenly reached across Gerry's lap and groped down by the side of his seat. 'Got it,' she muttered, and jerked upwards. The driver's seat collapsed backwards, crashing onto the rear passenger seat, carrying Gerry down with it. Sonja climbed onto him, hitching her short, tight skirt higher on her thighs. Sitting astride him, she unbuttoned her cotton blouse and pulled it off. Her bra was very pale against her tanned skin. Reaching behind her, she unclipped it and dropped it onto the seat. Opening Gerry's shirt down to his navel, she leaned forward, brushing her hard nipples against his flesh.

'Why. . .? he asked. 'Why are you doing this?'

'Because I want to,' Sonja smiled, teeth flashing whitely in the gloom.

Margaret Haaren was astonished to discover her own arousal. She could feel a heaviness in her breasts, the almost painful touch of her nipples against the pyjama top she wore, the tightness between her legs.

Tilting her head back, squeezing her legs tightly shut, she stared at the ceiling. The first time she'd made love – no, not the first time, the first time was a fumbling disaster – but the first time she'd made love properly, when a man had penetrated her, had been in a car. She'd been nineteen, already training to be a police officer. He'd been a police cadet. They'd borrowed his brother's car and gone out for a drive in the country. They'd left Hendon in glorious sunshine, but less than an hour down the road it had started to rain. It had continued to rain for the rest of the day, but they were young and thought they were in love, and it didn't matter what the weather was like. They'd had their picnic in the back of the car and then spent the afternoon making love.

The police inspector was reaching for the book again when she stopped. She couldn't remember the young cadet's name.

Sonja pressed a rectangular foil packet into Gerry's hands. 'Here, put this on. You do know what it is?' she added, as he turned it around and around in his hands.

'Yes, yes, of course . . .'

'But. . .?' Sonja prompted.

'But, I've never worn one before,' Gerry confessed. 'Oh, I've seen it done,' he continued, 'but, I've never actually put one on . . .'

'I'll do it,' Sonja giggled. 'I can't believe I'm actually making love to a virgin.' Tearing open the package, she pulled out the rubber sheath.

She couldn't remember his name.

The inspector closed her eyes. She could remember everything else about that day. The weather, the smell of the interior of the car, the odours of their picnic, wine and cheese and chocolate, the salt fragrance of sex, the thick, rubbery smell as he'd produced the condom . . .

What was his name?

She could still *feel* the touch of his mouth on her nipples, the swelling pressure as he'd finally slid into her, the weight of his body atop hers. And then, instants before he'd shuddered in his own pleasure, the sudden – almost painful – series of tremors that had flowed through her body.

The inspector found her breath coming in great heaving gasps. The book slid from suddenly nerveless hands as an orgasm swept through her body.

Sonja gasped as Gerry slid into her body. His eyes were shut, but his blindly groping hands found her breasts and squeezed tightly. Arching his back he carried the young woman upwards with him. The girl's fingers tightened on his shoulders, her long polished nails scoring his flesh, putting her mark on him.

'Gently, gently,' she hissed, using her weight to push his hips back onto the car seat. 'Take your time.' Flattening herself along his body, she nipped his ear, the sudden pain snapping open his eyes. 'Stop moving,' she ordered. 'We've plenty of time. I want to come with you,' she added.

Gerry stopped his thrusting. Sonja began moving

gently then, sliding herself up and down the length of his body, her breasts brushing his chest, her nipples hard against his skin. He began moving of his own accord when he heard the change in her breathing, felt the tension quivering in her thighs, the tautness across her stomach muscles. Sonja swallowed hard and nodded, wisps of blonde hair coiling across his face. 'Now!' she grunted, digging her nails deeply into his shoulders, drawing blood, but he didn't feel the sting. 'Now! Now!'

It had been a long time since she had slept with a man, Margaret Haaren realised, a long time since she'd wanted to. A relationship needed time, and in the last few years there had been precious little free. She was a woman in a man's world, doing what was generally perceived as a man's job. If she was going to succeed, she didn't have to do it as well as any man, she had to do it better – much, much better.

And police work wasn't a job that finished when you clocked off. If you were committed, it was twenty-four hours a day, seven days a week. There was no time left for a personal relationship.

Picking up the book again, she thought of the young couple making love without a thought in the world, joining in the ultimate act of pleasure simply for pleasure's sake . . . and she envied them their freedom.

Sonja came first, sitting straight up on top of him, arching her spine, her face pressed to the roof of the car as her orgasm shuddered violently through her, muscles spasming and jerking. Gerry came seconds later, lifting himself in the last instants to drive deeper into Sonja's body.

A blast of cool air wafted across his sweat-damp

flesh, but he barely registered it.

Sonja slumped forward with a whimper of pleasure, and he clutched her tightly, arms wrapping themselves around her body, sliding across soft, slick flesh ... touching cold metal ... eyes opening ... feeling the sting of metal in his own flesh below his left nipple ... the sting turning to raw, searing agony ... registering the shape that loomed up out of the night.

For long seconds the couple continued to shudder and spasm in an obscene parody of lovemaking.

Even though she'd read it before, the brutal ending shocked her anew.

Margaret Haaren read the last line again: 'For long seconds the couple continued to shudder and spasm in an obscene parody of lovemaking,' and then she turned the page, but this was a completely new chapter, unrelated to the brutal killing.

Her own passion which the book had aroused abruptly drained away, leaving her chilled and sickened. She felt cheated, almost soiled by the ending. For a brief moment, she had been the girl enjoying a moment of ultimate passion, and then that image had been violently snatched away. The inspector flung the book on the floor. She was reaching over for the light when the phone rang. Glancing at the clock – two-ten – she picked it up. It was Stuart Miller. 'There's been another killing,' he said quietly, 'a young couple, killed as they . . .'

'. . . were making love in a car,' the inspector finished. 'I know.'

His face washed crimson in the light of the computer screen, Robert Hunter slowly read the words again. The tears in his eyes were the colour of blood.

Chapter Forty-One

EMMA Hunter awoke suddenly. A sour, sick feeling was lodged in her throat. She pulled her sodden nightdress away from her skin, her flesh damp with the icy sweat.

The nightmare had been terrifying.

And appallingly vivid.

She had been in a car with Robert – except that it wasn't Robert . . . or maybe it had been Robert, but younger, much younger – and they had been making love. It was like the first time they had made love. The first kiss. She had taken the initiative then. She had known for ages that he was interested in her, but too afraid to make any move. She remembered the look on his face when she had leaned across and kissed him, and the sudden hunger in him as he had returned her passion. That had happened in his car, on a wet Friday afternoon . . .

Emma threw back the covers and slid out of bed. Pulling off the nightdress, she screwed it up and dropped it on the floor. Stepping into the en suite bathroom, she lifted a towel off the heated rail and patted herself dry, quickly beginning to shiver as her flesh cooled.

The dream had been so vivid, so real. And yet it was ten years – more – since she had first kissed Robert.

Since that first kiss a lot had happened, but she regretted none of it. It hadn't been easy initially – and their first year together had been terrible. But the last ten years had been more than she could ever have asked for.

Emma stopped and looked at herself in the mirror. Could she have asked for anything else?

Robert was everything a good husband should be: a good provider, he was great with the girls, and a considerate lover. But at times he could be so cold, so distant, lost in the terrible worlds of his own imagination, where death and cruelty were common-place. That world frightened her. And lately he had been spending so much time in his own world, staring fixedly at the computer screen, his doorway into that world.

Robert frightened her.

Her image in the mirror blurred as tears stung her eyes. She had finally admitted it. Robert frightened her. In the last couple of weeks he had become so forbidding, so cold, and she had felt more and more isolated. They had spoken about it on a couple of occasions, but he had always blamed pressure of work, the ever-increasing demands of publishers and a reading public that demanded more and more excesses. At one point, when he had become almost a stranger to her, she thought that he might be having an affair, but her theory fell down when she realised that he left the house so infrequently.

Emma stepped back into the bedroom and switched off the bathroom light. Slipping naked in to the cool bed, she pulled the covers to her chin and stared upwards, brief images of the dream fluttering across the ceiling.

She had been making love to Robert in the car and

something had happened, something bad, something very bad. She remembered pain and tearing white fire.

She was still trying to interpret the dream as she fell into an uneasy sleep.

Katherine Norton stood in the shadows and watched the car. It was rocking gently from side to side, creaking on its springs, and she knew that the couple inside the steamed-up interior were making love. The woman was on top. She caught the occasional flash of white flesh as the woman reared up and down.

Peter was in the car. She knew he was there. She knew he'd been having an affair, seeing another woman. That was why he had stolen the money. He hadn't taken it for Katherine and the children, he had stolen it to keep a mistress, set her up in a home or a small business of her own. They probably even intended to run away together.

Well, it was going to end now. She was going to confront him and his mistress.

Opening her shoulder bag she took out the seven-inch-long kitchen knife. Holding it flush against her right leg, she approached the car.

He had forgotten her name.

Peter Norton pulled the woman closer, feeling her hard nipples rasp against his chest hair. What was her name? He had forgotten her name, but he knew she couldn't be more than eighteen. He had met her when he'd been called in to liquidate a car wholesalers in Nottingham. They'd clicked immediately, they'd had dinner and on the way back to her house, they stopped in a lay-by and made love in the car. It had only happened once, but it had been the most passionate encounter of his life.

Oh, Katherine was a good lover, but after ten years, much of the sparkle had gone out of their marriage, and their lovemaking had become so mechanical.

Katherine never got on top.

Sometimes when he made love to Katherine he fantasised about the encounter. The woman climbing on top, guiding him into her, then leaning forward, stretching her body along his, moving very, very gently.

Her hair had been blonde; he remembered that. When she rested her head on his shoulder, he had looked through a veil of honey-blonde hair at the misted-up car window.

A shape moved outside the window.

She still couldn't make out his features, but she knew it wasn't Robert she was making love to. She'd had other boyfriends before Robert, but they'd all been boys of around her own age, and she had never really loved them. It had been sex that had bound them together and when they'd become bored with one another, they'd drifted apart.

Emma Hunter moaned as the man moved beneath her, sending ripples of pleasure through her body. She wished she could see his face, but her blonde hair draped across his face.

She could hear the cries of pleasure now. Both his and hers. Katherine Norton gritted her teeth and clutched the knife tighter. Peter never moaned like that when he was making love to her. He usually took his own pleasure, then rolled off her, leaving her frustrated and unsatisfied. He was a selfish bastard.

Katherine walked up to the rocking car and peered in through the window.

255

Jesus Christ! There was someone outside. Dark circles of eyes in a white face peering in. Some pervert, getting his kicks watching them doing it.

Peter Norton was pushing the woman off him when the door was jerked open and a shape was lunging into the car, something long and silver reflecting the distant streetlights.

There was a wet, broken sound, and the blonde gave a quick gasp and shuddered in her orgasm, wetness flowing across his thighs as she slumped forward, clutching at him with clawing fingers, scoring his flesh. He was trying to push her off to get at the figure now filling the car, but she was too heavy.

And then he felt the pain in his chest. Ice-cold, red-hot, it seared into his lungs, scraping off ribs, driving the breath from his body, spots of red fire dancing across the roof of the car . . . but it wasn't red fire, it was blood. Blood spurting from the huge, wet wound he could feel in the blonde's back. Blood spattering onto the ceiling, then dripping down onto his face, hot and salt.

He knew what had happened then.

And now he could make out the face. The blonde and the killer. And they were one and the same.

'Katherine,' he screamed aloud.

Peter's agonised cry brought Katherine awake. As she reached blindly for the light, she realised that there was copper in her mouth where she had bitten into her lips and her right hand was so tightly closed that her nails had cut into her flesh, a long tendril of dark blood curling down her arm.

'A dream,' Peter whispered hoarsely, pressing his

hands to his chest. 'Indigestion . . . a dream.'

On the other side of the city, Emma Hunter shuddered as the pleasure turned to pain and back to pleasure again, the man penetrating her replaced by the blade piercing her back, then replaced again as the man entered her.

When she awoke, Robert was moving gently on top of her.

Chapter Forty-Two

THERE had been a time when it had fed often off the flesh of the human-kind. Those times were gone now.

But not completely and not forever.

Nothing was forever.

It still occasionally tasted the flesh and blood of the ape descended, savouring their pain, relishing their terror. And when it could not taste the rich copper blood, it took a little of the dreams of the human-kind, sowing tiny terrors in the grey otherworld that the human-kind called sleep, watching those terrors grow and blossom into nightmares.

And the terror of a true nightmare – the sweat-inducing, heart-thundering, soul-chilling terror – was a heady delicacy, a rare delight.

The perfect nightmare took reality and shifted it only slightly, so that on the surface it was as if nothing had changed ... like a perfect fruit which concealed a crawling maggot. To create the perfect nightmare, to blur the dividing line between what was real, what could have been real and what might be real, was the sign of a craftsman ... and the creature known as Lucifuge Rofocale was a master craftsman.

Lucifuge Rofocale fashioned dreams, crafted nightmares and, when invited, made the dream a terrible reality.

Although it existed in a place beyond time, it knew how the human-kind measured the passage of the seasons. It knew how important the concept of time was to them.

And it knew that events were drawing to a close.

It was gorged now – it had fed off the flesh and terror of the slain, and tasted the rare delicacy of the nightmares, each one separate, yet joined by a common thread.

Now it was sated.

But it would hunger soon.

Chapter Forty-Three

'THIS is your evidence,' Detective Chief Inspector James Maddox snapped, tossing the envelope across the desk. Margaret Haaren caught it before it tumbled to the floor. 'Is this what we're using as evidence now – horror novels?'

Haaren took a deep breath, forcing herself to keep smiling. Lack of sleep and the events of the previous night had left her edgy and short-tempered. 'You've read my report. You've seen where I've correlated the details of the killings with the text of Hunter's book, you've seen the photographs of last night's butchery . . .'

'Killing,' the Chief Inspector said, 'killing or murder or slaying, but not butchery. Butchery is such an emotive word.'

'What took place last night *was* butchery,' the inspector insisted. 'A young couple making love in a car, impaled with a short sword, then sliced open and mutilated in the most grotesque way, their organs swapped around. The girl's womb had been placed into the boy's stomach cavity.' She stopped and swallowed hard. She had seen many dead bodies, but the sacrificial killing of the two teenagers had truly sickened her; even now, ten hours later, her stomach was still churning.

'I'm surprised at you, Inspector Haaren.' Maddox leaned across the desk, sunlight shimmering off his carefully combed, silver-grey hair. 'Your record is excellent and you have a reputation to match . . .' He paused and touched the typewritten report again. 'And so I find it all the more appalling that an officer of your experience should come to me with this . . . this joke.'

Haaren sat back into the uncomfortable office chair and took a deep breath, carefully stilling the anger that was bubbling up within her. This was an attitude she could cope with; she had been coping with it ever since she had joined the force, it was a variation on the 'woman-doing-a-man's-job' routine.

'Tell me what you find so offensive about it,' she asked mildly. 'Can you find any faults in my investigation?'

Maddox flipped open the report. The inspector was sure she caught the glint of clear lacquer on his manicured fingernails. 'You have conducted an exemplary investigation, following every lead to its logical conclusion . . . I have no problems with that.'

'So what do you have a problem with?' she persisted.

'With your ultimate conclusion' he said. 'Based on this renegade priest's interpretation of the wounds on the bodies, you say . . .' Perching a pair of half-frame reading glasses on his nose, he read: ' ". . . *the killer believes that he is sacrificing the victims to a medieval demon called Lucifuge Rofocale."* ' Maddox looked up. 'This is the twentieth century, not the Middle Ages.' He turned another page and continued reading. ' "*The extraordinary level of coincidences between the killings and the text of Robert Hunter's book,* Zodiac, *leads to the inevitable conclusion that the author is somehow involved in*

261

or indeed directing the killings." ' He closed the report and pulled off his glasses. 'That's quite some stretch of the imagination.' Sitting back into the sighing leather chair, Maddox folded his hands behind his head. 'I fear that this investigation has been too much for you, Inspector Haaren. You are obviously overwrought. The extraordinary brutality of the crimes, the fact that all the victims have been women . . .' He shrugged. 'I am suggesting that you step down and allow another officer to continue.' He pressed on as Haaren shook her head. 'Let me rephrase that. I am ordering you to step down before you embarrass all of us with your suggestions. If you refuse, I will be forced to remove you from this case.'

Haaren smiled, almost relieved that the threat had been made. 'I will not be stepping down, chief inspector.'

'You leave me no alternative, then,' Maddox sighed. 'I'm relieving you of the . . .'

'*Ordo Templi Nuctemeron.*' Margaret Haaren said, without ceremony.

Maddox sat forward slowly, colour dancing on his thin cheekbones, small, cold eyes fixed on her face.

'*Ordo Templi Nuctemeron.* Is that how you pronounce it? I believe that is the name of the organisation you belong to . . . or should that be church? The Temple of the Order of Night, or some such.' Maddox opened his mouth to speak, but the inspector continued forcefully. 'I've uncovered a lot of bits and pieces during the investigation, including, for example, the thirteen top-ranking satanists in London. There were some interesting names on the list.'

'The priest Carroll, I suppose.'

'I cannot divulge my sources,' said the inspector.

Chief Inspector Maddox broke the long silence that

followed by reaching for the intercom on his desk. 'Angela, some tea for Inspector Haaren and myself, and hold my calls. I am not to be disturbed. Resting his forearms on the polished leather desk top, he leaned forward. 'What do you want?' he asked simply.

'I don't want you,' Haaren said. 'I don't care who – or what – you worship. If I can bring this investigation to a conclusion without implicating you in any way, I'll be happy. However,' she added, 'if you impede me, I'll bring you down. I have the evidence.'

'Ah. A threat,' Maddox said.

Haaren shook her head. 'A promise.'

'It seems your reputation for ruthlessness is well founded.'

'I make a very bad enemy, chief inspector.' She tossed the copy of *Zodiac* onto Maddox's desk. 'Now, let's talk about this again.'

There was a knock on the door. Maddox covered the garish jacket of the hardback with paper before calling out, 'Come.'

The door opened and a rail-thin, middle-aged woman entered carrying a tray.

'Thank you, Angela. I'll pour,' Maddox added.

'There were some media people looking for you,' the secretary said, 'BBC and NBC want interviews. The Press Office wants you to approve a statement, and *Le Monde* also want to interview you.'

'Later, Angela, when I'm finished with the inspector.'

'You have a luncheon appointment with Mrs Maddox in ten minutes,' she reminded him.

'Cancel it,' he snapped, his eyes fixed on Haaren's face.

The secretary looked from the man to the woman, wondering what was going on. She had never known

Maddox to refuse the opportunity to appear before the press before, and his weekly lunches with his wife were a ritual he never broke.

'That will be all, Angela,' Maddox said.

'Yes, sir.'

James Maddox rose out of his chair and came around the desk to pour tea from a small ceramic pot into two cups.

'I believe you are afraid to allow me to pursue this investigation to its logical conclusion in case it throws up anything which might harm you or your group,' Haaren continued. Maddox's hand trembled as he poured the tea. 'I simply want the killer stopped,' she added.

'So do I,' Maddox said. He handed her a cup of tea. 'The . . . the organisation I belong to has attempted to discover his identity using its own methods.'

'Occult methods,' Haaren said quickly.

Maddox nodded. 'Something like that.'

'Do you believe in what you worship?' Haaren asked. James Maddox looked startled. 'I mean, really believe . . . or is it just another excuse for an orgy.'

'Yes, I believe,' Maddox said. He returned to his chair and sank into it, putting the barrier of the table between them.

'You believe in Satan, and worship him,' Haaren stated flatly.

'You're making a judgement, inspector. My church is no worse than any of the other established religions; indeed, in many respects, it is superior because it is honest. It recognises what humans look for in a religion.'

Haaren sipped her tea. 'And what is that?'

'They want their gods to keep their promises.'

'Most gods don't look for payment in blood.'

'All religions are founded in blood,' Maddox said. 'When you take communion, you are partaking in an act of cannibalism: *"eat my body, drink my blood . . ."* '

'But no flesh is consumed, no blood is drunk,' Haaren said. 'The service isn't conducted using the naked body of a woman as an altar, and it doesn't end in an orgy.'

'You've been reading too many Sunday newspapers, inspector,' the chief inspector smiled. 'How much do you know about what is popularly called "the occult"?'

'Enough to know that it works. Enough to know that there are creatures – elementals, spirits, demons, call them by whatever name you choose – that exist at the very edges of human consciousness and can some-times penetrate into this world.' She smiled at Maddox's shocked expression. 'I have come up against organisations like yours before.'

'You destroyed the renegade satanist group that snatched thirteen newborn babies.'

'I experienced something then,' the inspector said slowly. 'I saw a creature that should never have existed walk through a slab of solid glass and slaughter those who had come to worship. You may worship the devil, Maddox, but I have seen him, or one of his spawn. And now something similar is stalking London. It is connected to Robert Hunter . . . but I think you already knew that.'

Maddox sighed. 'I know very little about this writer, except that he is – or was – involved in one of the fringe groups. Yes, inspector,' he smiled, 'even amongst the occult there is a lunatic fringe.' The implacable look on the woman's face wiped the grin from his lips. 'What I do know, however, is that something incredibly old and powerful has been active of late. Last Thursday, the day the young girl was slain, three of my group attempted to make contact with the creature.' He shook his head. 'It was a foolish, ill-considered thing to do, and if I'd been there I would never have allowed it to happen. I got a call just after midnight. One of the men was dead, a heart attack, one of the women had to be sedated – and is still under sedation – and a third suffered a broken nose, cheekbones and jaw when she was pushed, face first, into the ground.'

'But were they successful? Did they contact the creature?'

Opening a drawer in his desk, Maddox removed a manila envelope. Without opening it, he tossed it across the desk.

When Haaren opened it, she discovered a ragged square of cloth. Beneath the crusted brown blood, she could make out pink satin. DeeDee Banks had been wearing a pink satin dressing gown on the night she had been killed.

'This was found in the mouth of the man who died,' Maddox said.

'This being, this Lucifuge Rofocale, is mocking you.'

'I know that. He is a deadly adversary,' Maddox answered.

'I know that.' Haaren came to her feet. 'I take it you have no objection if I continue this investigation as I see fit?'

'I don't seem to have a choice.'

'None at all.'

'What are you going to do?' he asked, standing up and coming around the desk.

'I'm going to see the priest first, then Hunter. Hunter is the key.' Haaren turned on her heels and left the room, leaving Maddox with his hand extended.

Chapter Forty-Four

FATHER Michael Carroll slept on a bed in the middle of a magical pentagram which had been painted in painstaking detail onto the bare concrete floor of the basement. The five-pointed star was enclosed in a perfect circle and within the circle the supreme name of God – Tetragrammaton – and the five names of power – Hally, Hallya, Ballater, Bellony and Soluzen – were etched in jagged runic script. Around his neck the priest wore a heavy silver crucifix alongside a polished stone etched with a minature representation of the Pentagram of Solomon. There was a loaded .32 Smith & Wesson beneath his pillow.

From the moment he had first exposed the evil of the occult organisations, he had become a target. Following the publication of his two-volume history of the occult, there had been attempts at blackmail, phonecalls that threatened to ruin his reputation, to expose him as a paedophile. He'd called their bluff and immediately contacted the newspapers with the story. He'd been attacked and badly beaten when it was announced that he was going to chair a Parliamentary Select Committee on the danger of cults. Wearing his cuts and bruises like badges of honour, Carroll had proudly appeared before the cameras and accused the satanic groups of being behind the attacks.

Then the nature of the attacks changed. Every night for a month, terrifying nightmares had alternated with highly charged erotic dreams. Each dawn found him trembling and exhausted. The occult attacks only ceased when he drew the ancient magical circle of power around his bed. Only once in the last seven years had he neglected to charge the pentagram. That night the dreams had been so bad, so full of despair, filling him with such self-loathing, that he had seriously contemplated suicide.

The dreams still came, but, shielded by the magical circle, he was only aware of them as a vague discomfort. Last night had been different, though. He had drifted in and out of an uneasy sleep, aware that he was dreaming, yet unable to bring himself to full consciousness.

He dreamt that he was in the midst of a forest clearing, crouched over a tiny flickering flame, while yellow-eyed beasts prowled in the shadows.

He dreamt that he was walking down a lonely country lane, holding aloft a flickering candle which bathed him in a warm, yellow light; the light was his only protection from the creature who followed him on clicking claws.

He dreamt he was sitting on a wooden chair in a bare room beneath a flickering low-wattage bulb. Two shapes that moved around the walls had teeth filed to points.

He dreamt that he was enclosed in a metal box that dripped blood onto his face, stinging his eyes, splashing his lips, curling down his cheeks.

When the priest awoke, the sun was streaming in through the window and he could tell by the position of the shadows that it was some time in the early afternoon. He had a pounding headache and his mouth was furred. When he sat up in the bed, he recoiled at the odour of stale sweat and urine, and he realised his bladder had emptied itself.

He knew then what had happened.

Something had come last night. Something powerful.

The beast, Lucifuge Rofocale, the Earl of Hell.

Climbing slowly out of bed, the priest pulled on his glasses, then turned to the east and described a five pointed star in the air, visualising it burning gold. 'Tetragrammaton,' he said solemnly. The oldest name of God, from the Old Testament. Facing south, he said, Adonai, then turning west and north, he pronounced the names 'Eheieh' and 'Agla'. Facing east again, he stretched out his arms in a crucifix pose, and completed the formula by calling upon the names of the Archangels, 'Raphael before me, Gabriel behind me, Michael at my right hand, Auriel on my left.' Only when he could clearly see himself surrounded by a whirling circle of fire did the priest allow his trembling arms to drop to his side. Then he knelt on the floor and examined the pentagram.

The magical star and circle around the bed were inscribed with the names of power, and nothing evil or controlled by evil would be able to pass it. And even if the beast had sent a human creature, the windows in the square basement room were heavily barred, and he had fitted new locks and deadbolts to the single three-inch-thick wooden door. If it got past those, he had the gun.

The pentagram had been disturbed.

Lying flat on the cold stone floor, Carroll stared at the thick, white paint. At the foot of the bed, four thin grooves had been scored into its rubbery surface. Matching the grooves with his fingers, Carroll imagined long-nailed claws. Crawling on hands and knees, the priest moved around the circle. In two other places, on the left hand side of the bed and again by his head, the edges of the circle were torn as if a beast had scratched at them.

Straightening, Carroll dusted off his hands as he examined the room, searching for anything that looked out of the ordinary. But everything was as he had left it. Finally, crossing himself, he stepped out of the circle, and examined the door, long, delicate fingers tracing the edge of the wood. It was unmarked. Nor were there any marks on the windows.

The priest laughed briefly, the sound harsh and ugly in the small room. Last night something had come for him, and had been thwarted. And if it had attempted to get to him, then it had undoubtedly touched the others. He knew then that the beast had fed again last night.

Reaching beneath the pillow, he lifted the gun.

There were some paperbacks spread out on a battered table beneath the barred window. Standing at the table, the priest looked over the garish, blood-soaked covers. The majority were by Robert Hunter. They were distinguished from the others by their attention to occult detail, the intricate accounts of torture and murder, the terrible abuse of women.

Evil always triumphed in Hunter's books. Satan and those who followed him were always victorious, their organisations were depicted as honourable, while the established churches were shown to be cowardly and corrupt.

Carroll stared at the books, trying not to think, simply allowing his thoughts and fears and ideas to flow and arrive at some conclusion. But there were no answers. Finally, he scooped six of the titles into a

paper bag and dropped the gun in on top of the books.
Hunter was the key.

Chapter Forty-Five

SITTING at the kitchen table, with a cup of coffee in her hand, Katherine Norton watched the one o'clock news on the BBC, listening to the diluted details of the double murder. Beneath the police floodlights, the red Mazda 323 glowed blood red, contrasting sharply with the pool of thick black liquid which had puddled beneath the open door.

Margaret Haaren gave a brief interview, completely dismissing a reporter's suggestion that this double murder was connected to the recent spate of killings. The inspector curtly pointed out the differences beween those murders of single women, and this murder of a couple, and then moved onto the next question.

Katherine reached for the copy of *Zodiac* which lay on the table before her, and leafed through the pages, looking for Chapter Forty. The editor sipped the coffee again, but the liquid was brackish, bitter in her mouth, and she pushed the cup away.

'Pull in here.'

Eddie Carter glanced sidelong at his passenger, blinking in surprise.

'You heard me,' Sara Hunt whispered huskily. 'Pull in here . . . under the trees.'

The young man eased the car in close to the kerb, allowing

the red Mazda 323 to glide to a halt in the pool of deep shadow
directly beneath the trees that lined the road of the small
suburban estate.

On screen, the red Mazda 323, now draped in a heavy tarpaulin, was being hoisted onto a flatbed truck.

Pushing away the open book, Katherine turned to the manuscript of *The Earl of Hell* and leafed through the loose pages. The incident she was looking for took place about half-way through the book. It had meant nothing when she'd read it the first time – it was just another piece of Hunter excess. But when she read *Zodiac*, her editor's eye had caught the similarity of the characters' names. However, she'd been astonished when she'd gone back to *The Earl of Hell* and discovered that the piece was almost identical. Almost. Katherine wondered if Hunter had realised that he was plagiarising himself.

'Pull in here.'

Eddie Carter glanced sidelong at his passenger, blinking in surprise.

'You heard me,' Sara Hunt whispered huskily. 'Pull in here . . . under the trees.'

The young man eased the car in close to the kerb, allowing the red Mazda 323 to glide to a halt in the pool of deep shadow directly beneath the trees that lined the road of the small suburban estate.

The beast hungered.

Its hunger was a terrible thing, a physical ache that lanced through the man's stomach, doubling him over, until he could only walk crouched over. The hunger drove daggers of pain up into his lungs, into the base of his throat until he found it difficult to breathe. If he didn't feed the beast, then the beast would feed off him.

Sara slid across the seat, her right hand moving up to cup the back of his head, her other hand inching closer to his groin. 'I saw you watching those other girls this evening,' she murmured, her tongue tracing a line cross his suddenly dry lips.

'There's no harm in looking,' Eddie mumbled. His heart was hammering in his chest and he was having difficulty breathing. He couldn't believe this was happening. ''Sides, they couldn't compare to you.'

'You were watching that tart in the white dress,' Sara breathed. She brushed her lips along his jawbone, her tongue moist against the flesh, then tilted her head to nip at his earlobe. She caught his hand and placed it on her left breast. 'You were watching her breasts. I'll bet you like big breasts.'

Eddie squeezed the flesh gently. He could feel her nipple beginning to swell, budding through the soft fabric of her cotton shirt. Before he could answer, Sara kissed him again, her tongue darting into his mouth, her hand locking into his groin, squeezing almost painfully.

In the beginning there had been time to prepare for the beast's hunger. To pick and choose a tasty morsel. But the beast had become more demanding. In the beginning it had taken sustenance once a year, then every six months, and in the last year, it was demanding a feeding every moon.

It had fed less than four days ago – and it hungered now.

The beast was taking control of him now, leading him, looking out through his eyes, hearing with his ears, using the senses denied it. Razor-tipped claws lurked in his soft flesh, needle-pointed fangs filled his mouth, hidden just behind his own teeth, a barbed tail coiled against his spine.

Prowling the streets, head thrown back, nostrils flared, tongue flickering, tasting the air, the beast foraged.

The driver's seat collapsed backwards, crashing onto the rear passenger seat, carrying Eddie down with it. Sara climbed onto him, hitching her short, tight skirt higher on her thighs. Sitting astride him, she unbuttoned her cotton blouse and pulled it off. Her bra was very pale against her tanned skin. Reaching behind her, she unclipped it and dropped it onto the seat. Opening Eddie's shirt down to his navel, she leaned forward, brushing her hard nipples against his flesh.

'Why. . .? he asked. 'Why are you doing this?'

'Because I want to,' Sara smiled, teeth flashing whitely in the gloom.

A scuffle in an alleyway attracted its attention. Two youths, with shaven heads, wearing industrial steelcapped boots, were kicking another youth who lay curled in a foetal position on the filthy ground. The air was rich with the potent aroma of blood and hate. The beast was moving into the shadows when it caught the unmistakable fragrance of sex.

It stopped, tongue flickering, moist on the warm night air, head turning from side to side. When it identified the direction, the beast in the body of the man moved towards the source.

Sara gasped as Eddie slid into her body. His eyes were

shut, but his blindly groping hands found her breasts and squeezed tightly. Arching his back he carried the young woman upwards with him. The girl's fingers tightened on his shoulders, her long polished nails scoring his flesh, putting her mark on him.

'Gently, gently,' she hissed, using her weight to push his hips back onto the car seat. 'Take your time.' Flattening herself along his body, she nipped his ear, the sudden pain snapping open his eyes. 'Stop moving,' she ordered. 'We've plenty of time. I want to come with you,' she added.

The street was quiet, lined with trees that still retained their leaves despite the long summer drought. The houses were set well back from the road, a few still showing lights in the upper floors, even though it was well past midnight.

The odour was unmistakable now. Rich and salt. Soft flesh, warm meat. A woman on heat.

The car was almost invisible in the shadows at the end of the road, but the beast fixed on it immediately, sorting through the odours, identifying the distinctive odours of male and female. It hesitated; it preferred the flesh and blood of the female. Sometimes, of necessity, it had taken the flesh and spirit of males, but it found the taste thin and unwholesome.

Tongue flickering, saliva streaking its damp chin, the hunter crept closer to its prey.

Male and female: it would take them both.

It would feast.

Eddie stopped his thrusting. Sara began moving gently then, sliding herself up and down the length of his body, her breasts brushing his chest, her nipples hard against his skin. He began moving of his own accord

276

when he heard the change in her breathing, felt the tension quivering in her thighs, the tautness across her stomach muscles. Sara swallowed hard and nodded, wisps of blonde hair coiling across his face. 'Now!' she grunted, digging her nails deeply into his shoulders, drawing blood, but he didn't feel the sting. 'Now! Now!'

Sara came first, sitting straight up on top of him, arching her spine, her face pressed to the roof of the car as her orgasm shuddered violently through her, muscles spasming and jerking. Eddie came seconds later, lifting himself in the last instants to drive deeper into Sara's body.

The beast touched the cool metal of the car.

A fragment of the human consciousness buried deep within it was aware of the danger in taking the couple, here in the open. But the beast was confident; it existed in a place without time. Without time, there is no future, no present, no past. It had seen itself taking this couple. It had watched itself feed off their flesh, feast off their spirits, relishing their single moment of fear and absolute terror.

It knew it would not be caught.

Holding its hand up to its face, the beast watched as its talons slid through the tips of the soft human fingers. Deep in its core the human howled its agony. When the dark, razor-tipped talons had stopped moving, it gripped the car door and silently eased it open.

A blast of cool air wafted across his sweat-damp flesh, but Eddie barely registered it.

Sara slumped forward with a whimper of pleasure, and he clutched her tightly, arms wrapping them-

277

selves around her body, sliding across soft, slick flesh . . .

There was no blood when the long nail first sliced through the girl's back. Driving deeper, it slid between the ribs, puncturing the lung. The girl shuddered in exquisite pain, but the beast took the pain, relishing it, stealing the breath from her body, rendering her mute. Then, with the fingers of its right hand pressed together, the talons forming a deadly cone, the beast drove into the righthand side of her back, shredding muscle and tissue, and it pushed its way through her body.

The spasming boy reached around the girl's body and touched cold flesh, cold metal. There was a moment of confusion, of terror.

The talons broke through the girl's flesh just below her right breast and pierced the skin of the boy's chest. The transition from pleasure to pain was immediate and absolute. He was dead even before the talons nicked his heart.

For long seconds the couple continued to shudder and spasm in an obscene parody of lovemaking, joined now by the beast. When it had savoured their pain and fed off their spirits, it opened them to hunt for the choicest morsels.

Katherine Norton swept the untidy manuscript into a bag and dropped *Zodiac* in on top of it.

It was time to talk to Hunter again.

And this time she wanted the truth.

Chapter Forty-Six

'I'M not sure what I expected. Something better,' Margaret Haaren said as Stuart Miller pulled the car in to the kerb. She climbed out of the car and looked up at the grimy three-storey building. A badly printed B&B sign peeled away from the front window, water stains bubbling the thick cardboard.

'It was a transient hotel until the local council pulled its licence for at least a dozen breaches of health and safety regulations,' Miller said, coming around the car. 'The listed occupier and owner is a Mrs Susan Gunning.'

'You're sure Carroll is here?' Haaren asked, climbing the filthy steps.

'Followed him here myself.'

The small, stout woman who opened the door on its security chain looked suspiciously at the tall, masculine-looking woman and the black man standing behind her. 'Yes?' she asked.

Haaren smiled professionally. 'Hello. We're here to see one of your guests: Father Carroll, Father Michael Carroll.'

'I don't keep guests any more,' the woman said, but her eyes betrayed her, and the inspector knew she was lying. She held her warrant card up in front of her face. 'Police, Mrs Gunning. Open the door.'

'I've told you, there's no one here,' the woman snapped and immediately started to close the door.

The inspector jammed her shoe in the opening and pressed the flat of her hand against the wood, pushing the door back to the fullest extent of its chain. 'I want to speak to the priest now.'

'I've told you, there's no one here. Now, piss off, or I'll call the police.'

'We are the police,' Haaren sighed, glancing over her shoulder, checking the dingy alleyway for prying eyes . . . before she threw her bulk against the door, tearing the safety chain from the frame. The force of the blow sent the woman staggering back. 'I've no time for games,' the inspector said, stepping into the hall. She loomed threateningly before the shaken woman. 'Now, where's Carroll?'

'You can't do this,' the woman stammered. 'You need a warrant.'

'Sergeant. Why don't you arrest Mrs Gunning for obstructing a murder investigation?'

As the sergeant stepped up, the woman said, 'Father Mike has rooms in the basement.'

'I thought you didn't keep guests,' Miller smiled.

'Father Mike is a friend, he's not a paying guest.' Susan Gunning straightened herself, smoothing her crumbled apron. 'He's an old friend of the family; he stays here whenever he's in London.'

'The room, Mrs Gunning?' Haaren said evenly.

The woman pointed along a dark, sour-smelling corridor. 'Down the steps at the bottom of the hall. Be careful, the lightbulb blew last night and I haven't had time to replace it.' As the two police officers moved down the corridor, the woman added, 'And I wouldn't want you to fall and break your necks.'

Before she tapped on the door, the inspector pressed

the side of her face against wood, listening for signs of movement inside. Glancing at Miller, she shook her head, then took a coin from her pocket and rapped on the door. 'Father Carroll? Father Carroll, it's Inspector Haaren.' She knocked again, then pounded on the door with her fist. The wood boomed solidly. 'Father Carroll!' There was no answer. 'Better get us a key, Stuart.'

Miller turned and discovered Susan Ganning standing at the end of the corridor, arms folded across her breasts. 'Did Father Carroll leave the house this morning?' he asked, approaching her.

'No. He went to his room after supper last night – about ten – and hasn't been out since.'

'Are you sure?'

'Yes, he always tells me when he's going out.'

'Has he had any visitors?'

'Father Mike never has any visitors.' The woman looked over the sergeant's shoulder to where the inspector was hammering on the door again. 'Is everything all right?'

'Do you have a key to the room?'

'There is a spare key, but Father Mike insists that no one enter his room.

Miller stretched out his hand. The woman looked at it for a moment, before reaching into her apron pocket and producing a small ring of keys. Extracting one, she twisted it off and handed it to the sergeant. 'Father Mike's not in any trouble, is he?'

'Father Mike . . . Father Carroll is helping us with our enquiries,' Miller answered. 'We're just checking to make sure he's all right.'

Haaren glanced over her shoulder as Miller returned. 'This door sounds solid,' she said, pounding on the door with her fist, 'it doesn't even vibrate in the frame.'

'It's a different pattern to the rest of the doors back

along the corridor,' Miller said. 'It looks newer, too.' He slipped the key in the lock. Both officers instinctively stood to either side of the door as he turned the key, then gently pushed the door open.

'Father Carroll,' Miller said, taking a quick look inside. 'Empty,' he said, looking at the inspector. She jerked her head into the room. Crouched double, Miller darted in. The inspector heard him whisper, 'Good Christ,' and when she stepped into the room, she found him staring at the enormous pentagram painted onto the floor. Miller slowly crossed himself.

'Do you know what it is?' she asked.

'A pentagram or a pentacle, I'm never sure which is which,' Miller said. 'All the best black-magic movies have them. Guaranteed protection against occult attack.' He knelt and rubbed his hand across the edge of the circle. 'Painted onto the floor. Touched up several times. You can see where the new paint has been laid on top of the old. This has been here for quite a long time.'

'You'd wonder why a Catholic priest felt he needed such protection,' the inspector said, moving around the room. The room smelt dry and musty, the air tainted with a slightly acrid sweetness, like incense. A crude homemade bookcase filled the wall behind the door. The bottom shelves were crammed with books and papers, but the top shelf held a dozen ancient-looking leatherbound volumes. She pulled one out, recoiling slightly at the odour of decay, blinking as dust curled into her eyes. There was no title on the spine, but when she opened it she discovered an ornate wood-block illustration opposite the title page. It bore a remarkable similarity to the circle painted onto the floor. Tilting the book, she read the crabbed, jagged printing. ' "Grimorium Verum." Grimoires are magical books,' she said. 'An interesting addition to any priest's library.'

'Carroll wrote books on the occult,' Miller reminded her. He pulled a thick hardback from one of the lower shelves. '*A History of the Occult*, by Michael Carroll.'

Haaren looked around the room. 'I wonder where he is. There's no sign of a struggle, no signs of forcible entry.'

'Maybe he went out for a walk. Maybe he had to celebrate mass or something.'

'But Mrs Gunning thought he was still in his room.'

Miller shrugged. 'He obviously slipped out.'

'There was a double murder last night. I'm surprised he didn't contact me looking for details of the mutilations.'

'Ma'am . . .' Miller said. He was standing before a wooden table. There were a dozen paperback novels scattered across it. Most of the titles were by Robert Hunter. The sergeant lifted one, *The Possessed*. 'Looks like he was doing a little research on our subject . . .' He stopped as a curl of thick liquid trickled off the cover of the book onto his hand. Bringing the book close to his face, he breathed in the oily aroma. Without a word he handed it to the inspector. Nostrils flaring, she inhaled the smell.

'Gun oil,' she said decisively.

'On Hunter's book,' Miller added.

Chapter Forty-Seven

BLINKING furiously in the late-afternoon sunshine, Katherine Norton stepped out of the Sloane Street Tube station and turned right towards Eaton Square. She had forgotten her sunglasses and squinting against the glare had given her a pounding headache. As she walked towards Eaton Square, she noted the early-evening newspaper headlines.

'POLICE HUNT SEX FIEND.' 'RIPPER HORROR.' 'DOUBLE SLAYING BAFFLES POLICE. NO CLUES TO KILLER'S IDENTITY.'

The heavy bag containing the manuscript of *The Earl of Hell* and the hardback edition of *Zodiac* bumped against her leg. She had the clues, right here in her bag. If only the police had listened to her, they might have prevented this latest killing.

She thought she knew what had happened. When the police had received her phonecall, they'd visited her as a matter of course. They'd listened to her accusations, visited Hunter – who'd obviously had an alibi for the killings – and then come to the conclusion that she was simply an hysterical woman and that her suspicions were without basis.

Katherine turned off Eaton Square and stopped at the entrance to the small private square, looking down the white-fronted houses towards Hunter's.

Maybe Hunter had managed to fool the police, but he hadn't fooled her. Katherine grimaced. Well, that wasn't entirely true: he had with his psychic bullshit. For a while she had believed him and she had actually felt sorry for him and his curse. But it was only when she was reading the piece from *Zodiac* and then comparing it with the manuscript of *The Earl of Hell* that she realised that if Hunter could see the killing . . . then he could also see the killer.

But he hadn't told her that.

And now she wondered why.

The demon's-head door knocker felt slick and cool beneath her fingers as she gripped it. She rapped firmly.

There was no answser.

She knocked again, turning to look out across the small square. This side was in shadow, while the white-painted houses across the small patch of burnt greenery were reflecting back the light blindingly. Blinking away the after-images, she turned back to the door . . . just as it opened.

Emma Hunter peered through the slit.

'Yes?'

Katherine stepped forward, forcing herself to smile. 'Hello, Emma, I've come to see Robert.' She stopped when the younger woman didn't move to open the door any wider. 'Is everything all right?'

'Yes, everything's fine.' Emma attempted a smile, but it was taut and strained, and Katherine realised that the woman's eyes were red-rimmed, as if she'd been crying.

'I can come back, if it's inconvenient . . .' she began.

Emma Hunter turned to look back into the shadowy hallway, then opened the door a fraction, leaving barely enough space for Katherine to squeeze through.

Puzzled by the woman's behaviour, Katherine stepped in. After the brilliant sunshine, it took her eyes a few seconds to adjust to the gloom. When she could see again, she discovered a tall, white-haired man standing behind the door, a hand resting lightly on Emma's shoulder. She was opening her mouth to speak when he raised his right hand and pointed a gun at her face.

'Inside.' He jerked his head towards the open sitting-room door.

Katherine felt her stomach lurch. She looked from Emma to the tall man and realised with a start that he was wearing clerical garb. But his blue eyes, magnified behind thick glasses, were cold and pitiless.

'Drop the bag and step away from it.'

Katherine allowed the bag to slide to the floor. 'Who are you?' she whispered. 'What do you want?'

The priest shoved Emma towards Katherine. 'Inside,' he said again. Catching up the bag he followed the two women into the sitting room.

Katherine discovered Robert Hunter sitting in a high-backed leather chair holding on tightly to his two sobbing girls. Emma went to stand beside him, lifting the youngest girl – Rose – up into her arms. The floor was scattered with books which had obviously been pulled from the shelves. Some had been shredded, the ornate leather snapped and broken. Glass from a broken vase crunched underfoot, matted into the fibres of the carpet.

The priest closed the door with his foot, then stood with his back to it. He pointed the gun at Katherine. 'Who are you?'

'I'm Katherine Norton.'

'What are you doing here?'

'I work for Mr Hunter's publishers.'

'Doing what?'

'I'm an editor.'

'An editor.' Something flickered behind the priest's eyes. 'Another book?' he asked. 'Another book. The thirteenth,' he said suddenly. 'Dearest God, the thirteenth volume, *Liber XIII*.' Crouching down he opened Katherine's bag and pulled out the copy of *Zodiac*. Spotting the bookmark, he flipped it open and read the first few lines. 'Ah, I see you've marked an interesting chapter.' Tossing the book aside, he lifted out the thick bundle of manuscript, turning it to read the title page. '*The Earl of Hell* . . . how appropriate,' he spat. Sliding a long-nailed finger into the pages, he opened it at the editor's second bookmark. 'Now, let's see what we have here.'

As the priest read, Katherine turned to Hunter. 'What's happening, Robert, who is this man?'

Hunter smoothed his daughter's hair as he looked at the editor. 'He said he was a priest – a fan,' he added bitterly, nodding to the bag of paperbacks on the floor at Katherine's feet. 'He wanted a few books signed so that he could auction them off for charity. Once he got into the house he pulled a gun.'

'But what does he want?' Katherine whispered.

'He wants me,' Hunter said simply. 'He wants to kill me. Looking into Katherine's eyes, he added. 'He thinks I'm the killer.'

'Fiend!' Carroll hissed, straightening up. 'Fiend! Here is the proof, if proof I needed.' He waved a fistful of manuscript in the air. 'You know what he is, don't you?' he demanded, looking at Katherine. 'You know him for what he is?'

'I don't know what you mean,' she said quietly.

'Why did you come here today, with this?' He held out the manuscript. 'The truth,' he added threateningly.

Katherine sank into the chair facing Hunter. 'I was going to ask Robert about the similarities in the two texts.'

'You know he's the killer, don't you?' Carroll said. 'You know he's killed those women and dedicated their bodies to Satan, his lord and master.' He nodded fiercely. 'Yes, you know. Why didn't you go to the police with your suspicions?'

'I did. They didn't believe me.'

Carroll nodded jerkily. 'I had hopes for the inspector. But in the end she failed me,' he said. The priest looked around the small group. 'There are two laws: Man's law and God's law – the law of the Old Testament. An eye for an eye . . . thou shalt not suffer a witch to lie,' he mumbled. 'How many have you killed, Robert Hunter? How many souls have you fed to your foul master?' Lifting the pistol, Carroll thumbed back the hammer. The double-click of metal silenced the two girls. Huge tears flowed silently down Emma's face.

'None,' Hunter whispered. He pushed Violet towards Katherine, out of the line of fire.

'He sees the killings,' Katherine said desperately, wrapping the girl in her arms. 'He's psychic. He sees them, then writes about them.'

Michael Carroll shook his head quickly, white hair flicking across his face. 'No; he's more than that. Do you deny that you are a satanist?'

The two women looked at the writer.

'I once attended some ceremonies purely for research purposes. Just like yourself,' he added, suddenly recognising the priest. 'Father Michael Carroll, the "occult priest", the newspapers called you.'

'You sold your soul to the demon known as Lucifuge Rofocale in return for success and fame as a writer,' Carroll said evenly. 'I believe you made a bargain with

288

the demon several years ago, and that contract has now run out. But the demon-kind are generous; they will always allow you a little extra time – just a little extra time – provided you pay for it. And the demon-kind take their payment in human flesh and souls.'

Hunter's expression was glassy. 'I don't know what you're talking about,' he whispered.

'Oh yes you do,' the priest whispered, knuckles whitening on the trigger, spittle flecking his lips. 'It ends today.'

Hunter's fingers closed so tightly on the leather arms of the chair that they burst through the material. Blood welled around his nails.

The priest abruptly lowered the gun. 'Where do you write?' Without waiting for an answer, he looked at Katherine. 'Where does he write?'

'In an attic at the top of the house.'

'On a computer?'

'Yes.'

Carroll lifted the crumpled pages again. 'So there is a copy of this on the machine?'

'Yes,' she whispered, glancing at Hunter. The writer's colourless eyes were fixed on the priest's face, the skin pulled taut across his cheekbones, tendons and muscles clearly visible in his back.

'Is there a basement?'

Katherine shrugged. 'I don't know.'

'There is a basement,' Hunter said.

'How many doors?'

Frowning, Hunter said, 'One.'

Stuffing the manuscript into the bag, Carroll stepped away from the door. 'Right, all of you, out into the hall.' His smile was a terrifying grimace. 'Please don't misunderstand me. I have come to kill only one, but I will kill you all if needs be.'

Carrying Rose, Emma inched past the priest followed by Hunter leading Violet by the hand. As Katherine approached she looked into the priest's wide eyes. 'Why are you doing this, father. Why?'

'Because he is evil,' the priest said simply. 'And if I don't kill him then he will kill and kill again.' He followed Katherine out into the hallway. 'You. Take the woman and children and lock them in the basement. Bring me the key.'

'The children are frightened of the dark,' Hunter said, 'and there's no light in the basement.'

'It will only be for a little while.' The priest attempted to smile at the two girls, but they both looked away, terrified by his expression. 'Do it,' he snapped at Katherine.

Katherine took Violet's hand and walked with Emma to the end of the hall. Neither woman spoke. The entrance to the basement was through a door beneath the stairs. The key to the basement was in the lock, the spare hanging from it, dangling on a curl of wire. Wrapping her hand tightly around the second key, the wire cutting in her hand, Katherine turned the key in the lock and pulled the door open. The dry odour of dust made her eyes water.

'Mama, I don't want to go down there ... Violet turned to her mother.

'It's just a game,' Emma said shakily. 'Just a game.' She held the child close.

Katherine hugged the younger woman, kissing her cheek. 'Get help,' she whispered, 'find Margaret Haaren.' She pressed the spare key she had pulled off the wire into Emma's cold hands. Then she closed the door to the cellar and locked it.

As she handed the key to Carroll, she asked, 'What happens now?'

'Now it ends,' Carroll whispered. He pointed the gun up the stairs. 'It's time to destroy the devil and all his works.'

Chapter Forty-Eight

KATHERINE Norton watched Robert Hunter straightening as he turned the key in the lock and entered his long study. It was almost as if he was drawing strength and confidence from his surroundings. He crossed the room and sat down in front of his computer, swivelling the chair around to face the priest, hands clasped before his face in his customary pose.

'Sit,' Carroll said, pushing Katherine away from the door.

Sitting in the swinging wicker chair, the editor watched as the priest twisted the key in the lock, then dropped it into his pocket. She felt her stomach heave: she realised then that none of them was going to leave the room. The priest was mad; he would kill Hunter, then her, then turn the gun on himself.

'So this is your lair.' Carroll prowled along the shelves, pulling out books and magazines, pages, charts, scrolls, scraps of paper, looking at them briefly before tossing them all onto the floor. He swept an arm along the table, pitching its contents off. Catching the end of the second table, he tilted it, allowing the books and notes to slide into a heap. 'Filth,' he spat, his eyes wild.

'You want me,' Hunter said evenly, 'you've no need for the woman. Let her go.'

Carroll shook his head. 'No, not yet. She knows what you are. She's read your books, she knows the secret of the thirteenth novel. You've probably contaminated her with your foul creed.'

Katherine started to shake her head, but the priest was staring intently at the writer. 'The time for lies is over. Why don't you tell me the truth – tell me you raised a demon . . .'

Hunter's thin lips curled in a smile. 'Why should I tell you anything? You've already made up your mind.'

'Don't toy with me,' Carroll hissed. He lifted the gun and pulled the trigger. In the confines of the room, the report was deafening. The fax machine exploded in a shower of sparks and foul black smoke. Paper spooled from it onto the floor, where it curled and blackened. Thumbing back the hammer, Carroll went to stand beside Hunter and pressed the smoking barrel of the gun against the writer's temple. 'I would like some answers, but I can live without them. You'll remain alive as long as you answer my questions.'

'What do you want to know?' Hunter mumbled, head twisted awkwardly away from the gun barrel.

'Did you invoke the demon?'

'Yes . . .'

'Tell me!'

With his eyes fixed on Katherine, Hunter spoke quietly, his voice barely above a whisper. 'There's little enough to tell. It was ten years ago, and I was desperate. I needed some money. I decided to write a horror novel, with an occult background. I was doing some research when I stumbled across a grimoire – a magical book – which contained dozens of spells, including one for contacting one of the Earls of Hell, Lucifuge Rofocale, who was supposed to grant success to artists, writers and poets. I don't know what I was thinking; I was half-mad with despair and self-pity at the time. I followed the ritual and invoked the demon.'

'And?' Carroll said eagerly. 'The demon came. You saw the demon, spoke with it?'

Hunter turned to look at the priest. 'No, I didn't. Nothing happened.'

'Liar!' Carroll drew back his arm as if he were about to strike the writer.

'It's true, I swear it. But maybe it's just a coincidence that my first book went almost immediately for a surprisingly large sum of money. Even though the book sold well, the publishers were reluctant to take on another ... until I repeated the conjurgation. They bought the book the following morning. And so it was with the third and the fourth. Since then, I've conjured the demon before every book.' He attempted a smile. 'But it was just my little superstition, a little ritual to give me confidence. Writing is supposed to be a hard, soul-destroying occupation, but I found it remarkably easy ... until I discovered that the horrors I was writing about, the images I was seeing in my mind's eye, were actually taking place. People were dying in ways similar – identical – to the deaths in my books. And as my books became more violent, more brutal, so too did the killings in the real world. When I wrote of a death, there was a death; when I wrote about rape and mutilation, they too followed soon enough. Eventually, it reached the stage where I was terrified to write just in case I was condemning another innocent to death.'

Carroll shook his head. 'I don't believe you.'

'I do.' Both men looked towards Katherine. 'I believe him. I was brought in because he was so far behind on this last book. The publishers were astonished because

Robert Hunter has always been such a professional author, delivering his books in plenty of time.'

'I couldn't write it, I was afraid to . . . and yet I had to. I needed the money.'

Carroll stepped away from the writer. 'I don't believe you,' he repeated. 'I know you're a member of one of the most active satanic covens in London.'

'I joined because I became convinced that I had called something to me with the silly conjurgation. I wanted to see if there was some way of dismissing the creature or its influence over my life.'

'Your excuses are pitiful.'

'Almost as pitiful as attending a black mass simply for research purposes,' Hunter countered.

Carroll fired into Hunter's laser printer, sending it flying across the room in shards of plastic. Coils of black powder spilled everywhere, and a thick wire spat multi-coloured sparks onto the floor. Some of the sparks ignited paper from the fax machine, which began to burn with blue-green flames.

The priest looked at Katherine. 'You came here today to make an accusation. Make it. Let us listen to him lie.'

Aware that her life was in the balance, Katherine chose her words with infinite care. She was shaking so hard that the chair she was sitting in was trembling in unison. 'I came here today because I discovered two identical pieces of writing, one in *Zodiac*, which is published, and the second in the unpublished novel.'

Hunter blinked in surprise. 'Identical?'

'Almost word for word. The published piece is the killing of a young couple in a car. The unpublished bit is the same killing, but it is intercut with sections where the killer, now possessed by the spirit of a demon, tracks and slays them.'

'Extraordinary,' the writer murmured.

'Last night a couple were butchered in their car. The killing matches your text,' she finished.

'The need to confess,' Carroll said, 'is one of the most deep-rooted of all the human emotions. Perhaps consciously you could never admit that you were the killer, but your unconscious mind betrayed you. You killed that couple.'

Hunter shook his head. 'I was working here all through the night. I never left the house. I swear it.' He looked from the priest to Katherine. 'Do you believe I was writing about myself, possessed by some . . . some demon?'

Katherine shook her head. 'I don't know what to believe any more.'

The writer turned to Carroll. 'But you do?'

Carroll nodded. 'I do.' He grinned wolfishly. 'Now call it!'

'What?'

'Call the demon. Bring it here so that I can see it.' He fished in his pocket and took out a circular host and a small bottle of water. 'Bring it here so that I can see it . . . and destroy it.'

The writer spread his hands. 'Look, I really . . .'

The priest jammed the gun into the hollow of Hunter's neck. 'Show me this demon. Where are your grimoires?'

'I haven't any.'

'Liar. How do you conjure the demon?'

Hunter leaned away from the gun and tapped the computer screen. 'The ritual and formulas are all in here.'

'Use them.'

Chapter Forty-Nine

'DO you really think the priest will go after Hunter?'
Stuart Miller asked, turning the car into Eaton Square.

The inspector sighed. 'He's not exactly your normal
priest, is he? We know he's got a gun. His knowledge
of the occult is too deep to be healthy. He sleeps inside
a magical circle, has an enormous library of magical
books, and the last time we spoke he told me that he
was beginning to doubt his faith and needed to prove
the existence of evil to show the reality of God . . .' She
shook her head. 'If he suspected that Hunter was
behind the killings . . . then yes, I think he would go
after him.'

'Would he kill him, though?'

'He didn't strike me as the type . . .' she began, then
stopped. They were coming up on Hunter's house.
The hall door had been flung wide open and a woman
with a child in her arms and holding another by the
hand was running down the steps. 'Oh shit,' she
breathed, 'wrong again.'

The computer screen showed the image of a magical
pentagram alongside a block of crabbed Latin text.
Hunter tapped the screen. 'I discovered that you don't
actually need the circle . . .'

'What?' Carroll snapped.

'You don't need the circle for the conjurgation to be effective.'

'You fool!' the priest snarled. 'The circle is to hold the demon when it arrives. Do you mean you've been calling this creature without any containment?'

'But it never came,' the writer protested.

'It did, you fool, it did.' Carroll glanced over his shoulder at Katherine. 'Push the tables out of the way. Clear a section in the centre of the floor, about six feet across.' Turning back to Hunter, he tapped the screen. 'What did you do with this? How did you work the ritual?'

'I simply called it up on the screen and repeated the words aloud.' He took a deep breath and said, 'El, Michael, Arahl, Elohim. Gabriel, Taliahad, Yahweh, Raphael. Chassan, Adonai. Auriel, Phorlakh. By the divine names of Earth and Air, Water and Fire, I conjure, command and invoke thee . . .'

With a shout of horror, Carroll struck Hunter on the side of the head, the gunsight tearing a long strip of flesh from jaw to temple. The writer crashed to the ground, blood curling down his face.

'You imbecile!' The priest was almost incoherent with rage. Spittle flew from his mouth as he spoke. 'What have you done? Dearest God, what have you done. . .?'

Called.

And this was good, for it hungered,

Although the ancient way of summoning was incomplete, the correct formula of words needed to set up the proper resonances to enable it to cross from its domain into the world of men was uttered. It had travelled the roads often enough to latch onto the human and pull itself into him.

It found the creature in turmoil, its emotions whirling,

confused, frightened. Stifling them, it looked through the eyes
of the human.
  It smelt blood in the air. It tasted fear.

While Katherine dabbed blood from Hunter's forehead, Carroll knelt on the floor, frantically scribbling arcane sigils onto the wood. He had driven a small, black-handled knife into the floorboards, tied one end of a length of string to it and the other to a black felt-tipped marker. Using this crude compass, he had described a perfect circle on the floorboards.

'I've spent my life in pursuit of evil,' he babbled. 'I've studied the darker lore from every country, every race, every creed. The similarities are remarkable . . . and in every case, when a demon is called, either it must be contained within a circle or the magician must protect himself within the circle.' He straightened, examining his handiwork. 'It'll do,' he muttered. Stepping out of the circle he kicked the tumbled books and papers aside and drew a smaller circle, the felt-tipped marker squeaking and squealing on the polished boards. 'But for maximum protection, two circles are required: one to hold the demon, the second to protect the magician.'

'You believe in all this,' Hunter said astonished, struggling to sit up. His closed left eye was swelling.

'Don't you?' Carroll hissed.

Hunter shook his head. 'No. Psychic phenomenon – yes. But not this . . . this demon-lore.'

'Do you believe in demons, father?' Katherine asked.

The priest straightened. 'I'm about to find out.'

Margaret Haaren stood in the doorway and watched the car pull away from the kerb. Emma Hunter turned anxiously in the back seat, while one of the little girls raised a chubby hand and waved goodbye.

The inspector glanced at her watch. It was a few minutes to five. The nearest reinforcements were thirty minutes away through heavy evening traffic. They'd want to seal off the square, evacuate the houses on either side, and then attempt to negotiate.

By then it would be too late.

Haaren closed the hall door and pulled off her jacket, tossing it over the end of the stairs. She looked through the open door of the library. The formerly pristine room was a mess, the beautiful leatherbound books scattered all over the floor, some cracked and broken.

There was blood on the arms of Hunter's chair. Upstairs, Emma had said, that's where the priest had been taking them, upstairs to her husband's study at the very top of the house. The inspector was stooping to lift a metal poker from the fireplace when the sound of a phone ringing shocked her motionless.

The answering machine clicked on. '*Bob, Bob, it's Tony Matthews. If you're there, pick up . . .*' There was a pause, then Matthews continued excitedly. '*All this publicity's done wonders for the books. We've got movie interest from three agencies. They're even clamouring to pick up the old titles. Give me a call as soon as you come in. We're going to see not one but two and possibly three Robert Hunter movies. There's also talk about you writing a documentary on the occult.*' The machine clicked and beeped, resetting itself.

Michael Carroll stood very still, almost mesmerised by the flashing light on the small machine. 'You see – this is how Satan spreads his message,' he said softly. 'Once it was by word of mouth, then by hand in secret, scrawling grimoires; then with the advent of print, it was possible to produce unlimited numbers of copies.

Nowadays, the cults use computers to talk to one another, spreading their evil on electronic bulletin boards. And now by cinema and television,' he added. He stared at the answering-machine. 'How many lives have you contaminated by your books, how many young souls have you blighted with your evil? How many more will you destroy when motion pictures are made of your work, when you can spread your message on television?' Raising the gun, he pulled the trigger: once, twice.

The gunshots sounded flat and distant, like bursting balloons.

Margaret Haaren raced up the stairs, attempting to move as quietly as possible, praying she wasn't too late.

Fearing she was.

The first shot had destroyed the computer screen; the second gouged a huge hole in the processor. Black smoke plumed from the screen and the air was filled with drifting dust motes, thick as soot. Sparks and smouldering shards of plastic scattered across the room. Tendrils of smoke began coiling upwards as papers smouldered and caught in half a dozen places.

'There will be no more Robert Hunter books,' Carroll snarled. Catching hold of Katherine's bag, he dumped it on the ground, manuscript pages spilling every-where. 'When I'm done with you, I'll burn this . . .' he began, and then stopped.

There were footsteps on the stairs outside.

Raising the gun he shot through the door. There was a muffled shout and the sound of a body tumbling down the stairs. Then silence.

'You,' Carroll said, pointing at Katherine. 'Come

here. Stand with me in this circle.' He dug in his pockets and pulled out two silver-tipped bullets. Swinging open the cylinder, he dumped the empty shell casings onto the floor and pushed in the two bullets. Snapping the gun closed, he pointed to Hunter. 'You, stand in the smaller circle, so that when the demon comes, we may see both of you together. Now . . . finish the invocation. Call the demon.'

It had seen enough.

It was time to act.

The beast was taking control of him now, leading him, looking out through his eyes, hearing with his ears, using the senses denied it. Razor-tipped claws lurked in his soft flesh, needle-pointed fangs filled his mouth, hidden just behind his own teeth, a barbed tail coiled against his spine.

Margaret Haaren lay at the bottom of the stairs and tasted blood in her mouth where she had bitten her lip in the fall. She sat up gingerly. She ached everywhere, but she was astonished that there didn't seem to be anything broken.

When the shot had burst through the door, the shock had sent her tumbling backwards and she'd lost her footing, catapulting her backwards down the stairs. The fall had probably saved her life. Picking up the poker, she pulled off her shoes and climbed the stairs again.

She could hear voices from inside. She recognised Carroll's first, shouting, demanding, then Katherine's, softer, and finally Hunter's, pleading.

Standing outside the door, Haaren peered through the bullet hole in the wood.

'Call the demon.'

Hunter shook his head wildly. 'I don't know how . . .'

Carroll raised the gun and thumbed back the hammer. 'Do it,' he said . . . then stopped, watching in blank astonishment as the gun fell from his suddenly nerveless fingers.

Holding its hand up to its face, the beast watched as its talons slid through the tips of the soft human fingers. Deep in its core the human howled its agony.

Margaret Haaren threw her shoulder against the door snapping the lock from the frame as the priest locked his left hand around Katherine Norton's throat, pulling her head back, stretching her throat, ignoring her flailing fists and feet. Scooping up the fallen gun, the inspector turned, levelling it at Carroll. 'Stop! Leave the girl. Leave her!'

Carroll raised his head . . . and in that instant Haaren knew that he was no longer human. The eyes were cold, dead slivers of stone, the pupils sulphurous slits.

Pulling the trigger, she fired into his chest.

Chapter Fifty

THE human died, and in that last instant of consciousness, it was grateful.

But the demon survived.

The host was still fresh, and the demon-kind had no need of a beating heart or pumping lungs.

The thing that had been Father Michael Carroll sat up.

Robert Hunter's terrified shout alerted the inspector, who was bending over Katherine Norton. Raising the gun, she calmly shot Carroll between the eyes at a distance of less than three feet. The force of the blow bounced what remained of the back of his head off the floor.

'It's over,' she whispered to Katherine.

But Carroll sat up.

The inspector pulled the trigger again, but the hammer clicked on an empty chamber.

The creature stood up and wiped its hand across its forehead, smearing blood into the fine white hair. It looked at the two women, mouth gaping, eyes dead and empty, then turned to Hunter. As it stepped past Haaren, she could see the gaping exit wound in the back of its head. Nothing could have survived that wound – nothing human. Stretching out her hand, she touched the poker she'd dropped.

The creature reached for Hunter with both hands . . . and stopped, fingers twitching and recoiling in the air a foot from the cowering writer's face.

'It's the circle,' Hunter shouted, 'it can't break through the circle.'

The creature reached for Hunter again, obviously straining against the invisible barrier, the tips of its fingers bruising red, then black, then the flesh burst apart as long, razor-tipped talons slid through. Throwing back its ruined head, it howled aloud a nightmare sound that no human throat could ever have produced. It began shuddering, spasming, growing, stretching, its head pushing forwards, hair receding, cloth ripping apart as unnatural muscles bulged, shredded material puddling around its feet. The pale human flesh was changing, darkening, wrinkling, turning the colour of stagnant water, then black, the cracked skin leaking a pale, viscous oil.

The creature shuddered and sloughed off its human form, like a snake shedding its skin, the flesh falling away like strips of burnt leather to reveal another form beneath. Thick thighs jutted forward, the calves turning back, ending in bovine hoofs. A ridged tail hissed across the floor.

'Demon-kind,' Margaret Haaren breathed, thankful she couldn't see its face. But she had seen the type before. Her fingers closed around the metal poker.

'You called me,' the creature said. Hunter shook his head. 'You called me. And I answered. I came and granted you your heart's desire. But you denied me, you denied the evidence of your own success. You birthed me, but rejected me.' The creature's voice was a liquid bubbling.

'Who . . . who are you?' Hunter breathed. He was

trembling so badly he could barely stand.

'I am the being known in this place as Lucifuge Rofocale.'

Katherine put her mouth to the inspector's ear. 'Fire,' she whispered, teeth chattering.

The inspector nodded. She had been aware that a dozen tiny fires were starting around the room. Burning globules of black plastic were dripping from the wrecked computer onto the floor, eating into the floorboards.

'You called me,' Rofocale said. 'I came and you denied me. But I found this pitiful creature, a man so obsessed with my breed that he was open to me. You forced me to use him to feed myself.'

Hunter shook his head. 'I never . . .'

'We have conversed, you and I, in dreams.'

Hunter's eyes were wild, darting around the room. The fire from the burning machine was growing behind him, while the beast stood between him and the door.

'You wanted more time . . . time to finish your book.'

'That was a dream,' Hunter whispered.

'From the beginning I have given you the images. The link between us was strong. As I looked through this host's eyes, you saw through my eyes, you felt what I felt, you tasted what I ate.'

Haaren gripped the poker tightly in both hands and rose up behind the creature. If it had a physical presence, it could be killed. She brought the metal bar down with all her might on the creature's hairless skull. The metal poker bent, but the blow only staggered the creature, and it turned.

She had been expecting the features of a beast, instead she found herself looking at the face of an angel set in the skull of a demon. In that instant when they looked at one another, she struck at it again, driving the poker into its smiling, red-lipped mouth, smashing the small square neat teeth, revealing a second layer of teeth, and these were jagged and needle pointed. She struck it again, ramming the poker into its eye, pushing until she felt the orb give, the metal grate off bone.

Rofocale stepped backwards with the force of the blow, brushing against the edge of the circle, opening its ruined mouth to howl in something like pain, then lashing out at the inspector with its barbed tail, catching her across the right side of her chest, the force of the tremendous blow sending her crashing against the shelving. Books tumbled down around her, bibles, talmuds, and korans mixed with grimoires, treatises on the occult, collections of occult folklore from around the world.

The beast turned back to Hunter. Black ichor dribbled down its chin, bloody syrup on its cheek. It crooked a taloned nail. 'Come to me. This host is useless, but I can reside in you, you can feed me, and I can give you what you most desire. Seal the bargain we made all those years ago.'

A licking blue flame danced across the floorboard behind Hunter, staining the golden wood black, approaching the edge of the felt-tipped circle.

'I called you as a joke, nothing more. I never wanted you.' He shook his head savagely, spittle moist on his chin. 'I never needed your help.'

'You needed me. You were nothing.' The beast swept its arm wide. 'How else did you achieve all this?'

'No,' Hunter whispered.

'It is not your talents which made your books different. It is my imagery. On an instinctive, emotive level, your readers relate to your writing . . . because they recognise the truth in the words.' Rofocale spread its arms wide, elbows bending at unnatural angles. 'Through your writings they experience a vague glimpse of the existence the human-kind call Hell. This they know to be true. You have denied me for too long; the host I used also denied me, though on a deep level he knew I controlled him. Accept me willingly and I will make you a lord amongst men.'

'No!'

'The circle cannot hold,' Rofocale hissed. It suddenly turned and wrapped its talons around Katherine's head, dragging her upwards. 'But I can wait. I can amuse myself.'

The pain in her chest was agony.

Margaret Haaren concentrated on her breathing, trying to draw in only shallow breaths, but her lung felt cold and wet in her chest, and there was blood in her mouth. More on her blouse . . . damp stickiness on the back of her head where she'd struck the shelving.

The creature could be killed.

Clinging desperately to that thought, the inspector levered herself into a sitting position with her back to the shelves. Smoke was beginning to fill the room. A plastic box of computer disks on the writer's desk was melting into a puddle, oily black smoke curling upwards.

The demon had Katherine Norton by the hair, its right hand at her throat, long nails resting against the taut skin. The inspector watched the demon's ruined face move, concentrating on the words.

'Do you want her before I feast off the flesh and spirit? No? Are you sure?'

Hunter shook his head, eyes wide and shocked.

The beast turned its huge head, a single muddy

yellow eye fixing on the inspector. 'I am saving you. You are destined for an eternity of agony.' Then the talons pressed gently, gently against Katherine's throat, the stretched skin parting like torn paper, blood welling in the wound. Opening its mouth, forked tongue flickering wildly, the creature lowered its head onto Katherine's neck.

Digging her heels in, Haaren levered herself upwards, holding tightly onto the shelves, scattering more books onto the floor. A scrap of paper covered with curling script twisted into blackened soot. Flames were dancing up across the wood, flickering across the shelves, the books – sacred and profane – popping alight, paper, parchment, leather and cloth blackening, crackling, the sound like gleeful laughter.

The inspector straightened . . . and felt the shelving shift slightly against her weight. From the corner of her eye, she saw the demon's bloody mouth gape wide, broken fangs prominent, razor-tipped talons beneath the woman's breast.

'No more,' Haaren whispered.

Catching hold of the edge of the heavy shelving, the inspector planted her feet and heaved it away from the wall. Pain blossomed in her chest, fire and ice, raw agony, blood filling her mouth. The shelving shifted. She pulled again, muscles cracking, tearing with the effort – and this time the pain rose up in a solid, black blanket and engulfed her. But as she was falling she realised the whole wall of shelving was coming with her, books and burning wood raining down . . . a burning bible fluttering open, like a huge bat, draping itself across the demon's face . . . an illuminated Medieval grimoire wrapping itself around an outstretched claw, golden inks running, eating into the flesh . . . a sacred talmud, blazing savagely, sinking into the beast's abdomen, the air was filled with burning pages striking at the creature, searing flesh and bone . . .

'The Word of God,' Margaret Haaren breathed.

Chapter Fifty-One

THERE was a hint of autumn in the air, but the two women carried their coats over their arms as they strolled along the Flower Walk in Kensington Gardens. After the blistering summer, much of the grass was still burnt ochre, although the recent rains had added patches of green amongst the brown.

'I've been meaning to get in touch with you,' Margaret Haaren said eventually, 'but when I got out of hospital, there was so much to catch up on. There never seemed to be the time.'

'I read about your promotion in the paper,' Katherine Norton said. 'Have you made a full recovery?'

The big woman patted her right side. 'I'm fine. Turns out I'd a punctured lung, a couple of broken ribs, concussion. You?'

'I'm fine,' Katherine said, turning to look out across the park towards the Albert Memorial. The inspector caught a glimpse of the white scar on her throat that was concealed beneath a silk scarf.

Katherine turned to look at the inspector – chief inspector now. 'I never got a chance to thank you for saving my life.'

'I thought I'd killed you too when the shelving came down,' Haaren admitted. 'My sergeant said when they pulled you out of the wreckage, a badly burnt, withered arm was still locked around your throat. It had been sheered off at the elbow. That's how close it came.'

Katherine stopped and turned to the chief inspector, putting her hand on her arm. 'What happened that day?'

Haaren shrugged. 'The report says that Carroll, believing that Hunter was the killer, forced his way into the house. In the struggle that followed, you and I were injured, the shelving somehow became detached from the wall and crushed the priest and Hunter. By the time the police reached the room the wooden shelving, leather binding and paperbacks were ablaze in a huge pyre. Their bodies were charred beyond recognition. We were lucky to get out alive,' she added.

'But what really happened?' Katherine insisted.

Haaren shook her head. 'You were there; you heard it all.'

'Much of it I've forgotten.'

'Maybe that's as well.'

'Tell me – what didn't your report say?'

'Ten years ago Hunter called the demon as a joke. It came but he didn't know it, and because he refused to accept it, it latched onto the priest, who was receptive to the concept of evil as a physical embodiment. It used the priest to kill; Hunter was aware of the killings and used them as material in his books.'

'Did he know?'

'I believe he suspected or at least was aware at a subconscious level.'

'Does that make him guilty, then?'

'He did nothing,' Haaren reminded her. 'In the eyes of the law he was innocent. Father Michael Carroll is the guilty one. But justice was served in the end; natural justice.'

They turned left off the Flower Walk, heading towards Palace Gate.

'I hear you've taken up writing,' the chief inspector said, glancing sidelong at her companion.

'Children's books,' said Katherine. 'It pays better; you work your own hours, and you don't have to answer to anyone. I've already sold a fantasy trilogy to Image.'

'Any demons in it?'

'None at all.'

The Top Ten Bestsellers

1. (1) *Zodiac*, Robert Hunter, Image Press

2. (-) *Tarot*, Robert Hunter, Image Press

3. (3) *October Moon*, Robert Hunter, Image Press

Notes

THE authors, books and publishers mentioned in *IMP* do not exist and any resemblance to authors, publishers, or titles in print, is purely coincidental.

Robert Hunter does not exist. Father Michael Carroll, however, is real.

Although virtually unknown today, Lucifuge Rofocale was one of the most invoked of the medieval demons because of its ability to grant wishes and reveal the whereabouts of hidden treasure, to grant longevity and success in business and the arts. Lucifuge Rofocale often appeared in place of the Master, Lucifer.

The full text for invoking this powerful demon is contained in the Grand Grimoire and the Grimorium Verum.

Like most demons, Rofocale enjoys human flesh, and occasionally feasts off the conjurer.

You have been warned.

☐	Image	Michael Scott	£4.99
☐	Reflection	Michael Scott	£4.99
☐	Irish Folk and Fairy Tales	Michael Scott	£6.99
☐	Irish Myths and Legends	Michael Scott	£5.99
☐	A Celtic Odyssey	Michael Scott	£5.99
☐	Death Trance	Graham Masterton	£4.50
☐	Mirror	Graham Masterton	£4.50
☐	The Walkers	Graham Masterton	£4.50

Warner now offers an exciting range of quality titles by both established and new authors. All of the books in this series are available from:

Little, Brown and Company (UK) Limited,
P.O. Box 11,
Falmouth,
Cornwall TR10 9EN.

Alternatively you may fax your order to the above address. Fax No. 0326 376423.

Payments can be made as follows: cheque, postal order (payable to Little, Brown and Company) or by credit cards, Visa/Access. Do not send cash or currency. UK customers and B.F.P.O. please allow £1.00 for postage and packing for the first book, plus 50p for the second book, plus 30p for each additional book up to a maximum charge of £3.00 (7 books plus).

Overseas customers including Ireland, please allow £2.00 for the first book plus £1.00 for the second book, plus 50p for each additional book.

NAME (Block Letters) ....

....

ADDRESS ....

....

....

☐ I enclose my remittance for _____

☐ I wish to pay by Access/Visa Card

Number ☐☐☐☐☐☐☐☐☐☐☐☐☐☐☐☐

Card Expiry Date ☐☐☐☐